THE HUNTING WIND

AN ALEX McKNIGHT MYSTERY

Steve Hamilton

THOMAS DUNNE BOOKS
ST. MARTIN'S MINOTAUR ⚹ NEW YORK

A THOMAS DUNNE BOOK FOR MINOTAUR BOOKS.
An imprint of St. Martin's Publishing Group.

THE HUNTING WIND. Copyright © 2001 by Steve Hamilton. All rights reserved. Printed in the United States of America. For information, address St. Martin's Press, 175 Fifth Avenue, New York, N.Y. 10010.

www.thomasdunnebooks.com
www.minotaurbooks.com

The Library of Congress has cataloged the hardcover edition as follows:

Hamilton, Steve.
    The hunting wind / Steve Hamilton.—1st ed.
      p. cm.
    ISBN 0-312-26894-7
    1. Private investigators—Michigan—Upper Peninsula—Fiction. 2. Upper Peninsula (Mich.)—Fiction. 3. Missing persons—Fiction. I. Title.
PS3558.A44363 H86 2001
813'.54—dc21   2001020247

ISBN 978-1-250-02577-7 (trade paperback)

First Minotaur Books Paperback Edition: January 2013

D 20 19 18 17 16 15 14 13 12 11

To Antonia

Acknowledgments

I want to thank all of the "usual suspects"—Bill Keller and Frank Hayes, Liz Staples and Taylor Brugman, Bob Kozak and everyone at IBM, Bob Randisi and the Private Eye Writers of America, Ruth Cavin, Matthew Shear, Cristina Gilbert, and everyone else at St. Martin's Press, Jane Chelius, Jeff Allen, Lisa Wasoski, Larry Queipo, former chief of police, town of Kingston, New York, and Dr. Glenn Hamilton from the Department of Emergency Medicine, Wright State University. God bless all of you.

In the end, I owe everything to my wife, Julia, who is more amazing than she'll ever know. To Nickie, who is growing up too quickly. And to Toni, who already has me wrapped around her little baby finger.

THE HUNTING WIND

Chapter One

When the left-hander found me, I was sitting in my usual chair in front of the fire, trying to stay warm. The calendar said April, but April in Paradise is still cold enough to hurt you, and I could feel the sting of it in my hands and on my face. I sat there by the fire, watching the baseball game on the television over the bar, nursing a cold Canadian beer as the left-hander made his way in the darkness. He knew where he was going, because he had a hand-drawn map in his back pocket, with a little star on the right side of the road as you come north into Paradise. The Glasgow Inn, that was his destination. He knew I'd be there. On a cold Tuesday night in April, where else would I be?

His trip had begun early that morning in Los Angeles. He boarded a 747 and flew to Detroit Metropolitan Airport. He had to wait two hours there, and he had already lost three hours in the time change. So the sun was going down when he finally got on the little two-propeller plane with twelve passengers, a pilot, and a copilot who doubled as the flight attendant. That plane took him first to Alpena, where he sat on the runway for a half hour while half the passengers got off. The copilot got out and sprayed the ice off the wings, and then they were in the air again.

The plane was noisy and cold, and it bounced around in the wind like a paper kite. It was after eleven o'clock at night when they finally touched down at Chippewa County Airport. There are only two flights per day that land there, two little airplanes like the one the left-hander was on that night. The funny thing is that those little airplanes land on a runway that's over two and a half miles long. It's one of the longest runways in the country, long enough to be on the space shuttle's emergency backup list. The left-hander asked one of the other passengers why the runway was so long, because that's the kind of thing the left-hander does. He asks strangers questions, as if he'd known them his whole life. And they always answer him, because he has this way of making them feel at ease.

"This used to be an air force base, aye," the stranger said. He was a local man from the Upper Peninsula, so he had that yooper rise in his voice. "Kincheloe Air Force Base, back in World War Two. Did ya know the Soo locks were the most heavily defended position in America back then? I guess they figured if the Japs or Germans were gonna bomb us, they'd start at the locks and cut off our ore supply."

"That's interesting," the left-hander said. I'm sure he said it in a way that made the stranger feel that it really *was* interesting, and that therefore the stranger must be an interesting man himself. That's the kind of thing the left-hander can do, with just two words.

The airport terminal itself is a one-room hut sitting next to that long runway. The left-hander went into the terminal and picked up his luggage. It didn't take long, because the copilot just grabbed the suitcases two at a time and carried them in himself. If the left-hander was worried about getting his rental car at such a tiny airport at eleven o'clock at night, he had no reason to be. A woman named Eileen was there waiting for him, keys in hand. That was her job, after all. When somebody reserves a car, she stays up late that night and waits for the plane to come in. The left-hander signed a form, took the keys from her, and thanked her. He thanked Eileen with a smile that she'd remember for months afterward, I'm sure. Then she went home to bed.

He found his rental car in the parking lot. Across the street from the airport, there is a factory where they recondition auto parts, twenty-four hours a day. The factory sends up a constant stream of smoke, and the light from the airport makes the smoke look silver against the night sky. He must have stood there and looked at the smoke for a moment, breathing in the cold air. The coat he had just taken out of his suitcase was not warm enough. He had started his day in California, where it was seventy-one degrees. Here in the Upper Peninsula of Michigan, on an April night a good three weeks after the official start of spring, it was twelve degrees.

He left the airport and drove down a lonely road with no streetlights. It must have seemed then like he'd come to the end of the earth. There were still piles of gray snow on either side of the road, what remained of the mountains made each year by the snowplows. When he found I-75, he took that north toward Sault Ste. Marie. The Soo, as the locals call it. But he didn't get to see the Soo itself that night, because the map he had laid on the seat next to him told him to take M-28 west, right into the heart of the Hiawatha National Forest. He passed through a couple of small towns named Raco and Strongs, and then he hit M-123. He took that road north. After a few miles, he could see Lake Superior in the moonlight. There was ice on the shore.

When he saw the sign, he knew he had finally reached Paradise. WELCOME TO PARADISE! WE'RE GLAD YOU MADE IT! He paused at the single blinking red light in the middle of town, and then he found the Glasgow Inn a hundred yards up on the right. He pulled his rental car into the lot and parked it right next to my twelve-year-old Ford truck with the woodstove in the back, covered in plastic.

I didn't know about any of this at the time, of course. About the plane to Detroit and then the plane to Chippewa County, about the words to the stranger or the smile for Eileen, the rental car lady. I didn't know he was coming all this way out to see me on that night. The Detroit Tigers were playing a late game out on the West Coast, the same coast Randy had spent all day flying away from. I was just sitting by the fireplace at the Glasgow Inn, watching the game on the television that hung over the bar. The place is supposed to resemble a Scottish pub, with the big over-stuffed chairs and footrests. It's a lot more inviting than most bars I've seen. And Jackie, the owner of the place, cannot be trusted to do anything right on his own, so it is my duty to stop in every night and share my wisdom with him. He never listens to me, but I keep going back anyway.

I own some land up the road, with six cabins my father had built back in the sixties and seventies. I live in the first cabin, the one I helped him build myself in 1968. The other five I rent out to tourists in the summer, hunters in the fall, and snowmobilers in the winter. Spring is the off-season in Paradise, a time to clean out the cabins and wait for the snow to melt.

There was a time when spring meant something else, the four years I was catching in the minor leagues. A lifetime ago. I didn't think about those days much anymore. A lot of time had passed since then, and a lot of things had happened. Eight years as a police officer in Detroit. A dead partner and a bullet still inside my chest. And then fifteen years up here in Paradise, spending nights like this one watching baseball on television and not even thinking about the days when I played the game myself. I certainly wasn't thinking about Randy Wilkins, a left-hander I had caught back in triple-A ball in 1971. When he opened the door and stepped into the place and shouted my name, I couldn't believe it was really him. If the Pope himself had come through the door wearing his big hat, I wouldn't have been more surprised.

Almost thirty years later, the left-hander had found me.

Chapter Two

"Wilkins," I said. "Randy Wilkins. I don't believe it." He looked about twenty pounds heavier, and the curly black hair he'd once had was mostly gone. What was left was cut close to his scalp. As if to compensate for the loss, he had grown a mustache and goatee.

The eyes, they hadn't changed. He still had that look in his eyes. Some days, you'd call it a twinkle; other days, you'd call it insanity. Which was totally appropriate, considering the side of the mound he threw from. There are some simple truths in baseball, after all. One of them, whether it would be considered politically correct these days or not, is that left-handed pitchers are not normal. They can't throw the ball in a straight line, for one thing. Everything a left-hander throws has a little movement on it, no matter how hard he tries to throw the straight fastball. A left-hander, being a total freak of nature, is fragile and more likely to hurt himself. One bad throw and the arm is done forever. I've seen it happen.

And left-handers think differently, too. They might be a little absentminded maybe. Or eccentric. Or downright crazy.

"Alex McKnight," he said. He grabbed my shoulders and didn't let go. "How long has it been?"

"It's what, almost thirty years?" I said. "How in the world . . . What are you doing here?"

"I was in the neighborhood," he said. "I thought I'd drop by."

"In the neighborhood, huh? You wanna try that again?"

"Do I get a drink first?" he said. "It's been a hell of a long day."

"A drink," I said. "Of course."

I introduced him to Jackie. "This man right here," I said, "played ball with me in Toledo, believe it or not. He was a pitcher."

"Pleased to meet ya," Jackie said, shaking his hand. "What are you drinking?"

"Whatever Alex is having," Randy said.

"Alex is having a beer," Jackie said. "A beer from Canada. Alex doesn't drink beer if it's bottled in America. He makes me go all the way over the bridge just to pick him up a case of beer every week."

"He doesn't need the sob story," I said. "Just get him the beer."

"You look good," Randy said to me. "You've been working out?"

"Working out, ha!" Jackie said from behind the bar. "Alex McKnight working out. That's a good one."

"I'll tell you something," Randy said. "This man right here was one hell of a catcher. I don't think I ever saw him give up a passed ball."

"Too bad he couldn't hit his weight," Jackie said as he brought the beer around.

"Just give the man his beer," I said. I sat him down in front of the fire and watched him take a pull right out of the bottle.

"So this is Canadian beer," he said.

"Can you taste the difference?"

"Um, sure," he said.

7

"You're lying," I said. "No matter how long it's been, I can still tell when you're lying."

He laughed. "I can't lie to my catcher."

"Damned right," I said. "But seriously. It's great to see you. Except for that mustache and that goatee thing."

"Makes me look pretty smooth, doesn't it?"

"Yeah, in a satanic, serial killer sort of way. What's that on your arm, a tattoo?"

He looked at the back of his left wrist. There were three parallel lines. The line farthest from his hand had a gap in the middle. "That's a trigram," he said. "You know, from the *I Ching*. It's called 'the joyous lake.' A Tibetan monk used a needle dipped in spider blood."

"You're lying again," I said. "I told you, don't even try it. I can see right through you. Even thirty years later."

"How about I got drunk one night in San Francisco?" he said. "When I woke up, I had no wallet, no shoes, and a brand-new tattoo?"

"That's sounds more like it," I said.

He laughed again. It was the same laugh. For one year of my life, I'd heard that laugh at least twenty times a day.

"So tell me already," I said.

"What?"

"What's going on? How far did you have to come to get here, anyway?"

"Well, I've been living in L.A. for the last few years," he said. "I was watching a Cactus League game a couple weeks ago, and the guy on TV was talking about how a good catcher is a pitcher's best friend. I said to myself, 'Ain't that the truth,' and I started thinking about the old days in Toledo. I was wondering whatever happened to you, so I started poking around on the

8

Internet to see if I could find you. I saw your Web site, man, and I figured, Hey, I'm gonna go see him!"

"Whoa," I said. "Back up. My Web site?"

"Yeah, I did a search on Alex McKnight and it came up."

"Randy, I don't have a Web site. I don't even have a computer."

"I'm talking about your business Web site, Alex. Prudell-McKnight Investigations."

I just looked at him for a long moment. And then it came to me. "Oh my God," I said. "What did he do now?"

"Your partner, Leon?"

I closed my eyes. "Yeah, my partner, Leon."

"Well, it looks like he's put a nice little Web site out there advertising your services. There's this drawing with two pistols on it, pointing at each other. It kinda looks like they're shooting at each other."

"Yeah, I know what you mean," I said. "He used the same thing on our business cards."

"I gave Leon a call," he said. "Real nice guy. He told me you'd be here. I made him promise not to tell you I was coming. I wanted it to be a surprise."

"Well, you certainly did surprise me. But why—"

"There's something on there about you having a bullet in your chest, too. Is that true?"

"I'm going to kill him," I said. "He is absolutely dead."

"So you do have a bullet in there?" He sneaked a look down at my torso, the same way everybody does when they first hear about it.

"Yes," I said. "It's a long story."

"All right, save that one, then. Are you married? You got any kids?"

"No and no," I said. "Married once, divorced. No kids. How about you?"

He looked at the ceiling for a moment. "I'm divorced, too. Three kids. Jonathan just passed the bar. He's a lawyer in San Francisco. His wife's expecting a baby soon. Can you believe that? I'm gonna be a grandfather! Annie's a chef, just got a new job at a really nice restaurant down in San Diego. And Terry just went off to school at UC-Santa Barbara. Hey, guess what." He reached over and punched me in the leg.

"Ouch. What?"

"Terry's a ballplayer. He's on the freshman team. Guess what position he plays."

"Oh great," I said. "Another pitcher. I bet he's a crazy left-hander."

"He's a catcher," he said. "Can you beat that?"

"That's even worse," I said. "He has to *catch* crazy left-handers."

"He's a switch-hitter," he said. "God, he can drive the ball, Alex. Just like you used to."

"I see your memory went along with your hair."

"Oh man, you haven't changed, Alex." He took another pull from the bottle. "Canadian beer. I can't believe I'm in Michigan drinking Canadian beer. And why is it so cold here, anyway? Haven't you guys heard of spring?"

"Sure," I said. "Just wait until June."

"Hey, Jackie!" he yelled. "Get your butt over here so I can tell you some stories about your boy Alex here. Stuff I bet you never heard before. And bring some more beer while you're at it."

Anybody else who came into the place for the first time and talked to Jackie that way, he'd be back out in the parking lot in ten seconds, wiping the gravel off his ass. But Randy had always had this knack for making you feel like you'd known him your whole life, even if you'd just met him. I saw it all the time when we were playing together, and even more when we became roommates. Randy had already gone through a couple of roommates by the time he got to me. Something about the way he'd keep talking all night, even if you had to get up early the next morning and ride on a bus all day to the next game.

But you couldn't hate the guy for it. As much as you wanted to kill him sometimes, he'd always say something funny and disarming, or, even worse, he'd put his arm around you and sing in your ear. "You know you love me, Alex," he used to say. "You've got the hots for me. You dream about me all night long. That's why I drive you crazy."

A whole busload of guys in their twenties, most of them from farms or little towns around the Midwest, all of them dirt-tough or at least trying to act like it. And I got Randy Wilkins for a roommate.

So now almost thirty years have passed, and out of nowhere he's sitting in the Glasgow Inn on a late Tuesday night in April. It's taken him exactly twenty minutes to feel comfortable. Hell, in twenty minutes, he owns the place. Even a crusty old goat like Jackie is treating him like royalty. I kept waiting for him to tell me why he had come so far to see me, after all these years, but he kept talking about baseball, the games we had played in, old teammates I had all but forgotten.

"So tell me, Randy," Jackie said at one point. "Did you ever make it up to the big leagues?"

There it was. I knew it would come up eventually. I certainly wasn't going to mention it myself.

"Why, yes," Randy said. "As a matter of fact, I did make it up to the big leagues. I pitched in one game." By this time, Jackie had pulled a couple of the tables over by the fireplace, and at least twelve men were sitting there listening to him. "You want to tell this story, Alex?"

"I wasn't there," I said. And that's all I said, because I didn't want to touch it. I had never even heard him tell it before, because after that September call-up, I never saw him again. Until tonight.

"September 1971," he said. "You guys know how they expand the major-league rosters from twenty-five to forty in September, right? The minor-league seasons are over by then, and most of the clubs like to bring up some of the players to the big club, let them see some action. You know, maybe think about them for the next year. Well, I got called up to Detroit in 1971. Alex should have been brought up, too. But they blew that one."

Everybody looked at me.

"Yeah, okay," I said. "Keep going."

"Detroit had a good team that year. They won like what, ninety-two games or something? But that was Baltimore's year and the Tigers were already out of it, with a couple weeks left. So Billy Martin—he was the manager then—he decides he's gonna take a look at this hot-shit left-hander up from Toledo, right? A lot of managers, they're not gonna start a guy right out of triple-A. They're gonna put him in to mop up a couple innings the first time out. But Martin gives me a start. God, I'm thinking, this is it. This is my big chance."

He paused to take a breath and a long drink. When he put the bottle back down, it was empty. Jackie hopped up to get him another one.

"It just so happens we're playing Baltimore," he went on. "Best team in the majors. And I'm thinking, Okay, no problem. If I can get these guys out, then I'm gonna make the roster next year for sure. It was a day game. A Saturday. I'm in the bull pen warming up—aw hell, they don't even *have* a real bull pen in Tiger Stadium. They just have this area down the third-base line. You're right out on the field. Anyway, I'm warming up and I just can't believe any of this is happening. It's like an out-of-body experience. And then when the game starts, I get right out there, because we're the home team, right? I throw my last warm-ups. Bill Freehan is catching me. You guys remember Bill Freehan?"

Which of course we do. The best catcher in Tiger history. And just one more reason why I didn't see any time in the big leagues. Not with Bill Freehan catching 150 games every year.

"Okay, so the first was Don Buford. First pitch I throw as a major leaguer, he takes right down the middle. Strike one. Next ball, he fouls off. Strike two. I nibble on the corner a couple of times; Buford lays off. Now it's 2-2. Freehan calls for the curveball. I shake him off. There's only one pitch I'm gonna throw now. Am I right, Alex?"

I cleared my throat. "The slinky."

"The slinky?" Jackie said. "What the hell's that?"

"Go ahead, Alex," Randy said. "Tell the man about the slinky."

"It was his money pitch," I said. "It was kind of a hard slider, but he'd sort of drop down and throw it sidearm. When he had it working, left-handed batters were dead meat. It wasn't exactly a treat for right-handers, either. It would ride right in on their hands." I stopped right there, because I didn't want to ruin his story. I didn't tell them that the slinky was once my worst nightmare, because when he started to lose it, he'd start bouncing it five feet in front of the plate.

"Buford fans on it," Randy said. "And I'm thinking, This is

gonna be easy. If the slinky's working, I'm unhittable. I'm already seeing the headlines in the paper the next morning. 'Unknown Rookie Throws No-Hitter,' something like that."

"I don't like this," Jackie said. "I got a bad feeling about what's going to happen next."

"Merv Rettenmund comes up," Randy said. "I throw him a couple right on the corner, but the umpire calls balls. I'm nobody, right? I'm not going to get a close one. I'm starting to get a little upset. So I bring the slinky again, but this time I bounce one in front of the plate. The slinky's a tricky pitch. It can get away from you once in a while."

Tell me about it, I thought.

"So now I'm a little rattled. It's a 3-0 count. I figure he's taking, so I put one right down the middle. At least it looked like it was right down the middle. Umpire calls ball four and now Rettenmund's on first. So I start yelling at the umpire and the umpire is looking at me like he wants to run me. Two batters, and I'm already this close to being ejected. So Freehan comes out to talk to me, says, 'Everything's okay. Calm down, kid, relax. Don't let the umpire get to you,' and all that."

Which was exactly the wrong thing to say to him, I know. But how was Freehan to know that? He'd never seen the kid before in his life. If it was me, I would have gone out to the mound, grabbed him by the jersey, and told him to stop acting like a two-year-old. Because getting him mad was the only way to get his head back in the game.

"Next batter is Boog Powell. God, I knew he was big, but not *that* big. He looked like a freakin' building standing next to the plate. But he bats left-handed, so I figure, What the hell, the slinky is what got me here. I'm gonna keep riding it. Freehan calls for a fastball; I shake him off. He calls for a curveball; I shake him off. I want the slinky. I see him sneak a look into the dugout, like Who the hell is this kid, anyway? But finally, he gives me the slinky. And I throw it."

He stopped and took a drink again. A born showman.

"So what happened?" Jackie said.

"Boog Powell hits it into the upper deck." He took another drink and gave everybody a chance to groan.

"Did they pull you out of the game?"

"No," Randy said. "They didn't. The pitching coach came out and talked to me. Then Frank Robinson came up and I threw the slinky again. Freehan didn't even call for it. I just threw it. Robinson hit it onto the roof in left field. Now it's three to nothing. Freehan comes out and just about tears my head off. Tells me the next time I throw that pitch, he's gonna break me in half. They've got two guys working in the bull pen already, and I'm in a daze by then. I walked Hendricks and then I walked Brooks Robinson, and it was just like a nightmare. I kept looking into the dugout, waiting for Billy Martin to come out and get me. But he's just sitting there looking at me. With that look on his face like he's got a bad case of gas. I walked Davey Johnson, and now the bases are loaded. Still, Martin's just sitting in that dugout. So Mark Belanger comes up. And I'm thinking, Okay, finally, here's the one guy in the lineup who doesn't hit. I'm gonna settle down and get this guy and get myself out of this. First pitch, Belanger hits this high pop-up down the left-field line. Any other stadium in the world, it's an easy out, but this is Detroit, so it sneaks over the fence. A grand slam. By Mark fucking Belanger. So finally, Billy Martin comes out and he says to me, 'Okay, that's enough, kid. We're gonna run out of baseballs.' "

When he stopped, nobody said anything. It was almost thirty years ago. Billy Martin was dead now. But you could still imagine what it must have felt like.

"So I gave up seven runs in one inning," Randy said. "Actually in one-third of an inning, because I only got one out. My lifetime ERA is 198. You can look it up."

And then he laughed. It broke the spell, and gave everyone else in the room permission to laugh with him. We had a few more beers. We talked some more, about what he had been doing since leaving baseball. Something about him selling commercial real estate, something about coaching baseball at a local high school. More about his divorce, his kids, especially his young son the catcher. He talked a lot that night, and made everybody around him feel glad to be there. Which was always his genius.

But he still never did tell me why he was there.

I had to wait to hear it. Back in my cabin, Randy sleeping on my couch, me in my bed because he wouldn't hear of kicking me out of it. And he didn't want to sleep in one of the other cabins, either. He wanted to sleep on the couch.

"Just like the old days, huh?" he said after the lights were out. "Just you and me."

"That's not a very comfortable couch, is it?" I said.

"It's perfect," he said. "Just like the beds we used to sleep in when we were on the road. You remember?"

"I remember," I said, and for a moment I was back in a small-town motel room, listening to my crazy roommate talk half the night away.

"So you want to hear it?" he said.

"Hear what?"

"Why I came all the way out here."

"I figured you'd get to it when you were ready."

"I've been thinking a lot about 1971 lately," he said. I couldn't see him in the darkness. There was only the sound of his voice. Maybe that's the way he wanted it. Just his voice and not having me look at him while he told me.

"About the game?"

"Not so much the game," he said. "Everything else that happened. You know, that was the best time of my life. Being called up to the big leagues, getting to go to Tiger Stadium, wearing the uniform, getting to sit in that dugout. You know, those dugouts in Detroit are *tiny*."

"So I've heard," I said.

"I'm sorry," he said. "I didn't mean to—"

"Go on," I said. "Tell me what you're gonna tell me."

"There was a lot going on that week. Outside of the ballpark, I mean. I'd never been to Detroit before. There was a lot to see."

"In Detroit?"

"All around Detroit," he said. "They've got a great art museum there, a pretty nice zoo. They've got that—what do you call it, the Boblo boat?"

"The Boblo boat," I said. "I haven't thought about that in years."

"You ever go on that?"

"Sure, when I was a kid." It was a big old-fashioned riverboat that would take you down the Detroit River to an amusement park on an island.

"And Greenfield Village? And the Henry Ford Museum? I'm going to all these things, and it's like everything is just great because I'm going there as a major-league baseball player. I mean, it's not like anybody's asking me for my autograph. Nobody even

17

recognizes me. But for the first time in my life, I felt like I was somebody important, you know? Everything was just... perfect."

"What was her name?" I said.

A long silence. "Maria."

"Let me guess," I said. "The museums, the zoo, the Boblo boat..."

"With Maria, yes."

"So what happened?"

"When I got shelled in that game, I sort of wasn't myself for a few days. I didn't want to see her. I didn't want to see *anybody*."

"So you didn't see her again?"

"No."

"And now, it's been almost thirty years..."

"I want to find her."

"Randy, you can't be serious."

"I want to find her, Alex."

"You came all the way out here..."

"To ask you to help me, Alex. You've got to help me find Maria."

Chapter Three

The woodstove almost killed him the next morning. Five hundred pounds of cast iron came hurtling off the back of my truck, turning the wooden ramp into splinters. If he had been half a second slower, Randy would have been flattened like piecrust under a rolling pin.

"I told ya those boards wouldn't be able to take it," he said. "Good thing I still have the reflexes of a jungle cat."

I had already torn the old woodstove, worthless piece of crap that it was, out of my second cabin and hauled it away to the dump. When I bought the new one, they wanted three hundred dollars to deliver and install it, so I told them just to put it in the back of my truck. It sat there for two weeks under a plastic tarp, waiting for me to figure out a way to move it. This was a great source of amusement for Jackie, and he never missed a chance to ask me if I was still hauling it everywhere I went. Jackie would have helped me himself, he said, for a flat fee of $350.

When Randy and I had finally muscled the thing into the cabin, he stood with his hands on his knees, catching his breath. "You see, Alex," he said. "I knew coming here was a good idea. It's already paying off."

He hadn't said a word about Maria that morning. I figured he'd get to it when he was ready.

"It feels good, doesn't it?" he said.

"What feels good?"

"Stuff like this," he said. "Having to use your body again."

"Yeah, I feel great," I said, rubbing my shoulder.

"You still got your glove?"

"What glove?"

"Your catcher's glove."

"Yeah, in my closet. Why?"

"And a ball?"

"Oh no," I said. "No way."

"Come on, while we're warm. Let's toss a few."

"You gotta be kidding."

"When's the last time you threw a baseball?"

I had to think about that one. Before I could answer, he was out the door.

"Come on, McKnight!" He was already jogging down the road. "I'll race you back to your cabin."

"Will ya wait a minute already," I said.

"All right, we'll walk," he said. "It's what, a whole quarter mile?"

"Something like that."

"And you got how many of these cabins?"

"Six in all," I said. "The old man built them."

We walked down the road, through the pine trees on what had once been an old logging trail. The sun was out, fighting a hard battle to warm up the heavy air. There were patches of ice that would slowly thaw during the day and then freeze again at night. It would be the middle of May before they were all gone.

"And you came up here when?" he said.

"1984," I said. "After I left the police force."

He nodded. "After you got shot."

"Yeah," I said. "After I got shot."

"You've been up here ever since?"

"I spend my winters in Monte Carlo," I said. "I have an estate there."

"No, really," he said. "You've been up here all this time?"

"Yes," I said. "Is that so amazing?"

He shook his head. "You still got another glove besides the catcher's mitt?"

"Yes, but we're not going to play catch, Randy."

Five minutes later, he had dug out my old catcher's mitt, along with my first baseman's glove. Every catcher has a first baseman's glove or an outfielder's glove, because every catcher dreams about the day when the manager sends him out into the field, where he can play standing up, without pads and a mask. We stood forty feet away from each other on the road in front of my cabin, and then he tossed the ball to me.

"Just a couple," I said. "This is crazy." When I threw the ball back to him, it felt like something I had never done before in my life.

"Since when do you throw like a girl?" he said.

"You'll have to forgive me," I said. "They took one bullet out of my rotator cuff, and the other out of my shoulder blade. You kinda lose a little zip on the ball."

He threw it back to me. "It feels good, right? Throwing the ball again?"

"No," I said. "As a matter of fact, it hurts a great deal." I threw it back, trying to use the turn of my body to take the stress off my arm.

"You just need to warm up," he said.

21

"By the fire, with a beer," I said.

"I tried looking her up," he said, throwing the ball back to me. "On my computer, I mean. Maria Valeska."

"Randy, that was her name in 1971." I threw the ball. The pain was starting to go away. Just a little.

"Yeah, I know," he said. "She could be married now."

"If she's married . . ."

"Alex, I'm not expecting that she's going to be waiting for me after all these years. I know she's not sitting up in a tower like Rapunzel or something."

"Then why—"

"Rapunzel was the one with the hair, right? The long hair?"

We kept throwing the ball.

"Although Rapunzel had blond hair, right?" he said. "Maria's hair was jet black."

"Randy . . ."

"Have you ever been in love with a girl with dark hair and dark eyes, Alex?"

I threw the ball. "Do green eyes count?"

"In California, there are blondes everywhere. Just gorgeous women, Alex. You look at 'em, and it's like you're looking right into the sun. But then you blink and you look away, and it's like you can't even remember what they looked like. Now a girl with dark eyes, the kind of eyes that just go right through you . . ."

"Randy . . ."

"That's the kind of girl that gets under your skin."

"She's not a girl anymore," I said. "She's gotta be what, in her mid-forties now?"

"About that," he said.

"Some woman in her mid-forties, probably been married for

22

a long time, probably has a couple kids. You're gonna walk up to her door and say, 'Hello, remember me?'"

"She'll remember me," he said.

"And then what?"

"I don't know," he said. "I really don't know, Alex."

"Randy, do you have *any* idea what this sounds like? I'm sorry, it just sounds so *stupid*."

"Yeah, yeah," he said. He backed up a few feet and threw the ball a little faster. It hit my glove with a pop, the same sound I used to hear a thousand times a day. It had been my entire life once, just catching a baseball and throwing it back, again and again.

"Take it easy," I said. "I'm not wearing a mask here."

"Just think about it," he said. "I look her up and I can't find her, but instead I find *you*. And it turns out you're a private eye now." He threw the ball again. *Pop!*

"No, not really," I said. But he wasn't listening. I tossed the ball back.

"And you used to be a cop in Detroit, which is where she lived."

"A long time ago."

"And you still live in Michigan now." Another throw, another pop in my glove.

"Detroit's six hours away from here, Randy."

"I could always count on you, Alex. You were my catcher, man. I mean, I threw to other guys, but you were *my catcher*." He backed up another few feet and threw a hard one. It gave my left hand a little tingle when I caught it.

"Okay, we're about done here," I said. I should have pocketed the ball right then, but instead I tossed it back to him.

23

"Don't you believe in fate, Alex? With you and Leon helping me, I know this is going to work out."

"Leon," I said. "About Leon . . ."

"He's expecting us today, by the way," Randy said. "I figure we can go see him after lunch."

"Expecting us?" I said. "For what?"

"To bring us up-to-date on the case," he said. "I talked to him a few days ago, you know, when he told me where to find you."

"Up-to-date?" I said. "On the case?"

"I feel a slinky coming, Alex."

"Randy, don't."

"I got to throw one, Alex. I'm bringing out the slinky." He went into a slow windup.

"Randy, so help me God, if you throw a slinky . . ."

"Get down, Alex. Here comes the slinky . . ."

I could have thrown my hands up in the air. Or turned my back to him. It probably would have stopped him. I don't know why I went down into the position, my glove in front of me, my right hand behind my back. Maybe it was just instinct. Or maybe part of me really did want to see him throw the slinky again, one more time.

He threw the ball, dropping down into that sidearm delivery. Just like the old days.

And just like the old days, the ball bounced five feet in front of me.

I didn't catch it, but at least I stopped it. That was the one thing I was always good at. Whatever it took, whatever part of my body I had to sacrifice, I could always stop the slinky.

"I think I hurt my arm," Randy said. We were sitting at the bar in Jackie's place, sitting in front of two big plates of his Wednesday corned beef.

I didn't say anything. I just sat there with a bag of ice against my right eye.

"Jackie, this is damned good," he said.

Jackie came over, looked at me for the seventh time since we had come into the place, and shook his head. "Alex, tell me again what happened."

I gave him as nasty a look as you can give a man with your right eye swollen shut.

"Are you telling me, Randy," he said, still looking at me, "that this man *forced* you to throw to him?"

"He wouldn't take no for an answer," Randy said.

"And he made you try to throw that pitch you used to throw? What was it called?"

"The slinky," Randy said. "On a cold day, without even warming up. I could have ruined my arm."

"Well, it serves him right," Jackie said. "He got what he deserved."

"If you guys are about done," I said, "I could use some more ice."

"Hurry up and eat, will ya?" Randy said. "We gotta go see your partner."

"Randy, I've been trying to tell you," I said. "He's not *really* my partner. I mean, he is, but it's because we have this arrangement. All his life, Leon has wanted to be a private investigator. His old boss fired him and talked me into taking his job. Don't even get me started on that. Let's just say it didn't work out very well."

"But you are still a private investigator," Randy said.

"I still have the license," I said. "But I don't do anything with it. Leon helped me out of a jam, so in return I agreed to be his partner. You know, just to have my name on the business cards."

"And in the phone book."

"Yeah," I said. "We're in the phone book. Like we're gonna get a lot of business up here."

"And on the Web site."

"Yeah, the Web site. I'm gonna have a little talk with him about that."

"I've got plenty of money, Alex," he said. "I plan on paying you for this."

"It's not the money, Randy. Are you listening to what I'm saying? I'm not really a private investigator. Two times now I've gone out trying to find somebody, and both times it ended up being a disaster. I'm not any good at it."

"You were always a good two-strike hitter, Alex."

I dropped the bag of ice and looked at him. "Say that again?"

"You were always a good two-strike hitter."

"Randy, we played a whole season together. Were you ever watching when I went up to the plate?"

"Of course."

"How many times did you see me go after a bad pitch with two strikes?"

"Offhand, I don't think I can remember you ever doing that."

"How about at least once a game, sometimes twice, sometimes three times. Hell, I remember doing it four times once. Swinging at a ball a foot outside and striking out. In fact, if you had to pick one reason why I never made it as a ballplayer, Randy, just *one* reason, that would be it."

It was all coming back to me, and after already taking one in the eye that day, it wasn't doing much for my mood. I was good behind the plate, I was *great* with the pitchers, especially the headcases like Randy, and I had a decent throw to second base. But I never batted over .240, mainly because I struck out swinging too much. It didn't take long for the pitchers to find out. If they got two strikes on me, I was dead.

I guess that says something about me. Two strikes and I'll try too hard to protect the plate. I'll swing at anything.

"Well, okay, then," Randy said after a long moment. "Here's your chance to make up for it."

"Seriously," I said. "We gotta talk about this."

"Hold that thought," he said. "I gotta hit the little boys' room before we go." He spun off the bar stool and started singing. "*L'amour, l'amour, oui,* ya da da . . .*"

"Where's Jackie?" I said. "I need more ice."

"How does it go?" Randy said, and then he started singing it again. "*L'amour, l'amour, oui, son* ah something . . . What's the next line?"

"I don't know."

"It's Romeo's song," he said. "From the opera, in French. It's beautiful."

"I don't know the words, Randy. Especially not in French."

"*L'amour, l'amour . . . Oui, son ardeur . . .* Is that it?"

"I don't know, Randy."

"You try to think of it while I'm in the bathroom, Alex."

When he disappeared into the bathroom, Jackie finally came over with the new bag of ice.

"What am I gonna do with him?" I said.

"What do you mean?" Jackie said.

"I mean, what am I gonna do? He really wants to find this girl he met in 1971. How crazy is that?"

"Doesn't matter," he said. "It's a moot point. You know you're gonna help him."

"Why do you say that?"

"Because you have to," he said. "You spend your whole life up here sitting in your cabin all by yourself. You don't even have a television, for God's sake. You're so desperate for human contact, you gotta come in here every day and make *my* life miserable. If a new face comes through that door and asks you for help, you're gonna do it, no matter what. I've seen it before, remember? In fact, you know what? One of these days, an alien spaceship is gonna land out there in the parking lot, and a couple of little green men are gonna come in here and ask you to help them. You know, take you back to their planet so you can help them ward off some other aliens who are trying to invade them or something. And of course you'll just get your ass kicked again, but it doesn't matter. Because *you'll go.* In two minutes, you'll be out that door and on that spaceship."

I just looked at him for a while, with the new bag of ice pressed against my eye. "That's quite a story, Jackie. Little green men, eh?"

"Yep. Right in that parking lot."

"And they'll come ask *me* for help. They'll speak English and everything."

"By the time they get here, yes. That's why they haven't landed yet. They're still studying you. They've already picked you out as the biggest sap on the planet Earth. Now they have to learn everything about you before they come get you. Hell, I bet they'll even have a case of Canadian beer in the spaceship waiting for you."

Randy came back out of the bathroom, still trying to sing his song. "What do you say, Alex. Are you ready to go?"

"Randy, you better take him quick," Jackie said. "While he's still available."

As he walked away laughing, I threw the bag of ice at the back of his head.

I followed Randy to the airport so he could turn in his rental car, and then he hopped in my truck for the ride over to Leon's house.

He was quiet for a few minutes, looking out the window at the passing trees. "There's not a whole lot up here, is there," he finally said.

"Besides trees?" I said. "No, there isn't."

"It's kinda nice," he said. "Big change from L.A."

"I imagine."

"Hey, we're headed for Sault Ste. Marie, right?"

"Yeah, Leon lives in a little town called Rosedale, just south of the Soo."

"I've never seen the Soo locks before," he said. "I think we should go up there first, while there's still daylight. Then we can go see Leon."

"What? I thought you said Leon was waiting for us."

"He's not going anywhere," he said. "Come on, you gotta show me the world-famous Soo locks. When am I ever gonna see them again?"

"Randy, the locks aren't even open yet. Not for another week."

"There's another reason why I don't want to see your partner yet," he said. "I sort of have to tell you a little bit more about Maria first."

"Why? What are you talking about?"

"It's just . . . some stuff," he said. "I want to tell you this myself, so you don't get the wrong idea."

29

"Just tell me."

"Take me to the locks, Alex. Some things you can't talk about unless you're looking at water."

I shook my head and kept driving. "Why is this happening to me?" I said. "What did I do to deserve this?"

Twenty minutes later, the truck was parked in front of the Soo Locks Park. In the summer, the lot would be full, and the observation deck would have maybe forty people on it. On this overcast April afternoon, with a cold wind coming up off the bay and blowing right down the St. Marys River, we had the place to ourselves.

Randy stood on the observation deck, looking down at the locks. There were still great blocks of ice floating in the water. He was already shivering, with that poor excuse for a coat wrapped tightly around his body. But it was his own damned fault, so I didn't feel too bad for him.

"This is it, huh?" he said. "The ships come right through here, and then what, they get lowered in the middle here?"

"Lowered if they're going into Lake Huron," I said. "Or raised if they're going into Lake Superior. Twenty-one feet."

"How long does it take?"

"Ten minutes maybe."

"Must be an impressive sight."

"When you've got a seven-hundred-foot freighter coming through here, it's pretty impressive, yeah."

"It opens up next week, you say?"

"Randy, are you gonna tell me about Maria before you freeze to death?"

He moved up onto the concrete bleachers, where there was at least a little bit of shelter from the wind. "This is going to sound

30

a little crazy," he said as he sat down. "Damn, this feels cold on my ass."

"It's gonna sound crazy? How much more crazy can it get?"

"Well, here it is," he said. "Just let me tell you the whole story before you say anything, okay?"

"I'm all ears," I said.

"Okay." He took a deep breath. "In 1971, when I went up to Detroit, there were a few of us who got called up together. You remember Marvin Lane, the outfielder, and Chuck Seelbach, the other pitcher? A couple guys from double-A, too. Anyway, we were all new in town and kinda overwhelmed by everything, so we ended up spending time together, just hanging out in the afternoons, before the games. One day, we're having lunch at the Lindell AC. It was a nice September afternoon in the big city, you know, so we're just walking around down there in Corktown, feeling like hot shit 'cause we'll be going over to the stadium in a few hours for the night game. And we see this place, with this sign on the sidewalk. A big hand, with all these lines on it. MADAME VALESKA, SPIRITUAL READER. I guess she'd call herself a psychic nowadays. But back then, the sign said SPIRITUAL READER. It was one of those buildings with the stairways that go up the side. We all went up there, thinking we'd all get our fortunes told. See if we'd see any game time that night. You know, just as a gag. I tell ya, Alex, this place was wild. It had this incredible red wallpaper, and all these strange paintings on the walls. One was a guy hanging upside down, like on the tarot cards, and another was a skeleton in a black robe— you know, with the big blade thing he carries around to harvest souls. Anyway, Madame Valeska was sitting in the back room, with a crystal ball, I swear to God, and she read our fortunes

31

one by one. All five of us. I was the last guy. By the time I got in to see her, I was already in love. This girl, in the lobby, sitting at a little table. She had black hair. And these eyes that just . . . God, I know what this sounds like, Alex. I don't know how to make this sound any different. But when she looked at me, it was like everything just stopped. I couldn't even breathe. I finally asked her what her name was. She said it was Maria. And that's it. That's how I met her."

We both sat there for a long moment. The wind picked up and whistled through the deck. The cold air was making my eye hurt.

"So what did Madame Valeska say?" I said. "What was your fortune?"

He laughed. "I wasn't listening too well. Although I do remember, she said some things that were pretty amazing. She knew that I was about to have the biggest test of my life."

"You were there with a bunch of other young baseball players," I said. "Of course she's going to say that."

"No, there was more than that. She seemed to know stuff about how I was trying to prove to my father that I could be successful doing my own thing instead of going into business with him."

"A son trying to impress his father. Another amazing revelation."

"All right, Alex. I hear ya. It's not like I really believed in that stuff. It's certainly not why I went back the next day."

"Let me guess."

"I left Maria a little note. Just like a high school kid. I was only twenty, remember. She was nineteen."

"How many times did you see her?"

"Every day for ten days. Until I got shelled and then . . . um, sort of left the human race for a while."

"You had your fortune told every day for ten days?"

"No, just a few times," he said. "Madame Valeska would have killed me if she'd known about Maria. And her father. And God, her older brother. His name was Leopold. He saw us walking together downtown once, and he just about strangled me right there. Maria had to go over and talk to him, calm him down. She must have made him promise not to tell their parents. We always had to sneak around, you know, meet in different places. I saw her every day, even if it was only for a few minutes before a ball game."

"Did you have sex with her?"

"Alex, come on."

"Did you?"

"It was 1971. Everybody was having sex back then."

"I'll take that as a yes."

"Yes," he said. "We had sex. Although really it was only the one time. A couple other times, we sort of just—"

"All right," I said. "I don't need the details. Let's go."

"Where are we going?"

"To Leon's house," I said as I stood up. "He's waiting for us, isn't he?"

"Does that mean you're going to help me?"

"How can I not?" I said. "It's such a heartwarming story."

"I told ya," he said. "I know it doesn't sound good."

I led the way down the stairs. "Did you say that Leon has already been working on this for you?"

"Yeah," he said as he caught up to me. "Actually, I had already tried a couple of those person-locator services, but all I had was

33

an address from 1971. I don't even know her birthday. Leon's been looking at some stuff, says we'll probably have to do some legwork in Detroit. And in his condition . . ."

"What condition?"

"You know, from his accident. Are you telling me he's your partner and you don't even know about his accident?"

"No," I said.

"He fell off his roof. He was trying to get the ice out of his gutters or something. I tell ya, you guys are crazy living up here."

"Yeah, we're crazy," I said. "Come on, let's go see what he did to himself. And see if he's got any ideas about how to find your fortune-teller's daughter."

Chapter Four

Leon's wife answered the door. Her name is Eleanor, and the first thing you notice about Eleanor is how large she is. You can't help it. There was a time when Leon hated me, back when he believed in his heart that I had cost him his job as a private investigator. In those days, I was honestly more afraid of Eleanor than of Leon. They're both bigger than I am, but something about Eleanor always made me think she'd move a lot faster than her husband.

Since then, I've gotten to know Eleanor a little bit, enough to know that she's a good woman, with a quick mind and a sense of humor. And a lot of patience about her husband's dream of being a practicing private eye. I'd still take her over Leon, though, if I needed some backup in a bar fight.

Randy kissed her hand when I introduced them. Another woman charmed right out of her socks.

"Don't mind him," I said.

"I don't mind him one bit, Alex," she said.

"What in hell happened to your husband?" I said. "Randy said he fell off the roof?"

She rolled her eyes and pointed behind her. There was an open door on the other side of the kitchen, and through it I could see Leon lying on the bed with both feet propped up on pillows. There were casts on both ankles. "Alex!" he called when he saw me. "Bring our client in here!"

The lights were off in the bedroom. There was a computer monitor set up on one side of the double bed, and Leon was bathed in the blue glow off the screen. It made his unruly red hair look downright frightening. He had a plaid flannel shirt on and gray sweatpants. The keyboard from the computer was in his lap.

"You must be Mr. Wilkins," he said, extending his right hand.

"Call me Randy." He shook Leon's hand.

"Leon," I said, "did you actually fall off the roof and break both your ankles?"

"I was trying to get the ice out of the gutters," he said. "Ellie's been carrying me around for the last week. Good thing I'm as light as a ballet dancer."

"Make that three ballet dancers," Eleanor said as she came into the room. "I should have just left him out in the snow." She was carrying a big wooden kitchen chair in each hand as casually as a pair of dinner plates. "You'll be wanting some chairs in here," she said, "seeing as how my husband isn't going anywhere."

When we were sitting on either side of the bed, he finished tapping something on the keyboard. From somewhere behind me, a printer sprang to life.

"Okay, then," he said. "I've put in a good twenty hours on the case, and here's what I've done so far."

"Twenty hours?" I said.

"Hey, what else am I gonna do?"

"I'm glad that you're keeping track," Randy said. "I'm going to be paying you both for your time."

"And getting your money's worth, I hope," Leon said. "You can count on our best efforts."

"Save the commercial," I said. "And speaking of which, remind me to ask you about that Web site...."

Leon moved his eyes over to Randy and kept them there. "As I said, here's what I've done so far. I know that you've already tried a couple of the locator services. For both Maria and her brother, Leopold. They can run the names through every database out there, but there just isn't enough information to go on. All we have are a couple names, an approximate year of birth for Maria at least—sometime in 1952, based on the fact that she was nineteen years old in 1971—and a very old address, where she worked with her mother and . . . you said they lived there, as well?"

"Yes," Randy said. "On the top floor."

"And you don't remember either of the parents' first names?"

"No, I don't," Randy said. "Her mother was just Mama to Maria and Madame Valeska to everybody else. I don't think I ever heard her father's first name."

"And it was just the one brother, you think? No other siblings?"

"Yes," Randy said. "She said her parents had a hard life before they came to America. They were already in their forties when they had Leopold and Maria. I think that's part of why they were so protective of her."

"And you don't know how old Leopold was in 1971?"

"I know he was older," Randy said. "But I have no idea how much."

"Those locator services," Leon said. "They usually need a date of birth, a Social Security number, or a recent address," Leon said. "Without any of those, they're not going to get very far. But then, you know that. That's why you're here."

"Absolutely," Randy said.

"The good news, right off the bat," he said, "is that she isn't dead. Not if she's in the Social Security system, anyway. There have been four women with that name who have died since 1971. All four of them were a lot older than she would have been."

"Okay," Randy said. "Okay, that's good."

"I didn't see a Leopold Valeska, either. For what that's worth."

"That's good, too," Randy said. "Even though he did hate me."

"She's not in prison, either. Not in a Michigan state prison, or a federal prison. Again, same thing for Leopold."

"Right."

"Our biggest problem," Leon went on, "is the amount of time that has passed since you last saw her. Obviously, a lot can happen in almost thirty years. A woman can get married. Leopold has the same last name, you would think, but Maria's name may be different now. She may have moved out of the area. How many people do you know who still live in the same neighborhood they did in 1971? What we have to do, in effect, is go back in time and try to trace her whereabouts from 1971 until the present. It's not going to be easy, but I think it can be done. The one thing we have going for us is her last name. If you were looking for Maria Smith, I wouldn't be optimistic. Maria Valeska is another story. That's gotta be what, some kind of Eastern European name? Yugoslavian maybe? Romanian?"

"I don't know for sure," Randy said. "I just know that both of her parents were born in Europe."

"You didn't even ask her where they came from?" I said. "Or were you too busy doing—how did you put it? What everybody else was doing in 1971?"

"I might have," he said. "I just don't remember."

"Alex," Leon said, "when the man is in this room, he's our client, okay?"

"Yeah," Randy said, "so treat me with some respect."

"What happened to your eye, anyway?" Leon said.

Before I could decide which one to strangle first, Randy told Leon to continue.

"I know those services must have already given you the numbers for every Maria Valeska listed in all the phone directories in the country right now. Just doing a quick search, I found five of them."

"Yeah, I think they gave me seven numbers," Randy said. "I called them all, but none of them was her."

"And Leopold..."

"They found two Leopold Valeskas," Randy said. "Neither was the right one."

"Life's not that easy," Leon said. "But the phone directories are still one way to go here. The name is still an important link. If we call every Valeska in the country, we might find another relative."

"Every single Valeska?" Randy said. "In the whole country?"

"Just counting the people who have listed numbers," Leon said, "I've found about three hundred of them. I did a search on the national directory. That's what's printing out right now."

"We have to call every one of them?"

"Well, exactly thirty-one of them live in Michigan, so I started there. I pretended to be a lawyer working on a class-action suit, told them I was looking for a Maria Valeska who lived in the Detroit area in 1971. I said she might be eligible to receive part of a large settlement."

"You couldn't just ask them up front?" Randy said.

"I could've, but you never know these days. People are suspicious. I didn't get anywhere. So we still have a good two hundred and seventy or so we can try. It's a lot of work. I think we should try to narrow it down first."

"How do we do that?"

"Well, a birth certificate would be nice, because then we'd have the parents' names at least. If they were immigrants like we think, there would be records. Problem is, birth certificates are very hard to get in Michigan. Most other states, all you gotta do is walk in the vital records office and ask for them. In Michigan, they're not *supposed* to give it to you unless you're one of the parents or a court officer. Although you never know. You're pretty sure she was born in Detroit?"

"She grew up in Detroit," Randy said. "I gotta think she was probably born there."

"They'd have it at the state office in Lansing. You could stop there on your way down. They'd also have it at the city clerk's office in Detroit. It's worth trying."

"We just go in the office and ask for her birth certificate?"

"I think you're gonna have to beg," Leon said, "and hope you get a clerk who's having a really good day."

"We'll just turn on the charm, right, Alex?"

I let that one go right out of the room.

"Once you get to Detroit," Leon said, "the first thing you have to do is go to that address on Leverette Street. The man who lives in that house right now is named—what was it?" He grabbed a pad of yellow legal paper off the bed and flipped through it. "Here it is. Henry Shannon."

"How did you find that out?" Randy said.

"The city directory," Leon said. "I called the Detroit Public

Library, asked them to look it up. That's the thing about librarians. Unlike most public servants, they actually *like* their jobs. So they're usually a lot more helpful. She gave me everything she could find on that whole block on Leverette Street. I'll give you a copy."

"So what about this Mr. Shannon? Did you call him yet?"

"I called him a few times," Leon said. "But he hasn't been home. I did try calling a couple other numbers on that block, but I didn't get very far with that. Somebody calling out of nowhere, asking about who might have lived on the block thirty years ago . . . it just doesn't work over the phone. That's the kind of thing you have to do in person. Go up to the door and let them see how nice a guy you are, tell them why you're there, what you're looking for."

"That'll work," Randy said. "We can do that."

"I did find out who owned that house in 1971," Leon said. "A man named Michael Kowalski. The librarian at the Business and Finance desk put me through to the Burton Historical Collection. They've got city directories going back to the 1920s."

"Wait a minute," Randy said. "That makes sense. They must have been renting the upstairs of that place. I remember . . ." He stopped for a long moment, looking into the past. "It's coming back to me now. She said her father was trying to save some money so they could buy a house. He loved America, but everything was so expensive. Food especially. Sausages. I remember that. He hated to pay a whole dollar for sausages."

"Write that down," I said. "Sausages."

"Needless to say," Leon said, ignoring me, "there are a lot of Kowalskis in Detroit. I tried all the Michaels, but no luck. I think your best bet is still going to be knocking on doors in that neighborhood. You're bound to find one person who's lived there a long time, or at least *bought* his house from somebody who lived there a long time."

"Sounds like a plan," Randy said. "This is going to be fun."

"And like I said, if you want to stop at the state office on the way down there, or maybe try the city office, you might get lucky on the birth certificate. Oh, and you've got to stop in at the library. Here's the name of the librarian I spoke to at the Burton Historical Collection. She said she'd try to think of some other ways we can trace Maria. Give her my regards when you see her. And buy her some flowers or something."

"You got it," Randy said. "Man, you really know what you're doing, Leon. I'm impressed."

"All part of the job," Leon said. "Just make sure you guys call me every day, let me know what's going on."

Randy pulled out a roll of bills. "Let me give you some money for what you've done so far," he said.

"You don't have to do that now," Leon said.

"I insist. You've already been working on this. You shouldn't have to wait. A couple hundred? Five hundred?" He started ripping off twenties and throwing them on the bed.

"Stop, already!" Leon said. But I knew he had earned that money. I wasn't going to stop Randy from greasing him.

"How about you, Alex?" Randy said.

"I haven't done anything," I said. "And if I go down there and help you, I'm going to do it for the hell of it, you understand? You're not paying me any money. If you were paying me, that would mean I'd have to take orders from you."

"I'm a great man to work for," he said. "Just ask my ex-wife."

I was saved by Leon's two kids in the doorway. Leon Junior

and Melissa, nine and eight years old, respectively. They stood there looking at Randy with big eyes, until finally Leon Junior said, "Were you really a major-league baseball player?"

"Sure was, kids," he said. "Come on in." A half hour later, we were all eating pizza around Leon's bed. Eleanor and the kids, Leon in the middle, spilling pizza sauce on himself, all listening to Randy tell his story again.

And me, not quite listening, wondering what the hell I was doing there, why I would be going downstate the next morning to help Randy find this woman, driving down like the northern wind, "the hunting wind," as the Ojibwa call it, hunting for the lost love of his life.

Jackie was right. I am the biggest sap on the planet.

It was dark by the time we left. If Randy was cold, he didn't show it. He was humming to himself all the way out to the truck.

"You guys really have casinos up here?" he said. "Real casinos?"

"The Indians do," I said. "The Sault tribe has the Kewadin here in town, and the Bay Mills tribe has a couple out on the reservation."

"What do you say we stop in for a little bit?"

"We've got to get up early tomorrow," I said.

"Come on, Alex. I'm feeling homesick here. I love driving across the desert to Vegas. I do it all the time."

"These casinos are nothing like Vegas," I said.

"One bet," he said. "One bet for luck."

One bet, my ass. Two hours later, he was still ruling the crowd at the craps table. I gave up and went over to the bar for a drink.

The bar they've got in the Kewadin looks as long as a football field. It's supposedly one of the longest in the country. To go with the long runway at our airport, I guess.

I sat there and nursed a scotch and water that was heavy on the water, wishing that the bar had a television so I could see if the Tigers were losing again. Three games into the season and they already had the look of also-rans.

But no. No televisions in there. Nothing to remind you that there was an outside world and it was almost midnight. Just table games and slot machines, and a lot more people than you'd expect on a cold April night.

Another hour passed. The crowd around Randy's table got bigger. I could hear them all the way over at the bar.

When he finally came over to me, he had a sheepish look on his face. I had a sudden flashback of seeing that look before. After all these years, even with the mustache and goatee he was sporting now, the look was the same. When he would shake off a sign and challenge a batter, if the batter ended up taking him out of the ballpark, I'd throw a new ball out to him while the batter rounded the bases, and Randy would have that look on his face. Most guys are mad at themselves then. Hell, *every* other pitcher who ever played the game is mad at himself then. But Randy would just look at me like the dog who'd crapped on the new carpeting.

"Sorry, partner," he said. "I got on a little roll there."

"How much did you win?" I said.

"I was up three thousand dollars," he said. "And then I gave it all back."

"Ouch."

"No problem, right? It's house money."

"Let's get out of here," I said.

He was quiet for a while, all the way down I-75 to M-28. When we got into the heavy pine trees, he started humming again. A few minutes later, he was laughing. "This is gonna be so great," he said. "It's like a big adventure."

"Randy, let me ask you something," I said. "Have you thought this through all the way to the end? Let's say you find out where she lives now. You go up to her door and knock on it. With what, flowers in your hand? She opens the door, and behind her you see her three kids, and her husband at the table, eating dinner. What are you gonna say?"

He looked out the window at a large doe that was standing beside the road. The white on her tail flashed in the headlights. "Hey, a deer," he said.

"Randy, what are you gonna say?"

"If she opens the door and I see three kids and a husband, I'm gonna say, 'Hello, remember me? I never got to give you these flowers at your wedding.' And then I'll ask her to introduce me to him, and to her kids."

"Okay," I said. "Good."

"But you know what?" he said.

"What."

"It's not gonna be like that. She's gonna be alone."

"How do you know that?"

"I just know it."

"Oh Randy. For God's sake."

"I'll bet you," he said. "That three grand I just lost. I'll bet you she's alone right now."

I shook my head. There was nothing else to say.

"You want to stop at Jackie's place for a nightcap?" he said.

"We gotta get up early," I said. "And I want to take this snowplow off before we go."

"Why do you leave it on so long?" he said. "When's the last time it snowed?"

"The day I take it off," I said. "It'll snow within twenty-four hours. Guaranteed."

"So leave it on."

"I'm not hauling a twelve-hundred-pound snowplow all the way to Detroit and back."

"So take it off."

We took the snowplow off. In the light from a single bulb outside my cabin, we took the snowplow off and left it sitting there in its springtime resting place behind the little utility shed, a block of wood holding the mount off the ground and a big plastic tarpaulin covering the whole thing.

By the time we got to bed, the snowflakes were already flying.

Chapter Five

The next morning, eight inches of new snow lay on the ground. After Randy got done rolling around in it, he helped me put the plow back on the truck, which only takes about forty times as much effort as taking the damned thing *off* the truck. You have to line it up just right, because technically I don't have the right kind of front mount to carry that plow. After an hour of monkeying around with it, we got the stupid thing on and plowed the road. Then we tore the stupid thing off again and put it back in its spot behind the shed. The sun was just coming up by then.

"Come on," I said when we were all done. "Let's get out of here before it starts snowing again."

"Don't you want some breakfast?"

"We'll grab some on the way," I said. "We got old flames to find, remember?"

We jumped in the truck and gunned it through Paradise. The sun shone on the new snow and blinded us. "Snow in April!" Randy said. "I love it!" And then he started singing again. *"L'amour, l'amour ... Oui, son ardeur ... Damn it, Alex, what is the next line to that song?"

"You just keep singing the one line you know," I said. "All the way down to Detroit. That'll make me very happy."

We made Mackinac by 9:30, rolled through a McDonalds, where we picked up breakfast and hot coffee. Then we settled in for the long haul on I-75, right down the middle of the Lower Peninsula. Ten minutes south of Mackinac, all the snow was gone.

"What did you say you're doing now?" I asked him. "Commercial real estate?"

"Yeah, you know, office buildings, retail space, that kind of stuff. My father started the business, did pretty well with it. I never thought I'd take it over, but when he died . . . I mean, I was already out of baseball."

"What do you do, build these places?"

"No, just make money off them," he said. "Buy and sell, talk on the phone, have lunch with the investors. That kind of thing."

"Sounds fascinating."

"It has its moments," he said. "Good and bad. Hey, I told ya about my youngest son, Terry, right? The catcher?"

"You mentioned him, yes."

"God, you should see him hit the ball, Alex."

"You mentioned that he's a good hitter."

"He drives that ball. Not bad behind the plate, but he's not a human sponge yet like you were."

"Uh-huh."

"That was you, Alex. The human sponge."

I rubbed the swelling over my right eye. Human sponge indeed.

"How long until we get to Lansing?" he said.

"Three hours maybe."

"God," he said. "Three hours." He laid his head on the back of the seat. Within five minutes, he was snoring. I kept driving.

"**Wake up,**" I said.

"What? What is it?"

"We're here," I said. "We're in Lansing."

"Lansing?"

"Yeah, the capital of Michigan," I said. "Didn't you learn your state capitals in school?"

He sat up and looked out the window. The truck was parked in a lot next to a complex of tall gray buildings. "Wow, we're here already?" he said. "I slept that whole time? You should have woken me up and made me drive some."

"It was the only peace and quiet I've had in two days," I said. "Come on, let's go."

We left the truck and went into the first building.

"Where are we going?"

I looked through the papers Leon had sent with us. "State Office of Vital Records," I said. We looked on the board by the elevator and found it. VITAL RECORDS, THIRD FLOOR. On the ride up the elevator, Randy started humming.

"Positive thoughts," he said. "Confidence. Charm."

"Thank you," I said.

"Make sure you mention that you're a private investigator. That should help, right?"

"I'm not telling anybody I'm a private investigator," I said.

"Well, then just look him right in the eye and smile. Or her."

It was a her. Maybe fifty years old, glasses on a chain around her neck. She looked like the attendance officer at a junior high school.

49

"Can I help you gentlemen?" she said.

"Yes, ma'am," I said. "I'm a private investigator. I'm looking for some information."

She looked at me.

"Here's my card," I said. I took out one of the cards Leon had given me, the cards with the two guns on them. I put it down on the counter in front of her.

She looked down at it, then back up at me. "What did you do to your eye?" she said.

"A little accident," I said.

"What kind of information?"

"There's a woman," I said. "We believe she was born in Detroit in 1952. Her name is Maria Valeska. Or was. It may have changed."

"Nice name," she said.

"Yes," I said. "We were wondering if we could see her birth certificate. It's extremely important."

"Birth certificates are not public records," she said. "Not in the state of Michigan."

"I understand that," I said. "I was hoping ..."

She kept looking at me.

"You see, it's very important. . . ."

Nothing. She was a statue.

"We really need to find her. . . ."

A statue carved in white granite. Wearing a blue cashmere sweater.

"I understand that marriage licenses are public," I finally said. "Could we try that?"

"Year of marriage," she said.

"I'm not quite sure of that," I said. I looked back at Randy.

"After 1971," he said.

"After 1971," I said.

"It costs seventeen dollars to do a search on a particular year," she said. "Four dollars for each additional year." She produced a form and put it on the counter. "Fill this out."

"Thank you," I said. I took the form and looked at it. The first line was for the name of the bride, the second for the name of the groom. "Do you need the groom's name?"

"Yes," she said. "We need the groom's name."

"We don't know the groom's name," I said. "We're not even sure she got married in Michigan. Or anywhere, for that matter. We were just hoping..."

She went into the statue routine again.

"Please," I said. "If you can't help us, just say so."

"I can't help you," she said.

So we left. I left my card there on the counter to torture her with guilt.

"You could have tried helping me," I said as we rode the elevator back down to the ground floor. "You could have thrown that famous Randy Wilkins charm into the situation."

"Wouldn't have worked," he said. "That woman was impervious to charm. You did good, though. You were smooth."

"I'm gonna smack you," I said.

He laughed. "Come on, I'll buy you lunch. We can celebrate our first total failure. Then it's on to Detroit!"

It was almost three o'clock in the afternoon when we made Detroit. The interstate goes straight into the middle of the city, then takes a big side step west, right behind Tiger Stadium, then remembers what it's supposed to be doing and turns back south toward Toledo. At least that's what it once did, before they

51

started tearing everything up to make room for the new stadium. With a big part of I-75 closed, we had to bail out at Gratiot and make our way down the side streets to Michigan Avenue. It was a strange feeling, driving around my old hometown. There's no traffic in the Upper Peninsula, no streets lined with buildings on either side for miles on end.

"One of the new casinos is gonna be over there," I said as we drove past First Street.

"Casinos in Detroit? Really?"

"The first one doesn't open until this summer," I said. "So relax."

"And a new stadium, too?"

"Next year," I said.

"It's like they're tearing up the whole city and starting over," he said.

"We might as well get a motel around Corktown," I said. "If that's where the old address is."

"Get someplace nice," he said.

"We're just gonna sleep there," I said. "We don't need the Hilton."

"Get the Hilton," he said. "I'm paying for it."

"Next stop, the Hilton," I said. As soon as the stadium was in sight, I pulled into the first motel I saw. The Motor City Motor Court.

"What is this supposed to be?" he said.

"The Detroit Hilton," I said. "Go check us in."

While he went inside, I stood in the parking lot, trying to shake out all the kinks in my body from the six hours in the truck. Across the street, a block away, the southeast corner of Tiger Stadium rose into the afternoon sky like a gray battleship. The Tigers were still losing ball games out on the West Coast,

52

would go to Minnesota to lose some more games there, then finally come back here to Detroit for their first loss at home.

"There she is," Randy said when he came back into the parking lot. "They're not really going to tear it down, are they?"

"I don't think they can," I said. "It's a national landmark. But they won't be playing baseball there anymore."

He shook his head. "Greatest ballpark I've ever seen."

"I know," I said. Tiger Stadium doesn't look like much from the outside. Just tall gray walls, rounded at the corners. When you go into the place, you realize why it *has* to look that way from the outside. Because the inside is a world of its own. It's totally enclosed, the only stadium in the majors with an upper deck that goes all the way around the field. With the overhang in right field, where Al Kaline played. The light towers on the roof, where Reggie Jackson hit that ball in the 1972 All-Star game. The broadcast booths in back of home plate, so close to the field that the guys up there can hear the catcher and umpire talking to each other. Eighty-one more home games, and then it would be all over.

"Come on," I said. "While we still have some of the day left. Show me where she lived."

We walked east on Michigan Avenue. There was a big car dealership across from the stadium, and then a little corner bar and a dry cleaner. We passed a block of little brick houses, where during the season the owners would sit outside on their lawn chairs, watching the people make their way toward the stadium. Some of them would make a little money by letting cars park in their driveways. With the new stadium opening up next season, that was about to end.

"Leverette Street," Randy said. "It's right up there. God, Alex, this feels kinda weird."

"I wonder why," I said.

"Lindell AC is one more block down, right? Whaddya say we go have a drink first?"

"We'll go there later," I said. "Show me the house."

We walked south on Leverette, right into the heart of old Corktown. It used to be a Polish neighborhood, and this street was probably the high end of the market back then. Most of the houses were two-story Victorians, and every single one of them looked restored and freshly painted. A sign on the corner read CORKTOWN, DETROIT'S OLDEST NEIGHBORHOOD.

"God, where's the house?" he said. "It was two forty-one. That much I remember. Here on the left side, in the middle of the block, close enough to Michigan Avenue that you could see the sign. . . ."

We passed a man mowing his lawn, which, from the size of the lawn, would take him about three minutes. There were thousands of blocks just like this one all through Detroit and into the suburbs. Just enough room for a house, a driveway, and maybe five hundred square feet of lawn in the front, another thousand square feet in the back. Just like the house I had grown up in over in Dearborn. Just like the house I had bought after I got married, over in Redford. If I had stayed down here, I'd still have the same kind of house.

Some kids were out playing catch. Another kid was riding a bike. This street happened to be mostly black now, the Polish immigrants long gone. We were the only two white faces on the block, but nobody seemed to notice. Randy walked slowly. He was trying to picture the place the way it had been almost thirty years before.

The house numbers progressed from 235 to 237 to 239. And then we stopped in front of 241. Randy stood there looking at the house. It was another Victorian, like every other house on the block. It was painted a rosy sort of pink, with green trim.

"This isn't it," he said.

"Excuse me?"

"This isn't the house. It can't be. There was an enclosed staircase on the right side, with a separate door."

"I thought you said this was the address," I said.

"It is," he said. "I mean, it was. Two forty-one Leverette. I'm sure it was."

A young black woman came out of the house next door, pushing a baby carriage. She didn't look much older than seventeen.

"Excuse me!" I said. "Is this Mr. Shannon's house?"

She just looked at us for moment. "Yeah," she finally said.

"Can I ask you a strange question?"

"How strange?" she said.

"Did this house once have a staircase on the outside of it?"

"What are you talking about?" she said.

We walked over to her. "I'm sorry to bother you," I said. "I'm a private investigator." I started to dig out one of my cards.

"Did somebody steal a staircase?" she said. "Is that what you're investigating?"

"No, no, ma'am. We're just looking for somebody who lived here about thirty years ago. We think there was a staircase on the outside of this house then."

"Don't know nothin' about that," she said.

"I understand," I said. "How about Mr. Shannon? We've been trying to contact him."

"He's gone to see his son in St. Louis," she said. "He's supposed to be back today, I think. Are you two really private investigators?"

"No, just him," Randy said. "I'm a normal citizen."

"Well, good luck finding your staircase," she said. There was a hint of a smile on her face as she pushed the carriage down the sidewalk.

I smacked Randy on the shoulder.

"Hey, come here, Alex," he said. "Look at this." He led me back to the front of Mr. Shannon's house. "You see how there's a little bit of extra space here on the right side? Between the house and the driveway?"

"You think they tore the staircase off?"

"They could have," he said. He walked down the driveway, took two steps up onto a small concrete front porch. He looked at the door, and then up at the window on the second story.

"This is it," he said. "This is the house. Maria lived right up there."

"Okay, good."

"I can't believe it, Alex. I'm standing right underneath her window again."

"All right, I hear ya," I said. "Now will you get off the man's porch before somebody calls the police?"

"So now what?" he said when he was back on the sidewalk. "You wanna start knocking on doors?"

"We could do that," I said. "Or we could see if Mr. Shannon gets home today, then cover the rest of the neighborhood tomorrow if we have to."

"What time is it, about four o'clock? Why don't we hit the city office, see if we can get lucky on her birth certificate. Maybe we'll get a human being this time."

"I wouldn't bet on it," I said. "But it's worth a shot."

"We could try the library, too," he said. "You know where that is?"

"I was a cop in this city for eight years, Randy."

"So lead the way," he said.

We walked back down the block, got in the truck, and headed east toward downtown. After turning onto Woodward Avenue, we were right in the middle of my old precinct.

Woodward Avenue. As I said it to myself, I felt something jump inside me. Woodward Avenue. It shouldn't have surprised me. It was just a gut reaction. Something I could never stop, no matter how hard I tried.

Woodward Avenue.

"You okay?" Randy said.

"Yeah," I said. "We're just heading down memory lane here. And here we are. City-County Building."

The building was down at the end of Woodward, right next to the waterfront. From where we stood, we could see the five towers of the Renaissance Center, the great metal fist of Joe Louis, the fountain in Hart Plaza. On a nice day, the sidewalks would be full of people walking up and down the river. Today, it was empty. We walked into the building, past the statue they called the *Spirit of Detroit*. Or as my old partner used to say, "the great big green guy holding the sun in one hand and the people in the other hand." When the Red Wings finally won the Stanley Cup in 1997, they put a giant jersey on him. My old partner would have gotten a kick out of that, if he had been alive to see it.

"Why don't you let me take a try this time?" Randy said.

"It's all yours," I said.

"Watch and learn, my friend."

As soon as we found the city clerk's office, I knew he had an unfair advantage. With the big windows letting in the late-afternoon sun and an assortment of Tigers and Red Wings posters all over the walls, this room was a hell of a lot nicer than the State Office of Vital Records. The young woman sitting at her desk looked almost happy to be working there. "Can I help you?" she said. She was smiling.

"Good afternoon," Randy said. "We finally made it! Do you know how long we traveled to get here?"

She smiled again. "What can I—"

"What are they doing to this city, anyway?" Randy said. "Every road is closed! Construction everywhere!"

"Tell me about it," she said. "It takes me over an hour to get to work in the morning now." This woman was much too friendly to be working as a public servant. How she ever got through the screening process was a complete mystery.

"Last time I was here in town was 1971," he said. "I was a pitcher with the Tigers."

"Really?" she said. Her eyes lit up.

"I didn't last very long in the majors," he said. "But at least I got the shot, right?"

"Are you serious? Did you really pitch for the Tigers?"

"Long time ago," he said. "So much has changed here. They got casinos coming in, too, isn't that right?"

"Ah," she said with a wave of her hand. "Don't get me started on the casinos. That's all we need."

"Not a gambler, I take it," he said. "Oh, I'm sorry. This is my friend Alex."

I woke up out of my trance. Watching the man do his routine was downright hypnotizing. "Good afternoon," I said.

"Alex was a Detroit police officer for—what did you say, eight years?"

"Yes," I said.

"Back in the eighties," he said. "Even Alex doesn't recognize the place anymore. Ain't that right, Alex?"

"Like a whole new city," I said.

"I'll tell you why we're here," Randy said. He moved closer to her desk and lowered his voice. "Alex is a private investigator now. Let me have one of your cards, Alex."

I took a card out and gave it to him. He put it down on her desk while he gave the room a quick once-over. "We're trying to locate someone," he said. "We're trying to help her, you understand. This could be a matter of life or death."

"Okay . . ."

"Her name is Maria Valeska," he said, letting it hang in the air, as if she were an international agent.

"That's a nice name," she said.

"Indeed," he said. "The problem is, the only information we have, besides her name, is an old address. And we think she was born here in Detroit in 1952."

"I don't understand," she said. "What kind of records are you looking for, then? We have only four kinds here. Birth, death, marriage, and divorce."

"The birth certificate would be extremely helpful," he said. "If we could possibly—"

"You can't see birth certificates," she said. "Not unless you're a parent or—"

"Or an officer of the court," Randy said. "I know that. I'm certainly not asking you to break the rules. But seeing as how this is such an *important* matter, I was hoping that maybe *you* could just take a look at her birth certificate, and tell us her date of birth."

"I don't know about that," she said.

"And her parents' names."

"Oh, no, I really don't think—"

59

"Teresa, I'm not asking you to get us a copy of her birth certificate. I wouldn't do that to you."

Teresa? How did he know her name?

"I'm just asking you," he said, "no, I'm begging you to just take a look at the record yourself, with neither of us around. We'll go stand out in the hallway while you look at it."

There, on her desk. A coffee mug with her name on it. Some detective I am.

"I'm kind of new here," she said. "I'm not sure if I'm allowed to do that."

"Maria Valeska," he said. "Probably born in 1952. In Detroit." And then he just looked at her. I couldn't see his face from where I was standing, so I'm not sure what he was doing, but somehow it made her stand up.

"I'll be right back," she said.

"We'll wait here," he said.

"You wait here," she said.

"Right here," he said.

And then she disappeared into the back room.

He turned around and winked at me. "What can I say, Alex?"

"You're the master," I said.

Randy's reign as the master lasted another ninety seconds. Then Teresa's supervisor came charging out of that back room, a woman who looked exactly like Alex Karras, the old Detroit Lions defensive lineman. Maybe Alex Karras on a bad hair day.

By the time she got done with Randy, I was already out the door.

It was almost five o'clock when we hit Woodward Avenue again. The rush-hour traffic was heavy, and it didn't help that half the roads were being torn up.

"Don't say a word, Alex."

"I'm not saying anything."

"We were close," he said. "We almost had it."

"Tackled at the one-yard line."

"You going to the library?" he said. "It's gotta still be open now, right?"

"We'll find out," I said.

We were driving north on Woodward. Woodward Avenue. The library was up by Kirby Street. I could feel my stomach tightening up. A few more blocks north and we'd be driving right by it. The building where it happened.

We drove by the new stadium, right across the street from the old Fox Theater. Comerica Park, they were gonna call it. Not quite the same ring as Tiger Stadium.

"There it is," he said. "Hell, you can see right into it."

"That's the way they build them these days," I said. "You're supposed to be able to see the city while you're watching a game."

"I don't get it," he said. "It's Detroit, for God's sake."

I let that one go. When we got to the library, it was obviously closed.

"How can a library be closed at five o'clock?" Randy said.

"Budget cuts," I said.

"Maybe when the casinos open up, the city will have more money," he said.

"That's right," I said. "Those casinos will be a godsend to the library."

He looked at me. "You all right?"

"It's been a long day," I said. "I could use a drink now, and some dinner. You still want to go to Lindell?"

"Let's go," he said. "Then maybe later you can show me around."

"Around where?" I said.

"Around Detroit," he said. "*Your* Detroit. This is your home-town, right? You gotta have a lot of memories here."

I drove south, back to the motel. I didn't say anything.

Memories, he says. You gotta have a lot of memories here. If he only knew.

Chapter Six

Its full name is the Lindell Athletic Club, but I've never heard anybody call it that. It's the Lindell AC. It used to be a few blocks east, over by the old Hudson's department store; then they moved it to the ground floor of an oddly triangular-shaped building on the corner of Cass and Michigan Avenue. If you didn't know better, you'd swear it had been there forever. The building itself looks like nobody's touched it since World War II, right down to the old metal awnings over the windows. Next door there's a barbershop where you can still get a shave with a straight razor and a splash of Royal Bay Rum.

As soon as you step into the Lindell, you see fifty years' worth of photographs and memorabilia all over the place. Right above the door, there's a huge black-and-white photograph of an old-fashioned hockey brawl, back when everybody could come off the bench to join in. The caption read "Detroit vs. Toronto, 1938." A lot of sports bars try to look like the Lindell AC, but they don't pull it off. You can't just open up a bar and try to stick all the sports crap you can find all over the place. It has to evolve naturally over time. A bat one week, a ball the next. The next week a jockstrap. Two thousand weeks later, you've got the Lindell AC.

We sat in a booth in the corner, right under the picture of Mickey Stanley going over the left-field wall. We ate our world-famous grilled hamburgers while the sun went down outside. I didn't say much. Randy was too busy soaking up the place to notice.

"God, this place hasn't changed at all," he said. "There's Johnny Butsakaris over there behind the bar. Think he remembers me?"

"You were here a couple times almost thirty years ago," I said. "You really think he's going to remember you?"

"You're right," he said, rubbing his mustache and goatee. "Not with this stuff on my face."

"I'm gonna go see if Mr. Shannon is home yet," I said. I had his number circled on one of the sheets of paper Leon had given us.

"You're gonna call him?"

"No. I'm gonna go walk back to his house," I said.

"Somebody's a little grouchy," he said. "I'll get you another beer. Then we're gonna go out and you're gonna show me around, right? You promised."

"I didn't promise that, Randy."

"I want to see where you grew up, Alex. I want to see the parking lot where you lost your virginity."

"I'm gonna go call him now," I said.

"Go," he said. "Go do your thing."

I went to the pay phone and called the number. I heard two rings and then a rough voice saying hello.

"Mr. Shannon?" I said.

"Speaking."

"My name is Alex McKnight. I'm a private investigator. I've got a question for you, and it's going to sound a little strange."

"A private who? What's this about?"

"Mr. Shannon, I'm trying to find somebody who lived at your address in 1971. I don't suppose you know who owned your house back then."

"Nineteen seventy-one? Are you serious?"

"Yes, sir. I'm sorry to disturb you this evening. The family's name was Valeska."

"No, no, stop. Nineteen seventy-one, I was nowhere near here. I've only been in this house a couple years."

"Perhaps the person you bought the house from?"

"No, he only had the place for . . . a year, I think. And before he had it, I remember him telling me, the place was sitting empty here for a long time. . . ."

"I understand, sir. Can I ask if you're aware of an old staircase that used to run up the right side of your house?"

"Matter of fact, yeah. It looks like there used to be something like that. They redid the whole place, knocked the back wall out. Looks like they put in a new staircase when they did that."

"That makes sense," I said. "That's kinda what we figured."

"If you know about that old staircase," he said, "then I guess you really *are* looking for somebody from that long ago. You're really a private investigator?"

"Yes, sir, I am. If I can ask you just one more question . . ."

"Ask away."

"Is there anyone on your block who may have been living there back in 1971?"

"I wouldn't think so. It's changed a lot around here."

"Well, okay, then. I really appreciate your time."

"I wouldn't swear to that. You could ask around."

"Perhaps I will, sir."

"Stop by the house if you do. I've never met a private investigator before. I'm here after three o'clock most days."

"We'll do that, sir. And thanks again." I hung up the phone.

When I got back to the booth, something had changed. That smooth little look Randy always wore, like he was ready to be amused by something, was long gone. His eyes were wide open.

"What happened?" I said.

"I got us another round," he said, sliding a draft my way. "No problem."

"There's a problem," I said. "What is it?"

"There's no problem."

"You're lying," I said. "I told you, you can't lie to me. You're the world's worst liar."

"I got into a little disagreement, that's all."

I looked around the place. There were a couple of young men seated at the bar, watching us. White boys from the suburbs, slumming it in the Motor City.

"With those guys over there, I take it?" They didn't look too happy. They didn't look too small, either.

"A couple local gentlemen with some misinformed opinions," he said. "They were talking about how badly the Tigers sucked, which is pretty much true this year, so I couldn't disagree with them. But then they started going on about how it didn't matter, because baseball wasn't a real sport and anybody could play it."

"Let me guess," I said. "You tried to straighten them out."

"I just asked them when was the last time somebody threw a baseball ninety-five miles an hour at them. That's all I said. Then I just paid for our drinks."

"I meant to tell you," I said. "Detroit's not the best place to be flashing a big roll of bills."

"They asked me about the tattoo on my arm. I told them my

66

cellmate gave it to me, the last time I was in prison. He also taught me how to kill a man using just my index finger." He pointed to the ceiling with the finger in question, on his left hand, of course, and then brought it down on the table like he meant to break it in two. Somehow, the table stayed intact.

"That's quite a story," I said. "I bet that put them in their place."

"I think it was the slinky that really got them going," he said, shaking his hand. Then he took a hit off a tall glass. Whatever he was drinking, it was brown and foamy.

"You told them about your old pitch?" I said.

"No, it's a drink I invented," he said. "I can't throw them anymore, so I have to drink them now."

"I'm probably going to regret asking this, but what's in it?"

"It's pretty simple," he said. "One part vodka and one part root beer. You wanna try it?"

"I'm gonna say no to that."

"Go ahead," he said. "You'll be surprised."

"No, Randy, nothing would surprise me now. I'll probably never be surprised again in my entire life."

"You know what this drink is good for?" he said.

"Killing rats?"

"You see a really nice-looking woman at the bar, you go up and stand next to her and order a slinky. It never fails."

I didn't say anything.

"The bartender doesn't know what it is, so I have to tell him how to make it. The best vodka you got, preferably Charodei, which isn't filtered through charcoal like other vodkas. And she's standing there listening to this. Vodka and root beer? What kind of a man drinks vodka and root beer? She turns around to take a look at me, and I just give her this smile. Like I'm drinking

67

the best vodka in the house because I'm sophisticated and successful, and I'm drinking root beer because I'm still a little boy at heart. And when she asks me why it's called a slinky, I tell her I was once a major-league pitcher and that was my money pitch. It works every time."

"Uh-huh. Are you gonna try the same game when you find Maria? Order up a slinky?"

"Come on, Alex, I'm just joking around. I drink it because I like the way it tastes. Here, try it."

"I told you, I'm not drinking that," I said. "Vodka and root beer, for God's sake. What next, Randy? Are you crazy *all the time*? Do you ever take a day off?"

"You would have backed me up, right? If those guys tried something? Just like the good old days. Remember that brawl we were in that one game? Where was that, Evansville?"

"It was Savannah," I said. It all came back to me. There was another side to Randy Wilkins. You didn't see it very often. It took a lot to get him to lose control of himself. But when he did, he lost it completely. "You hit two straight batters in the head. What did you expect?"

He took a long drink and then put the glass down. "I think I know what your problem is," he said. His voice had changed.

"What?" I said. "What's my problem?"

"The problem is that I got a shot and you didn't. And it doesn't help that I got to play right here in Tiger Stadium. How many times did you go and see games there when you were a kid? How many times did you dream about playing on that field someday?"

"Randy, do you really think that I'm upset because you got to play in Tiger Stadium and I didn't?"

"It's got to bother you," he said. "*Something's* bothering you."

"Let's go," I said, standing up.

"Where are we going?"

"You wanna see the sights?" I said. "You wanna see where I grew up and where everything else happened in my whole life? Fine, I'm gonna show you."

I got up. As I walked out of the place, I heard Randy saying something to the boys at the bar, something cute about how they could go ahead and jump him now that I was leaving. I stood outside on Michigan Avenue, breathing in the night air. A spring night in Detroit, cold but not painful. I waited twenty seconds and then headed back inside, figuring I was going to get that bar fight whether I wanted it or not. But Randy came popping out the door and almost ran me over. He was alone and without a mark on him. Either he had talked his way out of another one or he'd killed both men with his index finger. For once, I didn't care. This whole escapade was starting to feel like a mistake. I looked at him for a long moment without saying anything, and then I started walking down Michigan Avenue. He fell in beside me, matching my silence with his own.

We walked past Leverette Street, the street where Randy'd had his fortune told in 1971 and met Maria and fell in love with her. Or whatever the hell had happened. Mr. Shannon, the man I had just spoken to on the phone, was probably sitting in his living room at that very moment, half a block down, watching the Tigers on television. Randy looked down the street but did not break stride. He did not say anything.

The stadium loomed above us. It was dark except for a blue neon sign at the very top. DETROIT TIGERS in blue letters. Tiger blue. And a sign that glowed white, with black letters that read HOME OPENER, APRIL 19 CLEVELAND INDIANS.

When we hit the motel parking lot, I opened up the door on

my side of the truck, leaned over, and unlocked the other door. Randy got in. I pulled out of the lot, took a right and then a U-turn to go west. Because long ago somebody had decided that you don't take left turns on major roads in the greater Detroit area. Thirty-four years, I'd lived down here, and probably one full year of that was making rights and U-turns to go left.

I took Michigan Avenue west all the way out of Detroit, past Roosevelt Park to Dearborn. I switched over to Ford Road, drove past River Rouge Park and the Dearborn Country Club. All the way to Telegraph Road, where I had to take another right and a U-turn instead of going left. I found the old street, took a left, an honest-to-God left this time, because I was leaving the main road, went down two and a half blocks. I pulled the truck over and stopped.

Brick houses. Just like the neighborhood back in Detroit. Maybe a little nicer. The lawns were watered a little bit better. The backyards were a little bigger. But the same idea. Brick houses in a row, with just enough room between them to drive your car into the detached garage.

"This is where I grew up," I said.

Randy looked out the window. "This house here?"

"Yes."

"Looks like a nice house."

"It's a nice house," I said. "When I was seven years old, my mother got pancreatic cancer. She lasted a year and a half."

He didn't say anything. He kept looking at the house.

"You think a seven-year-old kid even knows what pancreatic cancer is? Or what a pancreas is? Where you even find a pancreas in your body?"

He didn't say anything.

"All I knew was that my mother kept losing weight and getting sicker and sicker and there was nothing I could do about it."

"I'm sorry," he said.

"My father worked for Ford Motors," I said. "Most people did back then. He got up every morning at five o'clock and took care of her and made me breakfast and got me off to school. We could actually walk to school back then. When school was over, I walked home. I would be alone with my mother for a couple hours. Just sitting with her. Watching her die a little bit more every day. And then my father would come home and make dinner. I never went to one baseball game the whole time she was sick, you know that? I never *played* baseball when she was sick. Not once. A couple months after she died, my father finally got all my baseball stuff out of the garage. I had outgrown my glove. He had to buy me a new one."

A car came down the street. For an instant we were blinded by the headlights. Then it was dark again.

"When I was in high school, my father bought the land up in Paradise. I remember wondering what the hell he was doing spending all that money for a piece of land six hours away, way up there in the middle of nowhere. He took me up there, and there was nothing but pine trees. Nothing. I finally asked him why he had bought that land. You know what he said? He said he bought it because my mother had always loved the smell of Christmas trees."

I pulled away from the curb, made my way back to Telegraph Road. I could see Randy's face in the light from the streetlamps. He was staring straight ahead.

"I assume you don't need to see where I went to school," I said. "Or the field where I hit my first home run. When I graduated, I went right to the minors, but you know that. That season in Toledo was as close as I ever got to making the big leagues. I was disappointed that I didn't get a call-up in September. I was envious of you, I'll admit that. But I got over it. As a matter of fact, I think I got off pretty easy. The next year, when they traded me to the Pirates and I spent that season in Columbus, I knew I was done. At the end of that season, I knew it was time to get on with my life. How many more years did you spend chasing that dream?"

He didn't answer. He didn't have to. I knew that he spent six more years bouncing around between double-A and triple-A, riding the same broken-down buses and sleeping in the same lousy motel rooms. The Tigers gave up on him, but then the Athletics picked him up, and then the Dodgers, and then the White Sox.

I was a catcher who knew how to handle pitchers but couldn't hit .240, so my destiny was clear. But Randy had the one unforgivable talent. He had a live left arm, and when he was throwing well, he could kill left-handed batters. There would always be another team waiting to give him a chance.

I drove north on Telegraph, all the way up to the edge of Wayne County. I did another right and U-turn to go west on Seven Mile Road. Another side street. Another row of brick houses. This neighborhood was somewhere in the middle of the scale between Detroit and Dearborn.

"Here's where I lived when I was married," I said. "My wife's name was Jean. You know, I can't even remember the last time I said her name out loud. The day we got married, I promised her I'd spend every day with her for the rest of my life. Now I couldn't even tell you what state she lives in."

"I've been married, Alex." It was the first time he had spoken in the last hour. "I know what it's like to be married."

"Okay," I said. "That one you know." I looked out at the window at the house. There was a light on in the living room. There was a family in there, watching television. Maybe one kid was doing homework. Another kid already in bed. They didn't know we were out here, looking at the house. They didn't know that this was once *my* house.

"We lived in that house for nine years," I said. "I was a police officer in Detroit for most of that time. We were going to have kids, and I was going to take them up to Paradise in the summers, show them the cabins that their grandfather was building."

"So what happened?"

"She was pregnant once," I said. "She had a miscarriage. I was on duty at the time. A night shift. She drove to the hospital herself. She could have called me. I would have come and gotten her in the squad car. But she didn't. She drove there by herself, bleeding the whole way."

"It wasn't your fault," he said.

"I know that," I said. "Just like my mother dying, right? It wasn't my fault."

"Yes, Alex. That wasn't your fault, either."

"Okay," I said. I pulled away from the curb again, made my way back down Seven Mile Road to Telegraph.

"This is the way I'd drive to work," I said. "In the morning or at night, whenever." This time, I got onto I-96, which runs southeast all the way into Detroit. "I was a cop in Detroit for eight years," I said. "I had a partner named Franklin. Big black guy, played football at the University of Michigan. We used to argue about sports all the time—you know, which sport was harder to play."

"Gotta be baseball," Randy said.

"Oddly enough, Franklin didn't agree with that. Go figure.

Anyway, one night we answered a call at the Emergency Room at Detroit Receiving Hospital. There was this . . . disturbed man there. He was bothering people, hiding behind things. Harassing the doctors and the nurses. He was wearing this big blond wig. One of the security guards at the hospital followed him back to his apartment."

"And?" Randy said.

"I forgot this stretch of I-75 is going to be closed up here," I said. "This is the way I'd go to get to the precinct. I'm going to have to get off, get back onto Michigan Avenue again."

"So what happened?"

"I'll be able to show you the precinct this way."

"You're not going to tell me what happened."

"You see a lot of things when you're a cop for eight years in this city," I said. "I saw women who had been murdered by their husbands. Or their boyfriends. Or whoever. I saw a lot of prostitutes. Some of them, God, they couldn't have been more than fourteen years old. A lot of drug dealers. Some of them were even younger."

Randy settled back into his seat. He let out a long breath.

"I saw kids who had been abused by their parents," I said. "Or by their mother's boyfriend. Or by their older brothers. Or hell, the worst one of all, by their older *sister*. This little baby, he was only four months old. . . ."

"Okay, Alex," he said. "You don't have to tell me all this."

"You came up here for one month, Randy. You got to put on a major-league uniform and pitch in Tiger Stadium. You had your fortune told by Madame Valeska and then her beautiful daughter fucked you so hard you're still thinking about it thirty years later."

He didn't say anything.

"To you, Detroit is like this dream you once had. It's Disney World and Fantasy Island all rolled into one."

"Okay, Alex. I get it."

"I don't think you do," I said.

"Yes," he said. "I totally get it. Detroit is a horrible, shitty place. With drugs and crimes and murders and the most god-awful boring little brick houses I've ever seen. Okay? I get it."

I let that one hang in the air for a while. I drove down Michigan Avenue, past the ghostly ruins of the old train station. As tall as a hotel, it stood out against the night sky, blacker than the darkness itself.

"Randy," I said. "The next time you say stuff like that about Detroit, I'm gonna punch you right in the face. I'm serious."

He looked at me. "Are you not giving me the grand tour of all the reasons why I should think Detroit is a bad, bad place?"

"No," I said. "No."

"Then why are you doing this?"

I kept driving, straight toward the lights of downtown.

"I don't know," I finally said. "I need to do this. I need to show this to you. All of it."

"Okay," he said. "I'm with ya. Hell, maybe you need to show it to *yourself*. Go back over your whole life. You ever think of that?"

"Thank you, Dr. Freud."

"I'm serious, Alex. Have you been back here since you got shot?"

I drove past Tiger Stadium and our little motel and the Lindell AC, where this whole evening had started.

"Where did it happen?" he said. "Is that where we're going?"

"The man at that hospital," I said. "He lived up here on Woodward. We went to see him. We went to tell him to stop bothering people at the hospital. That's all we wanted to do."

I drove north on Woodward, past the City-County Building, where we had been that afternoon, straight toward the corner of Woodward and Seward.

"He shot us," I said. "He shot Franklin first. Then me. I watched Franklin bleed to death on the floor next to me."

We drove through Grand Circus Park, empty on a cold April night.

"I should have drawn my weapon sooner," I said. "I didn't do it in time."

We stopped for a red light at Adams Street.

"They took two bullets out of me, but they had to leave the third one," I said. "Franklin had a wife and two little girls. I didn't go to the funeral. I was in the hospital. When I got out . . ."

The light turned green. I didn't move.

"I drank a lot. Jean divorced me. I took disability, moved up to my father's cabins in Paradise. It took me fourteen years to be able to sleep at night without taking pills."

From behind us, a horn blew.

"I finally saw the man who shot us," I said. "In prison. I finally saw him face-to-face."

The horn blew again. I took my foot off the brake, touched the accelerator.

"This is the first time I've seen the building. Where it happened. This is where it happened."

Grand Boulevard. We were a few blocks away. I held on tight to the steering wheel.

"I could have drawn my weapon, Randy. I could have shot him before he shot us. It was my fault that Franklin died."

We came to Seward Street. I stopped in the middle of the intersection. The same horn blew behind us again. But I didn't care.

Where the apartment building had once stood, there was now only a construction fence. The ground inside the fence was covered with straw.

"It's gone," I said. "The building is fucking gone. They tore it down."

We were two blocks away from where they were building the new stadium. This whole corner had been mowed down. The whole block. Half the city, it seemed. Torn down to make way for a new stadium and casinos and God knows what else.

The horn kept blowing behind me.

"Can we get out of here before we get killed?" Randy said.

I drove through the intersection, hung a left on Euclid and another on Cass, back to Michigan Avenue. Back to our motel and the Lindell AC. We'd sit right at the bar this time. If those two men were still there, Randy would buy them drinks. If we were lucky, we'd catch Johnny Butsakaris's eye and call him over, and I'd get to hear Randy's story again.

"Alex," he said, "I'm sorry about what I said."

"Don't worry about it."

"I'm sorry I lied to you in the bar. I'll never do it again."

"Okay."

"I'm sorry you couldn't hit a curveball."

"Randy," I said. "I've got a question for you."

"Ask away, my friend."

"Was that really vodka and root beer in that glass?"

"It was indeed. The slinky."

"You really are crazy, you know that? I mean, I've said it a million times, but you really are crazy."

"Of course I'm crazy," he said. "Why else would I be here?"

Chapter Seven

We didn't get up quite as early as we had planned the next morning. But then we hadn't planned on staying so late at the Lindell AC. My head was throbbing when I got up, and it didn't look like Randy was feeling any better. The one thing I had going for me was the fact that I had refused to try his stupid slinky. So at least I wouldn't be tasting vodka and root beer all day.

And whatever had happened between us the previous night, that was done and gone. Like when you have a rough game one night and you forget all about it before the game on the very next day.

After a couple hot showers and some aspirin, we were new men. We headed out into another Michigan April day, with gray clouds and a cold wind whipping down Michigan Avenue. We went east to Woodward, then north toward the library. We stopped at a flower shop and Randy went in to pick out something nice for the lady at the library who had been so helpful to Leon. Randy came back out with enough flowers for a wedding reception.

"First-class all the way," he said. I just shook my head and kept driving. A few blocks later, we parked in front of the Detroit Public Library. It was a massive building of stone, the same shade of gray as the sky. When we walked into the main lobby and asked about the Burton Historical Collection, we were sent to the opposite side of the building, where the doors opened onto Cass Avenue, on either side of a huge globe. We took a right and found the room. The collection itself, mostly reference material from an entire century, was stored in bookshelves both here on the ground floor and above, on a balcony that ran along three of the walls. The fourth wall was all windows. Across the street, we could see the Detroit Institute of the Arts. There were flags advertising a van Gogh exhibit. Somewhere in the back of my mind, I remembered reading that van Gogh was left-handed. Another crazy southpaw.

We found the librarian who had worked with Leon over the phone. She was a trim black woman in her fifties, with the eyeglasses and the hair in the bun that all librarians are required to have. But there was a sparkle in her eye that said something a little different. Randy buried the poor woman in the flowers before I could even tell her who we were.

When she had jungle-chopped her way out of the flowers, I introduced ourselves and gave her Leon's warmest regards.

"Such a nice gentleman he was," she said. "I'm sorry I couldn't have been more helpful."

"Nonsense," I said. "You gave him a lot of information."

"Yes, but I promised I'd keep thinking about it," she said. "I took it as rather a personal challenge. Finding someone you haven't seen in thirty years. And with such a rare last name like Valeska, I was sure I'd be able to find something. I'm afraid the only other option I have left is to go through the old newspapers to find a birth announcement. As Mr. Prudell and I were discussing, if we had the parents' names we'd have a good chance of finding some immigration records."

"We tried to find her birth certificate," Randy said.

She laughed at that one. "Not in this state," she said. "You wasted your time."

A few minutes later, we were both sitting in the microfilm room, looking through all of the birth announcements from September 1951 to October 1952. If she was nineteen in September of 1971, we figured her birth would have to be in there somewhere. I took the *Detroit News* and Randy took the *Detroit Free Press*.

A couple hours later, we both emerged, blinking like mole rats, into the light of day. We had found nothing.

We went back to the desk to thank the woman. She had found half a dozen vases from somewhere and was busy subdividing Randy's flowers.

"I'll keep thinking about it, boys," she said. "A good reference librarian doesn't sleep until she finds what she's looking for."

On our way out to lunch, I gave Leon a call. I didn't have much to tell him, but I was sure he was sitting there in the Upper Peninsula, wondering what we were doing.

"Mr. Shannon hasn't lived in the house for long," I told him. "And he didn't have any leads going back more than a couple years. We're going to go try the rest of the neighborhood after lunch."

"You guys must be having a great time," he said. "Working the leads, trying to pick up a trail that's thirty years old. God, I wish I was down there with you."

"It's a thrill a minute," I said. "We just got done looking at a year's worth of old newspapers, and now we get to go knock on strangers' doors and ask them if they remember a fortune-teller and her family from 1971."

"That's what a private investigator does, Alex. He digs in the dirt until he finds the bone."

"That's beautiful, Leon. I'm gonna write that down."

"Go get it, partner," he said. "Go find that bone."

With those inspirational words ringing in my ears, I was ready to face the rest of the day. "Come on, Randy," I said. "Let's go get dirty."

We grabbed a quick lunch at a little restaurant down the street, then headed back to Leverette Street, parking the truck against the curb, right in the middle of the block. "How do you wanna do this?" I said. "You wanna split up or stay together?"

"Let's split up," he said. "I want this side." He pointed out at the side where Maria had lived. "For old time's sake."

"Good enough," I said. "Don't bother hitting that house next door."

"That lady who thought you were trying to solve the case of the missing staircase? I thought she was great."

"Fine," I said. "You go have tea with her. I'm gonna go do this and try not to think about how stupid I sound. If somebody asked me if I remembered a fortune-teller who used to live across the street thirty years ago, I'd slam the door in his face."

"Alex, you live in a cabin in the middle of the woods."

"You do this on purpose, don't you?" I said. "Just go."

I went down to the end of the block and knocked on the first door. A black teenager answered. He had headphones on. I started talking. When I got to the first question, he just stood there looking at me. Then he took the headphones off. I started at the beginning again.

"I'm looking for someone who used to live on this block in 1971," I said. "I know you weren't even born yet, but is there anyone else living here who might have been around then?"

"We just moved here," he said. "Last year."

"Are your parents around? Can I ask them if they remember who lived here before you?"

"Nobody else here," he said. "They all gone until Monday."

"Okay," I said. "Can I leave a card?"

"Sure," he said. He took the card from me and looked at it. "You're a private investigator, it says?"

"Sort of," I said.

"Do you carry a gun?"

"No."

"You've got two guns here on the card."

"That wasn't my idea," I said. "Look, I'll let you get ready for the party. I appreciate your time."

"Party?" he said. "What party?"

"You said your family's gone until Monday. A teenager alone in the house, I figure the party's gotta start at sundown, right?"

"Oh man," he said. "Is *that* what this is about? My mom's sending around a private investigator to see if I'm having a party when she's gone?"

"No," I said. "Please. I'm just looking for somebody. I swear."

By the time I left there, he still wasn't convinced. Which would probably ruin his party, because he'd be expecting me to spy on the place. So having spoiled one person's day, I went on to the next house.

This time, I got an older black man, and felt better about my chances. He certainly looked old enough to have been around in 1971. But it turned out he had just moved there in 1994. And he didn't remember who had lived there before him. I thanked him and moved on, and by the time I got done with the next house, I was beginning to see a trend. Everybody was new to the neighborhood. Within the last ten years at least. Nobody had any ties to the place before 1990.

When I got through my entire side of the block, I walked back to the truck and waited for Randy. He took a lot longer to do his side, because of course he's gotta stand there and talk about the weather and the tattoo on his arm and the Detroit Tigers, and for all I knew, he'd tell every last person the story of his one inning in Tiger Stadium.

I looked up and down his side of the block, but I couldn't see him. He's probably inside one of the houses, I thought, having a cold beer with somebody. I could have gone and found him, and helped him finish up his houses. But my eyes were still hurting from looking at all the microfilm. I sat in the truck and waited for him. And eventually, I started to doze off. He scared the hell out of me when he came back and knocked on my window.

"What the hell took you so long?" I said when he got in. "You didn't have to get everybody's life stories."

"We got talking," he said. "There's a lot of nice people in this neighborhood."

"Did you find out anything?"

"About Maria, you mean?"

"Randy, don't make me hurt you."

"No, Alex. I didn't find out anything. Nobody's been around here for very long. How about you?"

"Same story," I said. "Although I did prevent a teenager from having a party and trashing his house."

"I didn't stop at Maria's old house. You know, Mr. Shannon's place. And there was one house a couple doors down where nobody was home...."

"Mr. Shannon wanted us to stop and say hello," I said. I looked at my watch. "He said he'd be home after three. You wanna go see him now?"

"Sure," he said. "We'll see if we can go upstairs. I'll show you where it all happened."

"Somehow, I don't think it looks quite the same now," I said.

"Yeah, but I bet you'll *feel* it. You know, the raw power in the place. I bet Mr. Shannon feels it all the time. He's walking around up there, you know, maybe putting all his laundry into his basket or something, and he stops in the middle of the room, and he says to himself, 'Damn, I always get the strangest feeling in this room. Like something wonderful and amazing happened here once.'"

"I'll let you ask him about that one," I said. "Come on, let's go."

As we got out, a car passed us on the street and turned into a driveway.

"Hey, that's the house where nobody was home," Randy said.

The car stopped in the middle of the driveway. A man got out of the car and slammed the door.

"He doesn't look like he's in the mood to talk right now," I said. But Randy was already jogging down the sidewalk toward him.

"Excuse me, sir!" he yelled to the man.

The man was on his front porch when he turned around to look at us. He didn't say anything.

"Can I ask you something real quick?" Randy said.

The man folded his arms in front of him.

"I'm sorry to bother you," Randy said, stopping in the man's driveway. I finally caught up to him.

"What do you guys want?" the man said. "I'm not buying anything, so don't waste your time."

"We just want to ask you something," Randy said. "Did you live here in 1971?"

"What kind of question is that?" the man said. "How's it your business to know where I lived and when?"

"We're looking for somebody who used to live down the street," Randy said. "We thought you might remember her. If you lived here then, I mean. If you didn't, then just say so and we'll be on our way."

"Be on your way, then," the man said. "I didn't live here in 1971. I probably wouldn't have been allowed to walk down this street in 1971."

"Fine," Randy said. "We're sorry to bother you. Have a good day."

Randy turned to go. I looked at the man one more time, and then I followed Randy.

"Hold it, guys," the man said. He came down the steps after us.

We both stopped on the sidewalk.

"Look, I'm sorry," he said. "I've had a bad day. I guess I don't need to take it out on you."

"It's all right," Randy said.

"Seriously, I've only lived here since 1993," the man said. "I can't help you with 1971. Although . . ."

"Yes?"

"The couple I bought this place from. I remember them pretty well. They were pretty old, the last white couple on the block, I think. The wife, she didn't want to move, but the husband, well, I think they had been fighting about it for a long time. All during the closing, in fact, I thought they'd go over the table at each other."

"Do you have any idea where they might be now?" I said.

"They said they were moving to an apartment over in Westland. One of those assisted-living places. Kind of like half a nursing home, you know what I mean? God, Mrs. Meisner just hated the thought of going there; you could tell."

"That was their name, Meisner?"

"Fred and Muriel Meisner," he said. "Imagine having to get married and change your name to Muriel Meisner."

"You don't remember where this place was they moved to?"

"No, but I'm sure it was Westland. I remember saying to myself, 'Look out, Westland. You don't know what's about to hit you.' If you ever meet them, you'll know what I mean."

We thanked the man, then walked down to Mr. Shannon's house and knocked on his door. When he opened it, we made our introductions and answered his questions. Yes, I was a real private investigator. No, I didn't carry a gun. Randy? No, he wasn't a private investigator, but he had pitched for the Tigers. While Mr. Shannon settled down to hear the story, I asked if I could use his phone book. And his phone.

I looked under "Assisted Living" in the Yellow Pages. It said "See Nursing Homes," so I did. There were two listed in Westland; Azelia Park and Peach Tree Senior Community. I tried Azelia Park first, asking if I could speak to the Meisners. They didn't live there. I tried asking if there had been any Meisners living there in the past few years, but the woman wouldn't go for that one. I was starting to get tired of people who wouldn't give me information *just because they didn't want to.*

I called Peach Tree Senior Community and asked for the Meisners. Three seconds later, my call was transferred. Six rings later, a man's voice answered.

"Hello."

"Mr. Meisner? Mr. Fred Meisner?"

"Speaking! Who is this?"

"My name is Alex McKnight. I'm a private investigator."

"A private what? Muriel, for the love of God, will you turn that thing off!"

"A private investigator, sir. I wonder if you could help me. I'm looking for—"

"Muriel, did you hear me? Am I just talking to myself now?"

"Mr. Meisner . . ."

"Excuse me, what did you say you were?"

"A private investigator, sir."

"Muriel, in the name of all that is holy, will you please turn that stupid thing off for one second! I have a man on the phone here! Can you see me standing here with the phone next to my head? Do you think I'm doing this just because I like the way it feels against my ear?"

"Sir, maybe we could just stop by. Would that be more convenient for you? I see you're on Cherry Hill."

"No, it's Peach Tree! It's the Peach Tree place! Not cherries!"

"I know, but it's on Cherry Hill Road, isn't it? I see it in the phone book here."

"The Peach Tree Senior Community! It's quite a place! Muriel, do you want me to drop dead right now? I swear to God, if you don't turn that thing off, I'm going to have a massive stroke right in front of your eyes! Is that what you want?"

"Mr. Meisner! We'll be there in twenty minutes!"

"You're coming over here? Do you know how to get here? It's on Cherry Hill Road!"

"We'll see you in twenty minutes! Good-bye!"

I hung up the phone. When I went to look for Randy and Mr. Shannon, they were nowhere to be found. And then a voice floated down from upstairs. "We're up here, Alex!"

I went up the stairs and found them standing in the guest bedroom.

"This is it, Alex. This is the room where I first met Maria. Tell me the truth, Mr. Shannon, do you ever get a strange feeling when you're in this room?"

"How about right now?" he said.

"Randy, we gotta go," I said. "I found the Meisners. They're expecting us."

"You found them?" he said. "The people who used to live right down the street?"

"Yes."

"Her old neighbors. They'll remember her. How could they not remember her? And her whole family."

"We'll see," I said.

Randy grabbed me and hugged me. He picked me up in a bear hug and spun me around Mr. Shannon's guest room. He put me down and went for Mr. Shannon, but the look of sheer terror on the man's face stopped him.

We thanked the man and left. What he must have thought of us by then, I couldn't even imagine.

As soon as we were out of there and in the truck, he started singing the song again. *"L'amour, l'amour . . . Oui, son ardeur . . ."*

"Randy, either learn the rest of the words or stop singing that."

"We're getting closer, aren't we," he said. "I've got a good feeling about this."

I didn't know it at the time, but he was right about us getting closer. That good feeling, however, would be long gone before the day was over.

Chapter Eight

The Peach Tree Senior Community was on Cherry Hill Road, just like the man had told us. Randy and I walked through the front door and right into a large room with a fireplace and lots of couches and chairs scattered around. We saw maybe fifty senior citizens in the room, either playing cards at one of the tables or just sitting there talking. Every head turned when we walked in.

"Looks like a nice place," I said.

"Reminds me of your friend Jackie's bar," Randy said.

"I don't see the resemblance."

"Bunch of people sitting around by a fireplace," he said. "You should make your reservation right now, Alex. A couple more years, you'll be ready for this place. You won't even have to change your lifestyle."

I thought about that one while he walked around the place, looking for somebody in charge. He finally found a nurse sitting at a table in the corner. She had the *Detroit News* spread out under a reading lamp.

"We're looking for the Meisners," he said.

"Two seventeen," she said. "Right down that way."

We went down the wing she had indicated. It looked like a

hotel hallway, with doors on either side. A woman passed us, pushing a walker. She smiled at us.

"Good evening, ma'am," Randy said.

"Such handsome gentlemen," she said.

"Hey, she included you, Alex."

I looked at him. "Two seventeen's right here," I said.

We knocked on the door. There was yelling from inside the room, and then finally the door opened. The man who stood there had to be in his eighties. Maybe ninety. Ninety and still standing—I could only hope to be so lucky myself someday.

"Mr. Meisner?" I said. "I'm Alex McKnight. And this is Randy Wilkins. We spoke on the phone."

"You're the private guy," he said.

"Um, a private investigator," I said.

A voice called out from somewhere behind him. "Who is it?"

"It's the man from the phone call," Mr. Meisner said.

"Which man?"

"Muriel, the man who was—" He stopped and rolled his eyes at us. "Come in, gentlemen."

We followed him into his apartment. It was well furnished, with a small efficiency kitchen attached to the main room, and a separate bedroom. There had to have been at least a hundred pictures in frames all over the place, on shelves, on the coffee table, on the walls themselves. Mrs. Meisner was sitting in a wheelchair in front of the television. She had the remote control in her lap.

"Turn the television off, Muriel! We have company!"

"Who is it?"

"It's a Mr. . . ." He looked at me.

"McKnight," I said. "Call me Alex."

"It's Alex!" he said. "And . . ." He looked at Randy.

"Call me Randy."

"And Randy! Alex and Randy!"

"Pleased to meet you!" I said.

"Stop yelling!" she said. "I'm not deaf!"

"Sorry," I said.

"Can I get you gentlemen something to drink?"

"No, thank you," I said.

"We have beer in the refrigerator!" Mrs. Meisner said.

"No, that's all right," I said.

"We're out of beer!" Mr. Meisner said. "I was going to offer them coffee!"

"Men don't drink coffee!" Mrs. Meisner said. "Give them beer!"

"Really, we're fine," I said.

"Of course men drink coffee!" Mr. Meisner said. "I drink coffee every damned day! Will you turn the television off already!"

"I'm sure they'd prefer beer!" Mrs. Meisner said.

"We don't have any beer!"

"Please," I said. "We don't want to trouble you folks. We just wanted to ask you about Leverette Street."

"We used to live there!" Mr. Meisner said. "Here, sit down already! You're making me nervous standing around! Muriel, turn off the television!"

We sat down on the couch. Mr. Meisner sat in the chair next to Mrs. Meisner's wheelchair.

"Mr. and Mrs. Meisner," I said. "You were living on Leverette Street in 1971, right?"

"Yes," Mr. Meisner said. His voice dropped down a couple notches in volume now that he was sitting down. "We bought that house in 1934, if you can believe it. Right after we got married." He reached over and took his wife's hand. "We raised four sons there. Here, you want to see pictures?"

91

For the next few minutes, we went through all four of the sons, their wives, the seven grandchildren, and the eleven great-grandchildren.

"That old house got to be too much for us," Mr. Meisner said when we were done looking at the pictures. "We had to sell it and move here."

"You are so full of crap," Mrs. Meisner said.

"Muriel, please, we have company here."

"I hate this place," she said. "Peach Tree Senior Community? There's not a peach tree within a hundred miles of this place. And please, senior community? Why don't they just call it a nursing home?"

"It's not a nursing home, Muriel. It's 'assisted living.' Would you rather I be back there at the house, mowing the lawn? Shoveling the snow?"

"You pay a kid to mow the lawn! And shovel the snow!"

"The ice used to freeze in the gutters, remember? I'd have to get up there and chop it out in the springtime!"

"Alex's partner just fell off the roof doing that," Randy said. "He broke both his ankles."

"Do you see?" Mr. Meisner said. "Do you see what happens? Do you want that to be me, falling off the roof and breaking both my ankles?"

"Mr. Meisner," I said, "Mrs. Meisner. Do you happen to remember a family that lived down the street from you? The Valeskas?"

"Valeskas?" Mr. Meisner said. "Muriel, do you remember the Valeskas?"

"They lived over the Kowalskis. They rented the upstairs, I mean."

"The Kowalskis," Mrs. Meisner said. "We know the Kowalskis."

"Mickey Kowalski," Mr. Meisner said. "And his wife, Martha. We still get Christmas cards from them."

"I think he's sick, isn't he?"

"Who, Mickey Kowalski? He's not sick."

"I think he's sick."

"He's not sick. Don't listen to my wife."

"How about the Valeskas?" I said. "The people who rented the upstairs. Do you remember them?"

"I don't remember the Valeskas," Mr. Meisner said. "Muriel, do you remember the Valeskas?"

"Valeska, Valeska, Valeska," she said. "No, doesn't ring a bell."

"She was a spiritual reader," Randy said. "A fortune-teller."

That hit them like a bolt of lightning. "The fortune-teller!" Mrs. Meisner said. "Oh my God, Fred! The fortune-teller!"

"Yes! Yes!" Mr. Meisner said. "And that family. What was their name?"

"It was Valeska," I said. "You remember the family?"

"Oh good heavens, yes," Mrs. Meisner said. "My, what a time that was. With that family down the street. And that sign she put out on the sidewalk! You remember, with the big hand?"

"Yes! The hand!" Mr. Meisner said. "Mickey rented the upstairs to those people. I think they were only there for nine months, maybe ten months. And then they were gone! Just like that! Mickey, he thought they were Gypsies or something."

"But they paid their rent," Mrs. Meisner said. "I remember Martha telling me that. And they kept the place clean."

"Ah, but they were the strangest people," Mr. Meisner said. "The husband—what was his first name?"

Here it comes, I thought. This is why we're here. Randy and I were both hanging on their words now.

"It was an interesting name," she said. "Something exotic."

"The whole family was exotic. What were their names? There were four of them."

"The man's name was . . ." she said.

We held our breath.

"Gregor!" she said. "That was his name! I remember wondering what happened to the *y* at the end!"

"Yes, Gregor," Mr. Meisner said. "And the woman was . . . Oh Lord, what was her name?"

"Arabella," she said. "I remember it. It's such a nice name, isn't it?"

"Yes," I said. I looked at Randy. He was lost in his own world, now that he had those names to think about.

"They had one boy and one girl," Mr. Meisner said. "The boy's name was . . ."

"Leopold," Randy said. "His name was Leopold, wasn't it?"

"Yes," Mrs. Meisner said. "That was his name. He was a tough-looking little guy, wasn't he?"

"Ha! I remember now!" Mr. Meisner said. "He painted that room for us, remember, Muriel? That's what he and his father did—they were painters!"

"That's right!" Randy said. "I should have remembered that!"

"They were good, too. They did a good job on the room. Anyway, when they were done, I said something like 'Thank you, Leo!' And he said to me—what did he say? He said, 'My name is Leopold! My name is not Leo! Leo is a name for American men who drink beer and sit on their front porches in their undershirts.' Lord, how did I remember that?"

"He was a strange one all right," Mrs. Meisner said. "Ah, but the daughter . . ."

"Maria," Randy said. He said it in a way that stopped them. Both of them.

"Yes, Maria," Mrs. Meisner said. "She was such a beautiful girl."

"I'm looking for her," Randy said. "That's why we're here."

They both just nodded. Apparently, it didn't seem like a crazy idea to them. Of course, they had both seen Maria. So maybe that was enough of an explanation. Or maybe when you live that long, nothing seems crazy anymore.

"Do you have any idea where they might have gone?" I said. "After they left the Kowalskis' house?"

"No," Mr. Meisner said. "They just disappeared. They left the last month's rent under Mickey's door, and just vanished."

"Well, we have the names now," I said. "That could mean a lot. And wait a minute—didn't you say that the Kowalskis still send you Christmas cards?"

"Mickey and Martha," he said. "Yes, every year. We don't ever talk or anything, but every Christmas we get a card."

"I tell you, he's real sick," she said. "I heard that somewhere."

"Nonsense, Muriel!"

"Would you happen to have their address, then?" I said.

"Oh, sure," he said. "We send them a card every year, too. It would be kinda rude not to, don't you think?"

"Could I trouble you for that address perhaps?" I said.

"Yes, of course," he said. It took him a little while, but he got up off the chair. "You'll have to excuse me. I turn ninety-two next month."

"How long have you been married?" Randy said.

He looked down at his wife. He touched her hair. "Seventy years."

"We'll get a divorce someday," she said. "We're waiting for the children to die."

"Ha! I love that one," he said. "All right, now where did you put those addresses!"

"They're in the box," she said.

"I know they're in the box! Where's the box?"

"It's where it always is! In the bedroom, on the dresser!"

"No, that's where *you* always put it! Oh, never mind. I'll find it myself!" He disappeared into the bedroom.

"I can't tell you how much we appreciate this, Mrs. Meisner," Randy said.

"It's nice to have the company," she said. "I haven't thought about the old neighborhood in a long time."

"I found it!" Mr. Meisner called from the next room. "Right where I put it!"

Mrs. Meisner gave us a smile and a shake of her head.

"Here it is," he said as he shuffled back into the room. "They moved to Arizona. Can you believe it? All the way out there with the desert and the cactuses. Let's see, Kowalski..." He looked through the index cards in the box. "Here, Mickey and Martha Kowalski. In Tucson."

I took the card from him and copied down the address. There was no phone number, but I figured we could look that up.

We stayed for another thirty minutes, listening to more stories about the old neighborhood and how wonderful or horrible this new place was, depending on who was talking. Mr. Meisner stood up to shake our hands as we left. We both bent over Mrs. Meisner in her wheelchair and gave her a hug and a kiss. We promised we'd come back and visit them again someday.

On our way back to the motel, Randy kept looking at the Arizona address I had written down for the Kowalskis, even though he could not read it unless we were passing under a streetlamp. Even though he probably already had it memorized.

"We're almost there, aren't we?" he said. "This is them. The people who rented the upstairs to the Valeskas."

"They may not be much help," I said. "You heard what the Meisners said about the way the Valeskas left. They probably have no idea where they went."

"I know," he said. "But it'll be good to talk to them anyway. They might help me remember something else. So much is coming back to me now. Like the fact that they were housepainters. It's like a fuzzy picture that's coming back into focus, you know what I mean?"

"A picture of the way things were in 1971," I said. "You can't forget that, Randy."

"I know, I know," he said. "I hear what you're saying."

When we were back in our motel room, I sat on one bed, Randy on the other. I called information in Tucson and got the number for the Kowalskis. Before I could dial it, Randy took the phone from me.

"Let me do this one," he said.

"It's all yours."

"What time is it, about nine o'clock? So in Arizona, it's seven o'clock? No problem."

He dialed the number, waited for a couple rings, and then said, "Hello! I'm looking for a Mr. Michael Kowalski! Or Mickey, I guess they call him!" He was wearing his killer smile, which doesn't work so well over the phone. The smile disappeared, and before he could say another word, he was looking at the phone like it had just stung him in the ear.

"They hung up," he said. "They told me that Mickey was dead and then they hung up."

"I guess Mrs. Meisner was right," I said. "Mickey *was* sick."

"What am I going to do now?"

"Call them back and apologize?"

"Yeah, I'll do that," he said. He dialed the number again. "Oh please, please, ma'am, I'm very sorry. Please, ma'am, don't hang up. I'm so sorry to hear of your loss and I'm sorry to disturb you. I just spent a couple hours with the Meisners up here in Michigan. They were very good friends with, um—I'm sorry, am I speaking to Mrs. Kowalski? . . . Their daughter. Oh, I see. If I could apologize one more time, ma'am. The Meisners had no idea about . . . Yes, in Michigan. With the Meisners. They used to live down the block, on Leverette Street. . . . Yes . . . Yes . . . And they told me to give your parents a call, and . . . Oh, your mother is there? That would be, um . . ."

He looked at me with panic in his eyes.

"Martha," I said.

"Martha," he said. "Martha Kowalski. Yes, we were all just talking about . . . Yes . . . Oh yes, please. If there's any way I can just speak to her for a moment . . . Oh God bless you. Thank you. . . ."

I listened to his end of the conversation with Martha Kowalski. It started out pretty simple, with the Meisners and the old neighborhood and Randy telling her how sorry he was to hear of the loss of her husband. When he got around to the Valeskas, a cloud came over his face. "Are you sure about that, ma'am?" he said at least three times. When he was done, he thanked her and then just sat there on the edge of the bed, looking at me.

"What happened?" I said.

"She remembers them very well," he said. "It was just like the Meisners said. They stayed there for nine months, and then in the middle of the tenth month, they disappeared."

"So what's the problem?"

"She said that Valeska wasn't their real name. It was Valenescu."

"Valenescu?"

"That's what she said. That's the name that was on their checks. She said she remembers Maria's mother using 'Madame Valeska' on the sign because it wasn't such a hard name for Americans."

"Okay," I said. "That kind of makes sense."

"It does," he said. "It makes sense. And this explains why we couldn't find her before. Or her parents and her brother. We didn't have the right name."

"Randy, this kind of tells you something, doesn't it?"

"What do you mean?"

"You didn't even know her real name."

"Yeah?"

"You spent one week with her, almost thirty years ago, and you didn't even know her real name."

"Ten days," he said. He picked up the Detroit phone book. "I don't see any Valenescus in here. What do we do now?"

"I don't know," I said, "but Randy—"

"Wait!" he said. The cloud was gone. "Let's call Leon!"

I let out a long breath, and then I called Leon. I gave him the new name. Maria Valenescu. Her parents, Gregor and Arabella.

"That's fantastic work!" Leon said. "Now try and tell me you're not a real private investigator!"

"It wasn't that hard, Leon."

"I'll run these names right now," he said. "You guys must be psyched down there! We're getting closer!"

"I'm not so sure," I said, looking at Randy.

"What's the matter?"

"Let me take him to dinner and buy him a slinky," I said. "I need to talk to him."

"What's a slinky, Alex?"

"It's vodka and root beer, Leon. Don't ask me to explain." I said good night and hung up the phone.

"Well?" Randy said.

"Leon's gonna work on those names," I said.

"Good deal," he said. "We're back on track. Come on, let's go to the Lindell."

"I'm gonna take you someplace else," I said. "Someplace a little quieter."

"It's your town," he said. "Let's go."

I took him to a restaurant I remembered on Telegraph. I was hoping he'd see it all himself, how ridiculous this whole thing was turning out to be. I kept waiting for it to sink in. It didn't.

I drove him back to the motel. When I turned out the light, he stayed awake, staring at the ceiling. From outside our room came the sounds of the traffic passing on Michigan Avenue. Then he started talking again. It was just his voice in the darkness, like that first night, the night he flew all the way up to Paradise to find me, waited until he was lying on my couch in the darkness to tell me why he had flown all the way up there.

"The day before the game," he said, "Maria and I got a hotel room. Maria told her parents that she was sleeping over at a friend's house. We got this room and we made love. For the first time, really. The first and only time. But then afterward...

That's what I really remember, Alex. I was just sitting on the bed, thinking about the game the next day. It was like my whole future was hanging in the balance, you know? I knew I wouldn't be able to sleep much that night. And Maria, she was just sitting there in a chair. And she was drawing a picture of me. She loved to draw. Did I tell you that?"

"No," I said.

"She wanted to be an artist. She always had this big pad with her and a little canvas box with pencils and charcoal and stuff in it. Sometimes in the afternoons, we'd walk along the waterfront and we'd stop and sit down somewhere and she'd draw something. But she never drew a picture of me until that night. And I was just getting so keyed up about the game the next day, I wasn't really thinking about it, you know? I was just sitting there not talking and she was drawing her picture."

He stopped. A big truck rumbled by outside, rattling the pictures on the walls.

"Did you ever see that painting by—who was it? Toulouse-Lautrec, I think. The painting of the girl who's just sitting on a bench along the wall in a bar? You can tell there's some kind of party or something going on, and there're some people right next to her. But she's just sitting there looking at nothing, like she's lost in her own world. You know the one I mean?"

"I think I've seen it."

"Well, the thing about that painting is that you just look at it, and you can *feel* how tired that woman is, you know? How *lonely* she is. I mean, hell, if they had cameras back then and he had just taken her picture, you wouldn't have felt it like that. It was the way he painted it. I'm sorry, it's not like I'm an art critic or anything."

"It's all right," I said. "I know what you mean."

"Okay, so Maria shows me this drawing she did of me sitting there on the bed. And when I looked at it, I was just . . . My God, I couldn't even speak. The way she drew that picture, you could *feel* how scared I was. Just absolutely terrified of what was going to happen the next day. I couldn't believe it."

He was quiet for a long moment. Perhaps he was picturing the drawing in his head again. I didn't say anything.

"It wasn't just that she was a good artist," he finally said. "She could draw that picture because she *knew* me. You know what I'm trying to say, Alex? At that moment, she knew me better than I knew myself. I didn't even know that I was that scared until I looked at the picture. How many times in your life does somebody know you that well? You wanna know how many times it's happened to me?"

"How many?" I said.

"Twice," he said. "There was you. And then there was Maria. Not my wife. Not the woman I slept next to every night of my life for eleven years. Lord knows, not my parents. Not my kids even. It was you and Maria. You were the only two people in this world who could see right through me. All the jokes and the games and the bullshit. I know it was only one season we played together, but when I was pitching and you were catching, it was like you knew everything that was going on inside my head. Everything. Even stuff I didn't know. You knew what I could throw better than I knew. Which is why I could never be the same pitcher with anybody else. I came all the way up here and found you all these years later and it was like I had just seen you the day before. Am I right?"

"I don't know about that," I said. "Maybe."

"And Maria," he said. "I swear to God, Alex, she knew me just as well as you did. It didn't matter that we only spent a week and a half together. No matter how long ago it might have been. Hell, it doesn't even matter that I didn't know her real name."

Another silence, and then another truck rumbling by in the night.

"No offense, Alex," he said. "You both knew me just as well, but she wins the evening gown competition."

I laughed. What else was I going to do?

"Do you think we'll find her?" he said.

"I don't know," I said. "I wouldn't put money on it at this point."

"Do you think we should stop looking?"

"Don't ask me that," I said. "Not unless you want the truth."

"Tell me."

"Randy, I've been telling you all along that this is crazy. I know you don't want to hear that. And I know that if I had stayed home, you would have come down here by yourself. So I figured I had nothing to lose. A couple days hanging out with my old teammate, just to see what happens. But now I think you should stop. I really do. I think this is a bad idea."

Another long silence. Another truck passing outside, and then the sound of him breathing in the dark.

Chapter Nine

When I woke up the next morning, Randy wasn't there. His bag was still in the room, and when I looked out the window, I could see my truck parked in the lot. So I figured he couldn't have gone too far.

I took a shower and got dressed, went down to the motel lobby and sat there reading the paper for a while. Then I gave up waiting for him and went outside. It was an overcast April day in Detroit, with a fine mist in the air that worked its way into your lungs and through your clothes.

I found him on Michigan Avenue, sitting on a bench across from Tiger Stadium.

"Good morning," I said as I sat down next to him. "Not a real nice day to be sitting out here."

"I just wanted to look at this place one more time," he said.

"You planning on going somewhere soon?"

He smiled and shook his head. "I'll let you go home, Alex. I've kept you away too long already."

"I'm sure Jackie's managing quite well without me," I said. "Hell, he probably feels like he's on vacation."

He looked back up at the gray wall of the stadium. "You know, if I had gotten Rettenmund out instead of walking him, then I would have had two outs, with Boog Powell coming up. I would have been in a whole different frame of mind. The whole game could have gone my way at that point."

I didn't say anything. I wasn't going to argue with him, or tell him to forget about it.

"And then after the game," he said, "I would have gone out to celebrate with Maria."

"Randy . . ."

"Maria Valenescu," he said. "Anyway, you can't undo the past, right? Only a fool would even try."

"Let's go, Randy."

I took him back to the motel so he could put some dry clothes on. When we got to the room, the message light on our phone was blinking. I called the desk. A Mr. Leon Prudell had called, they said, and left a message to please call him back.

"What do you have for us, Leon?" I said when I got him on the line.

"Not a whole lot. I've only found three Valenescus in the entire country. They're all in New York City. I don't see any Gregor or Arabella or Leopold or Maria. It's worth calling these numbers, though. There might be a connection. You want to call, or should I?"

"I'm not sure we'll need them," I said.

"What are you talking about?"

"Ah hell, give me the names," I said. "I'll call you back later."

"All right, let me know how it goes!"

I thanked him and hung up. Randy came out of the bathroom with a towel wrapped around his neck.

"He found three Valenescus," I said. "You want me to call them?"

"It's up to you," he said. He sat down on the bed.

105

I dialed the first number and asked if they knew any of the four names. They didn't.

I dialed the next number. Same question. Nothing.

I dialed the last number. Whoever answered couldn't speak English very well. I think I got the idea across, and the answer seemed to be a firm no.

"No go," I said when I hung up.

"Okay," he said. "Time to pull the plug. Let me give Leon a call so I can thank him myself."

I didn't say anything. I sat there with the phone still in my hand.

"We played it out," he said. "That was our last card. What else could we do now, anyway?"

"Just hold on," I said. "Give me a minute here." I grabbed the Yellow Pages. "How old would her parents be right now?"

He looked at me. "What are you doing?"

"Humor me," I said. "How old would they be?"

"Eighties at least. Maybe nineties."

"Like the Meisners," I said. "So maybe they're living in the same kind of place right now."

"Assuming they're still alive, and assuming they're still in the area, then yes."

I looked up "Nursing Homes" again. I had just seen the same pages the day before, when we found the Peach Tree Senior Community.

"Alex, you're the one who told me this is a bad idea."

"I know," I said. "I just want to do this one thing. Otherwise, it's gonna bother me."

"You're gonna call every one of them, Alex? How many are there?"

"A lot," I said. "This might take awhile. Why don't you go get us some breakfast?"

A couple of hours later, I dialed the last number. I went through the routine for the hundredth time. Ask for Mrs. Valenescu, figuring there would be more chance of her being alive than her husband. In the obituaries, it's always men who are survived by their loving wives. The women die alone. Even if I was wrong on that, they'd probably catch me on it and tell me that there was no Mrs. Valenescu there but that there was a Mr. Valenescu. The name would stick out in their mind.

"Okay, thank you," I said, and hung up. I stood up and stretched.

"You're something else, you know that?" Randy said.

"It was worth a shot," I said.

"Thanks, Alex. Now we can stop."

"Not so fast," I said. "I got one more idea."

"Now what?"

"Her brother," I said. "What did he do for a living in 1971?"

"He was a housepainter. Like his father."

"Mr. Meisner said he was good at it, right?"

"Yeah, so?"

"So what do you think he's doing for a living right now?"

"I suppose he could still be a housepainter."

"Let's say he is," I said. "Do you think he still lives around here?"

"He might."

I grabbed the Yellow Pages again. "I don't see him listed here under 'Paint Contractors,' but that doesn't mean much. Most of those guys just work on word of mouth. So let's say that's what he does. What do you think he's doing right now?"

"Painting something?"

"Okay," I said. "You think he still makes people call him Leopold?"

"I would bet on it, yeah."

"So what happens when Leopold runs out of paint?"

"He buys more paint."

"He buys more paint," I said. "And where does he buy it?"

"At a paint store?"

"And how about next week," I said, "when he needs *more* paint?"

"At a paint store?"

"At the *same* paint store," I said. "I see about forty listings here for the whole Detroit metropolitan area. Why don't you go get us some lunch?"

When he was gone, I started working through the numbers. It was a long shot, but I'd be thinking about it for weeks if I didn't give it a try.

When I got through to the first number, I went into my spiel. "Hey, have you seen Leopold over there?" Thank God for strange names. If his name were Al, I'd have no chance.

"Leopold?" the man said. "Don't know no Leopold, sir."

"Ah, okay, wrong place. Sorry to bother you."

I did ten of the numbers.

I did twenty.

And then on number twenty-one . . .

"Leopold?" the man said. "Not today. He was here on Monday, I think."

I froze. My God, I've got a bite.

"Hello? Sir?"

108

I was about to play it straight, tell him who I was and why I was looking for Leopold. But then I thought about Leopold, and what Randy had told me about him. How much he hated Randy. Almost killing him on the street in 1971. I had two seconds to decide how to play it. I went for theater.

"Oh, uh, sorry," I said. "Hey, I'll be perfectly honest with you." Honest, my ass. "I've got one of Leopold's thirty-foot ladders here, and if I don't get it back to him today, he's gonna have my head on a platter. You know how he is."

"Oh man," he said. "Do I ever. I can't believe he even let you borrow it."

"Hey, I know he's been working on that job over there. Where was that again? Maybe I can just run it over to him."

"No, he didn't say."

Damn! Think, think.

"Oh man, I'm dead," I said. Okay, let's go for the home run here. "Hey, I know. Maybe if I just run it over to his house, you know? Leave it there. Hell, maybe he'll even forget he loaned it to me. You think that would work?"

"I still can't believe he loaned it to you."

"Yeah, tell me about it. I must have caught him on a hell of a good day. I was over at his house one time. God, where was it? It was over on . . ."

I let it hang. I was sweating. Come on, take the lead here.

"On Romney Street," he said.

"Yeah, that's right! On Romney Street. I'll just go over there right now and put that ladder in his garage."

The guy started laughing. "That'll never work, my friend."

"You're right," I said. "But at least this way, I'll have a running start."

"Good luck to you," he said.

109

"Hey, um, just one more thing. I appreciate you helping me out here. I'm just trying to remember which house it was on Romney. It was like a sort of white kind of—"

"Hell if I know," the man said. "I sure as hell never been to the man's house. I just know it from the address on the bills."

"Oh yeah, of course. Ah, well, never mind. I'll find it."

"Here, let me see," the man said. God bless this man. "Seventeen forty Romney Street."

"That sounds familiar," I said. "Man, you're really helping me out here. I appreciate it."

"Hey, no problem. Just don't tell him I helped you do the drop and run."

"Ha! You got it! Thanks a lot."

I hung up and let out a big breath.

By the time Randy came back with the McDonald's bags, I had already looked up the street in the index and found it on the map. It was in Farmington Hills, an upper-middle-class suburb to the northwest. "Looks like Leopold moved up in the world," I said.

"What are you talking about?"

I held up the piece of paper where I had written his address. "Let's go," I said. "I'll show you."

I remembered Farmington Hills as one of the nicer suburbs of Detroit. It was what they called "semirural," with four-bedroom houses on half-acre lots. A good old-fashioned mailbox on the street, with the little flag you raised when you had a letter to be picked up. I couldn't believe how much had changed.

"I remember this corner," I said as we drove past a strip mall. All the usual suspects were there now: Blockbuster Video, Sub-

110

way, TCBY. "I swear to God, there was nothing here but one gas station."

"Yeah, the owner used to come out, pump the gas himself, wash your window, and then turn the crank on the front of your car for you."

"Randy, I'm talking about fifteen years ago. It's like an entirely different place now."

"Progress," he said. "That's what I'm supposed to say, right?"

There was a lot of traffic on Halstead Road now. It used to be a lazy little two-lane road through nothing but weeds and dirt. We found the new subdivision we were looking for, right next to about five other new subdivisions, and turned in. We drove past a few dozen houses that looked like they had all been built that morning. We passed Corriedale Street and then we found Romney Street.

"Sheep," he said.

"What?"

"Corriedale and Romney. They're types of sheep. They must be running out of names."

We followed the numbers on the mailboxes until we came to 1740. The house was a split-level ranch, set back about a hundred feet off the road.

"Nice lawn," Randy said.

"I don't see a name on the mailbox," I said.

"So what do we do?"

"We'll just go knock on the door and ask," I said. "No big deal."

"Yeah, you're right," he said. "No big deal."

We drove down the driveway. It was asphalt, with what looked like a new coat of sealer on it. I stopped my truck behind a little red compact.

We got out. We walked to the door, passing a row of rhododendrons that had a long way to come back from a hard winter. We rang the doorbell.

A young girl answered. She was sixteen or seventeen years old, dressed in a softball uniform. There was an *F* on her jersey. Farmington High School. She smiled at me. She looked at Randy and her smile got a little bigger.

"Hi there," I said. "Is this the Valenescu residence?"

Her smile faded. "No, I'm sorry," she said. "There's nobody here by that name."

"There's nobody in your family who used to have that name even?" I was really reaching now. "Somebody named Maria? Used to live in Detroit? Her parents were Gregor and Arabella?"

"No," she said. "I'm sorry."

I looked up at the sky. "Okay," I said. I suddenly felt very tired. "We're sorry to bother you. You play softball, eh?"

"Yes," she said. "I'm a pitcher."

"Hey," I said, hitting Randy in the chest. "Another pitcher. Just what the world needs."

The look on his face stopped me.

"Randy?"

He was staring at the girl.

I looked at her, and then back at him. "Randy," I said. "What is it?"

He didn't take his eyes off her. "What's your name?" he finally said.

She swallowed. "Delilah."

"That's a beautiful name," he said.

"Thank you," she said. She sneaked a look at the doorknob.

"Delilah," Randy said. "Can I ask you something?"

112

"I need to get to practice," she said. "I came home to get my uniform."

"You're Maria's daughter, aren't you," he said.

She shook her head. "I told you, there's nobody here by that name."

"You're Leopold's daughter, then," he said. "That could be. You're Maria's niece."

"No," she said. "No, I told you. My name is Delilah Muller and I have no idea what you're talking about." She started to look a little scared.

"I'm sorry," I said, stepping in front of him. "I'm sorry, please excuse my friend." I turned to face him. "What the hell are you doing?"

"This girl," he said, and then he looked at her again over my shoulder. "This beautiful angel..."

"Is not who you're thinking," I said. "You heard her. What are you trying to do?"

"Alex, I know she is."

"Come on," I said, grabbing his arm. I pulled him back to the truck. As I turned to apologize again, the door was already shut.

Randy shook me off and got in the passenger's side. I got in, slammed the door, and backed up all the way down the long driveway to the street. I dropped the truck into drive and got us out of there.

I was already back on I-275 when I finally looked over at him. He had his hands together between his knees. He was staring out at the hood of the truck.

"What the hell is wrong with you?" I said.

He didn't say anything.

"You scared that girl," I said. "You really scared her. She's all alone in that house and you gotta go freaking her out like that."

He said nothing, so I let him just sit there. The interstate went down to one lane, so we had to slow down to a crawl. More construction.

"That's her daughter," he finally said.

"Were you listening to what she told you?"

"I don't care what she said. That's Maria's daughter."

I would have pulled over if I could have, but we were barely moving anyway. Two seventy-five has five lanes going north, five lanes going south. We were going south on the one lane that was still open while the construction workers tore the hell out of the other four.

"Randy, despite the fact that she *told* you she wasn't, why are you so sure that she's Maria's daughter?"

"You're the one who found the house, Alex. A housepainter named Leopold lives there. Is that just a coincidence?"

"As a matter of fact, yes."

"No," he said. "No."

"She's what, sixteen years old? Seventeen? You haven't seen Maria since 1971, right?"

"Right."

"You haven't heard from her? Or about her? You know nothing about Maria after 1971?"

"Right."

"So that girl was born around what, 1983?"

"Yeah, that sounds about right," he said. "That's when Maria gave birth to that girl."

I moved the car up another few feet. Then I stopped again. At this rate, we would be on I-275 until September.

"Why didn't she seem to know that, then? You'd think she'd know who her mother is, right?"

"She knew," he said. "She was lying."

I didn't say anything. There were no words to say. The man was out of his mind. I moved the car forward another few feet.

"Alex, we have to go back."

"Oh good God," I said. "I can't believe this."

"We have to," he said. "Turn around."

"I'm not turning around."

"Turn the truck around."

"Randy, so help me, I am *not* turning this truck around. Not that we're moving anyway." I could have gotten out of the truck and taken a long piss against the back tire if I had wanted to. I watched a couple construction workers walk past us.

"I have to talk to her again," he said. "Just one more thing I have to say to her."

"What? What do you have to say?"

He paused for a moment. "I have to tell her that it's okay. If she's lying because her mother told her to, then I understand. That's all."

"Let me get this straight," I said. "You think Maria told her daughter to be on the lookout for you, just in case you came back thirty years later? She's supposed to tell you she's not her daughter to throw you off the trail?"

"I don't think it would be exactly like that, no."

"Why not? Maybe she called her this morning to remind her."

"Alex, we turn around. We go back. I apologize to the girl. We leave. You take me to the airport and I fly back home. The end."

I had another ten minutes to think about it, while the machines slowly turned four of the southbound lanes into something that looked like the surface of the moon. Finally, we reached an exit and I took it.

"Thank you," he said.

"You apologize for scaring the hell out of her," I said. "And then we leave."

"You got it."

"I had to do it," I said. "I just had to try out one more thing. Call the paint stores. What a wonderful idea that was."

We worked our way back to Telegraph and took that all the way back up to Nine Mile Road. There were some traffic lights to sit through, but it was better than I-275. We found the same subdivision again, the same street, the same house. As we pulled into the driveway, we saw the same little red compact, and next to it a white truck with a rack of ladders in back.

"Looks like Leopold is here," he said. "This is good. Hell, he might even remember me."

"Well, we already know it's not the same guy," I said. "But I almost wish it was. Hi, remember me? I got lucky with your sister when she was nineteen."

"Yeah, that's funny, Alex."

We got out of the truck and went to the front door. Randy stepped in front of me and rang the doorbell.

We waited.

He rang it again.

We waited.

Finally, the door opened. A man looked out at us. He was short and dressed in white painter's overalls.

"Leopold?" Randy said. "Is that you?"

The man just looked at us.

"I'm sorry to bother you!" Randy said. "We were here earlier. We spoke to ... um ..."

The man opened the door. "You spoke to Delilah."

"I don't suppose you remember me."

He looked at Randy. He had dark eyes. "No, I don't."

"I'm, um . . ." He cleared his throat and looked at his shoes for a moment. "Leopold, I'm actually an old friend of Maria's. Your sister." I stood there watching the whole thing, not quite believing any of it.

The man smiled. He opened the inner door all the way, and then he opened the storm door. "Gentlemen," he said. "Please, come in."

Randy wiped his shoes on the little mat, and then I did the same. I followed him into the house, and when we were inside, I got my first good look at Leopold. He couldn't have weighed more than 160 pounds, but he had arms like a boxer. That's exactly what he looked like, one of those tough little bantam-weights.

He just stood there smiling at us. And then the door moved. Another man stepped out from behind it. He was younger. And a lot bigger.

He hit me once before I could even think about what was happening. I tried to duck out of the way of the next one, but he caught me on the side of the head. I went down with my ears ringing and a metallic taste in my mouth, a mixture of blood and adrenaline and sudden fear. I didn't know what was happening to Randy at that point. I tried to get up. The man was standing above me, ready to hit me again, I was sure, so I picked a spot in the middle of his body and drove my shoulder into it. He gave ground, but not nearly enough. I felt hands on my neck. A grip stronger than human.

He's choking me.

I grabbed at his hands, at his arms. Useless. You're going to die right here, Alex.

No, there's something you can do here. One way out. Some-body showed you this a long time ago . . .

I brought my right arm up and over his wrists, got as much leverage as I could, and then dropped to the floor. He went down with me, his forearms pinned against my chest. I heard him swearing. I felt his hot breath in my face. He drove his forehead into mine and pulled his arms free.

Did it work? Did I break his wrists? Before I could catch my breath, I got my answer. He hit me on the back of the neck with either one fist or both of them, or maybe it was an iron safe. It didn't matter. I was done fighting back.

A hand on the back of my shirt. Another one on my belt. I am lifted or dragged or God knows what and then there's a long flight of stairs leading down. I hit every one of them, five hundred steps or a thousand. And then I am at the bottom lying facedown on something soft. It is carpeting, thank God in heaven for carpeting at the bottom of the stairs and then I am out.

Chapter Ten

I opened my eyes. White ceiling tiles. Bright fluorescent lights. I thought about the hospital, waking up and seeing the doctor looking down at me. "He's lost a lot of blood," I heard them say. "We had to leave one of the bullets inside him."

No. I wasn't in the hospital. My eyes focused on machines. Stacks of metal plates, gleaming bars. A mirror on the opposite wall.

The basement. I was in the basement. It was filled with every kind of barbell and dumbbell and weight machine. All the fluorescent lights were on above us, so bright it hurt. My back against a wall. My left arm, hanging above my head. I looked up. A handcuff on my left wrist, looped through a D ring bolted to the wall. A hand in the other cuff. Someone else's hand.

Randy was sitting right next to me. "Hey buddy," he said. "Welcome back."

"Randy," I said. There was blood on my lower lip. I felt with my tongue where the lip had been split open.

"How ya doin'?" he said.

"What happened?"

"You don't look so good."

"Randy, what the fuck happened?"

"I'm not quite sure," he said.

I took a deep breath. Okay, I could breathe. I moved my legs. My left knee ached, but I could bend it. I moved my arms, as much as possible with the cuff on. The metal bit into the skin. I had forgotten how much handcuffs hurt when you put them on too tightly. I moved my neck. "God," I said. "That hurts."

"You gonna be okay?"

"I think so," I said. "How about you?" I looked at him. He didn't have a scratch on him.

"I'm fine," he said. "They didn't touch me."

"Wait a minute," I said. "The big guy, behind the door . . ."

"He jumped on you," Randy said. "Leopold just picked up this shotgun and pointed it at my head. I tried to stop the big guy from pounding on you, but Leopold told me he'd shoot both of us."

"That's beautiful," I said. "He picks me to beat up on and throw down the stairs."

"You were closest to him," Randy said. "Luck of the draw."

"Have you figured out why they're so mad at us?" I rubbed my neck with my free hand.

"No idea," he said. "He still can't be that mad at me thirty years later, can he?"

"Well, whatever it is," I said, "they obviously want us to stick around awhile. Where are they, anyway?"

"They went upstairs. They put these cuffs on us and said something about making ourselves at home."

"Did you say anything to them? Did you ask them why they were doing this?"

"I did," he said. "They said I shouldn't even have to ask."

"I don't get it," I said. "Does this make any sense to you?"

"There's gotta be some way out of these, right?" He shook the cuffs.

"Stop doing that," I said. "It hurts like hell."

"There's gotta be some way to pick the lock or something," he said. "There's always a way out."

"These are real handcuffs, Randy. We're not gonna pick them with the paper clip you happen to have in your pocket. This isn't a TV show."

"You used these things when you were a cop, right? You gotta know a way out of them."

"There is no way," I said. "Unless...Can we stand up?"

I put my weight against the wall, tried to get my feet underneath me. My knee hurt, the muscles under my right arm, my neck, my head. God, my head. I had to stop halfway up and wait for the pounding to go away.

"This thing is bolted in here pretty good," he said, giving the D ring a tug. "We need a wrench to get it out. Do you see a wrench anywhere?"

"I'm about to pass out here, Randy."

"If we see a wrench, maybe if one of us stretches real far..."

I lifted my head. Big mistake. "Oh God," I said. "This is not good."

"I don't see a toolbox, do you?"

"All I see are weights," I said. "And machines."

"That must be how that guy got so big," he said. "Look at all this. He's got a whole gym down here."

"Yeah, believe me," I said. "He hasn't missed many workouts."

"That's what this ring in the wall is for, I bet. Look, there're a few of them here. It must be some sort of exercise thing."

"I'm gonna sit back here," I said. "I really have to sit down."

I rubbed some of the feeling back into my left arm, and then I slid down the wall.

He sat down next to me. We heard voices above us, but we couldn't make out what they were saying.

"It's a nice basement," Randy said.

I let that one go.

"They did a nice job down here. I wonder if they did it themselves."

"Randy, what the hell are you talking about?"

"I'm just saying it's a nice place they've got here. If you have to get beaten up and thrown into a basement, this is the basement you want to be in."

"Randy, do you think this is some kind of joke?"

"I'm just trying to keep us psyched up, Alex. We can't give in to these guys."

"'We can't give in to these guys'? Are you really saying that? Are you out of your mind? We're beyond giving in to these guys, Randy. They've got us chained up in their fucking basement and God knows *what* they're gonna do to us when they come back down here. We've got one chance of getting out of this. We have to convince them that they made a mistake. They did make a mistake, right? They obviously think we're somebody else. Am I right?"

"We're just trying to find his sister," he said. "What else would they think?"

"You tell me," I said. But before he could answer, we heard footsteps on the stairs.

We saw the legs first, the white of Leopold's painting overalls, and then the bigger man coming down behind him. It was my first good look at him. He was at least six foot three, and I would have guessed 240 pounds. It was hard to tell. Muscle weighs a lot more than fat, and this guy had plenty. He was wearing baggy gray sweatpants and a white shirt with the collar torn open. The standard bodybuilder's outfit.

"Gentlemen," Leopold said. "I trust you're comfortable."

"We'd like our check now," Randy said. I would have jabbed him in the ribs, but it would have hurt me more than him.

"That's good," Leopold said. "That's real good." He had dark eyes and a certain Mediterranean intensity about him. But his words came out in a level midwestern accent. The shotgun was tucked under his right arm.

The bigger man sat down on a weight bench. He had the same eyes, the same black hair. This had to be Leopold's son. He was massaging his wrists. I must have hurt him when I tried that arm lock. Somehow, I didn't feel too bad for him.

"There's been a mistake," I said. "I don't know who you think we are, but—"

"I know exactly who you are," Leopold said. He put the shotgun down on another weight bench, then rummaged through the big pockets in his overalls and came out with two wallets. "Let's see," he said, opening the first wallet. He held it away from his face and squinted. "Alex McKnight. Says here you're a private investigator. Prudell-McKnight. Investigations. It's got a nice ring to it, but this business card is kind of second-rate, don't you think? What's this, two guns on here? They look like they're shooting at each other."

"I'll tell my partner," I said.

"Yeah, your partner," he said. "Where is he, anyway? I assumed this man was your partner." He looked at Randy as he opened up the other wallet. "But it turns out this is a Mr. Randall Wilkins. From Los Angeles. You came a long way, Mr. Wilkins."

"I told you," Randy said. "I just wanted to find your sister."

123

"Yeah, about that," Leopold said. "Tell me a little bit more about why you'd like to find my sister."

Randy hesitated. "I met her in Detroit," he said. "A long time ago. In 1971, when I was called up to the Tigers."

"You were a ballplayer?" Leopold said. "For the Tigers?"

"Yes. I met her when she . . . When you were all living over on Leverette Street. You don't remember seeing me with her? We ran into you one day on the street down by the waterfront."

"In 1971? That's a long time ago."

"I just wanted to find her again," Randy said. "I came back here to Michigan to do that. My friend Alex was helping me."

"Your friend, the private investigator."

"He's a private investigator, yes," Randy said. "But mostly, he's just a good guy helping out an old teammate. We used to play ball together."

Leopold looked at me. "You were a Detroit Tiger, too, I suppose?"

"No," I said. "I never got called up."

"That's a shame," he said. "Isn't that a shame, Anthony?"

"A real shame," Anthony said. These were the first words he had spoken.

"Anthony," Randy said. "You're Leopold's son?"

"I am," he said.

"And Delilah? Is she your sister, or is she—"

Leopold took a step toward us. His eyes darkened. "Do not speak her name again," he said. "Isn't it enough that you come here and terrorize her? That you grill her with questions about—"

"About her mother," Randy said. "She's Maria's daughter, isn't she."

Leopold turned away from us. He went through a pile of

weights and gloves and belts and finally pulled out a dumbbell. It was about eighteen inches long. As he held it up, the polished metal gleamed.

He stopped himself. He closed his eyes for a moment. And then he stood and came back to us—slowly—the bar hanging in his right hand.

"He sent you," he said. "Didn't he."

"Who?" I said.

"You know who."

"We don't," I said. "Randy is looking for Maria. Like he told you. He hasn't seen her in thirty years."

"It's true," Randy said. "I just wanted to—"

"Is that the best you can do?" Leopold said. "Baseball players from thirty years ago? Let me guess. You both wanted to say you played in the major leagues, but you figured that would sound too far-fetched. So you drew straws, right?" The bar began to sway in his hand. He was slowly twirling it like a baton.

"You're making a mistake," I said.

"Where is he?" Leopold said. "Where is he right now?"

"We don't know who you're talking about," I said.

"In Los Angeles?" Leopold said. "Is that where he is right now? He sent you out here to find her. And you hired this guy to help you."

"No," Randy said. "It's like we told you."

"How long have you been watching our house?" Leopold said. "How long have you been sitting out there on the street watching us?"

"No," I said. "We haven't."

"Leopold," Randy said. "We're telling you the truth."

"First, it was a white Cadillac," Leopold said. He twirled the bar a little faster. "A big white Cadillac sitting out there on the street. How stupid do you think we are, anyway? You think we're not going to notice a big white Cadillac?"

"That wasn't us," I said. "We just found you today."

"This thing weighs five pounds," Leopold said. He dropped the bar into his other hand. "It'll break right through the bone if I hit you with it. Whatever he's paying you, you know it's not worth having every bone in your body broken. You guys gotta realize that. I'll do it if I have to. I don't want to, but I'm a desperate man. We've been playing this game with Harwood for too long. It's time to make a stand."

"For the love of God," I said. "He didn't send us. Whoever he is. Harwood, you said? Is that his name?"

He shook his head. "Don't make me do this," he said. "I am not a violent man."

He raised the bar over his head. It looked like I would be first. I tensed my body, ready to move. But he was looking at my left arm. With the handcuffs, there was no way I could avoid it. I picked a spot on his leg, just below the knee. One more step and he'd be close enough for me to kick him there.

He dropped the bar. It hit the carpet with a soft thud.

"I got a better idea," he said.

I shook my head. "You're making a mistake."

He went back and picked up the shotgun. "Who gets it first?"

Neither of us said a word. It was a classic breach-action shotgun, with the two big barrels. It was the kind of gun that makes you nervous just being in the same room with it.

"How about you?" he said, pointing the gun at Randy. "Where do you want it?"

"Don't shoot him," I said.

He pointed the gun at me instead. "I thought you were just the hired muscle here. How much is this guy paying you?"

"He's not paying me anything," I said. "He's telling you the truth."

"Have you ever seen what this kind of gun can do to a person?"

"Yes," I said. "I was a police officer."

"If I put this gun against your left knee and pulled the trigger, how much knee would you have left?"

I didn't say anything. I kept looking at those two barrels. Very slowly, he lowered them to my knee.

"I think we could safely say that your left knee would be more or less completely eliminated. Don't you agree?"

I closed my eyes. I waited for the blast.

"Leopold!"

The voice came from upstairs. I opened my eyes.

"Leopold! What are you doing down there?"

"My God," he said. "Anthony, go see what your grandmother's doing."

Anthony sprang off the weight bench and started up the stairs. He got about halfway up, it sounded like, before he stopped. "Grandma, what are you doing?"

"Get out of our way," she said. "We're coming down."

"You can't come down here," he said.

"Like hell I can't! Now move out of the way! And put some real clothes on!"

Anthony came down the stairs backward, his hands raised in helplessness. Leopold just stood there for a moment, listening as one stair creaked above us, then another. Whoever was coming down was doing it slowly. When he finally pulled the gun away and started up the stairs himself, he didn't get further than the first three steps.

"Leopold! Who do you have down there?"

"Mama, go back upstairs! Delilah, take your grandmother back upstairs!"

"She'll do no such thing! What are you doing with that gun? What's going on down here?"

"Mama, please! I'm begging you! You shouldn't be up!"

"You're destroying the house! Did you see the living room? What in the name of Mary and Joseph is wrong with you? You're making enough noise to wake the dead."

"Mama, I *order* you to go back upstairs right now!"

He stood there frozen. We heard the creak of two more steps, then the woman's voice, softer now. "Leopold, dear, get out of our way."

He stepped back. The woman took the final two steps, holding on to Delilah. She had to be ninety years old. Her white hair was tied back, a single strand hanging over her face. She kept holding on to her granddaughter, even after they had cleared the stairway. She had brought the sharp smell of menthol down into the basement with her.

"Who are these men?" she said.

"Harwood sent them," Leopold said. "They're looking for Maria."

"Is that true?" she said to us.

"It's true we're looking for Maria," Randy said. "You're Madame Valeska. I remember you."

"But we don't know this man Harwood," I said.

"They're lying," Leopold said.

"Let me look at them," she said.

"Don't go near them," he said.

"Leopold, shush."

Delilah kept in step with her grandmother as they came toward us. Delilah looked scared of us, but the old woman's face was calm. Leopold stood behind them, biting his lower lip. Anthony had picked up the dumbbell, and now he stood holding it as if he would throw it at us if we so much as blinked.

The woman stopped in front of Randy and looked down at him. "I know your face," she said.

"My name is Randy Wilkins."

"Names, I don't remember. Your face, I remember."

"I came to you in 1971," he said. "To have my fortune told."

"You . . ." she said. She looked at him for a long time. "You were one of the baseball players. You're the one who came back."

"A few times, yes."

She moved over a couple steps and looked at me. "You I don't know."

"No," I said. "We haven't met."

"He's my friend," Randy said.

She came a step closer, close enough to touch my face. "Who did this to you? Did my son do this to you?"

"I did," Anthony said. "But not the eye. His eye was already swollen when he got here."

"Not the eye, he says. Everything but the eye. My grandson would make a good lawyer if he didn't dress in his pajamas all the time." She gave me a little wink.

"Mama, you don't understand," Leopold said.

"Let these men go," she said.

"Mama, we can't let them find Maria."

"Who says we're going to? Maria is safe. You know that. Now bring them upstairs so we can give them some tea."

Five minutes later, I was sitting at the dining room table, across from the same men who had thrown me down the stairs and had threatened to blow away a piece of my body. I couldn't stop the adrenaline. My hands were still shaking. Randy sat next to me, and for once, all of the charm and the jokes and the genius for making people like him were turned off. Madame Valeska sat at the head of the table, watching us with her dark, careful eyes. There was a thin tube running under Madame Valeska's nose and down to a tank of oxygen on the floor. The soft hissing of the tank filled the silence.

Randy finally spoke up, giving Madame Valeska the quick version of why he was there, minus the details about how intimate he had become with her daughter. He said it like a teenager explaining himself to his parents, while Madame Valeska watched his face, without so much as nodding her head. Delilah stood behind her, gently rubbing her grandmother's shoulders. When Randy was done talking, he sat back in his chair, his hands in his lap.

"That is quite a story," she said. "That you would think of my daughter after all these years and try to find her. It would be romantic if it wasn't so foolish. So much has happened since that time. Surely you don't expect to find the same person."

"No, of course not," he said. "I know that."

"So you say, and yet the image you have in your mind is of Maria as a young girl, with her whole life in front of her. This business with Harwood, it has changed Maria a great deal. He is evil, that man. He is a demon. He killed her husband, you know."

She reached up and touched one of Delilah's hands. "Delilah was born six months after Arthur's death," she said. "She never even got to meet her own father."

Delilah stared at us. She didn't say a word.

"Maria has endured so much sadness," Madame Valeska said.

"Beauty is a great burden, you must understand. The gods punish you for it. And those around you. Even you, Mr. Wilkins. Thirty years later, you come all this way just to see her again. And you, Mr. McKnight, you helped him do this?"

"Yes," I said.

"You are a true friend," she said. "And this is the reward you get. Are you badly hurt?"

"I'll be fine," I said.

"I think you are in more pain than you will allow us to see," she said. "If you were to call the police right now, I wouldn't blame you."

"I'm not calling the police," I said.

"My son and grandson owe you more than an apology," she said. "But under the circumstances, I hope an apology will be enough. My daughter's experience with this man has touched all of us. Perhaps it has made us a little deranged. Especially the men. You know how men are." She looked at Leopold and Anthony. They didn't look back at her. "My husband, Gregor. I believe it killed him, too. Another man Maria has lost. He could not sleep at night, thinking about Harwood."

She stopped talking for a moment. The room was silent.

"In any case," she said. "Maria is far away from here. It is hard for her to be away from her daughter." She stroked Delilah's hand again. "But this is the best way for now. Delilah will finish school here, and then perhaps in time things will be different."

"Is that why you changed your name?" I said. "Valeska. Valenescu. Today, Delilah told us her last name was Muller."

"It is easy to change your name in America," she said. "A name on a mailbox doesn't mean much anyway. Your real name stays in your heart. We know who we are."

"Who is this man Harwood?" I said. "Maybe we can help."

"That you would even say that after what has happened to you in this house," she said. "You are very kind. But he is our demon. He is not yours."

"You're not going to tell us where Maria is," Randy said.

"I cannot," she said.

"I understand," he said. "Can you at least tell her that I was here?"

"I will tell her."

"I don't know what else to say," Randy said.

"I believe that's all there is," she said.

And she was right. We left the place soon afterward. There was an uneasy peace between the men, Randy and I trying to forgive Leopold and Anthony for what they had done to us, or at least to understand their state of mind. And Leopold and Anthony trying to believe that we really weren't connected to this demon named Harwood, that our motives were innocent, if not sensible. I got the feeling that neither of them was completely convinced. The light rain had started again, the same light rain from the morning, which now seemed like a year ago.

I drove us to the first bar I could find. We both had a couple quick shots, without saying a word to each other.

"That was interesting," he finally said. "Wouldn't you say?"

"*Interesting* is one word for it."

"God, Alex . . ."

"What now?" I said.

"You feel like taking me to the airport?"

It was another hour's drive to Detroit Metro, avoiding the freeway. Randy looked out the window the whole time. I kept turning the wipers on and off as the rain stopped and then began again.

When we were at the terminal, I pulled into the loading zone and stopped the truck. "Do you know the schedule?" I said. "When's the next flight?"

"I'm not sure," he said. "I'll go see."

"You want me to go in there with you?"

"No, that's okay," he said.

"It might be a long wait."

"You should get home," he said.

"I'm in no rush."

"Alex, I'm sorry. I'm sorry I got you involved in this."

"Don't be sorry."

"How bad did they hurt you? Are you gonna be okay?"

"I'll be fine," I said. "I've been beat up worse before, believe me."

"I'm gonna pay you," he said. He pulled out his roll. "I'm gonna give you . . . let's see . . ."

"No, you're not," I said. "You're not giving me anything."

"Come on, for everything you did."

"If you want to send Leon more money, send it to him. Me, I was just helping out my old pitcher."

"Gas money," he said. "Let me give you gas money. And meal money."

"One hundred bucks," I said. "That's it."

He flipped off five twenties. "Terry's got a ball game today," he said, the spark finally coming back to him. "They're playing UCLA. Did I mention he's a catcher?"

"You mentioned it."

"He's gonna be a good one."

"Tell him hello for me," I said. "Tell him to watch out for left-handers."

"You think Maria's family will really tell her I was there?"

"I think so," I said.

133

"Nothing's gonna come of it, I don't think."

"Probably not," I said. "It sounds like she's got a lot of other things to worry about. You never know. Maybe someday. Hell, you know where her family lives now. Maybe you'll come back."

"I don't think so," he said. "I think this was my one shot at it. Just like my one shot at the big leagues. Another spectacular failure."

I left him on that note. I said good-bye and watched him walk into the terminal. And then I started for home.

I settled in for the six-hour drive. I knew it would be well after dark by the time I got there, but I wanted to be in my own bed when I woke up the next morning. That would be the worst day, I knew. My knee would be swollen, my wrist would burn where the handcuff had been, every muscle in my neck would feel as tight as piano wire, and my head would hurt more than the rest of my body put together. But at least I'd be home with my aspirin and my hot-water bottle and my Canadian beer.

I stopped outside of Saginaw for dinner, my body already stiff after two hours of driving. It got colder and colder as I drove north, as if I were driving backward in time, from spring back to winter. When I hit the Mackinac Bridge, the temperature was below freezing. Another hour of driving in the Upper Peninsula, the snow still on the ground, and then finally I was home. I went inside my cabin, lit the woodstove, and fell into my bed.

After one bad day, just as bad as I thought it would be, although nothing I hadn't lived through before, and then another night, I started to feel like myself again. I went to see Leon, still confined to his bed. I told him everything that had happened, the situation we had stumbled into. He wanted to jump right onto that one, call up Maria's family and find out more about this man named Harwood. "Private eyes solve problems, Alex! Let's help these people!"

I told him I wished we could. But I knew they wouldn't accept our help.

Then I dropped in at the Glasgow, answered all Jackie's questions. No, we didn't find her. Yes, I did get beat up. Yes, you were right. You told me something like this would happen again. And so on into the afternoon and evening. Another April day in Paradise, sitting in front of the fire. And yet it felt different somehow, without Randy's running commentary in my ears. A couple days with him and then everything was suddenly too quiet.

Then the phone call. In the middle of the night. A cold, raw night, with me stumbling for the phone and standing on the rough wooden floor, listening to a voice from far away.

"Alex McKnight?"

"Yes. Who is this?"

"I called your partner first. He told me to call you."

"Who is this?"

"You know a Randall Wilkins?"

"Yes, I do. Who is this?"

"My name is Howard Rudiger. I'm the chief of police in Orcus Beach."

"I don't know where that is."

"Well, right now, I'm at the Butterworth Hospital in Grand Rapids. You know where Grand Rapids is?"

"Yes. Wait. You're at a hospital?"

"Butterworth Hospital," he said. "Or that's the old name, I

135

guess. It's called Spectrum Health or some damned thing now. It's right on Michigan Street downtown. Your friend Mr. Wilkins is here."

"In Michigan? Randy's in Michigan? I don't understand."

"I'll explain it when you get here, sir. It'll take you what—about four, five hours to get here? I'll see you here at ten."

"Just tell me what happened," I said. "How bad is it?"

"It's bad," he said. "Mr. Wilkins was found about six hours ago. He was shot, and he's lost a lot of blood. We brought him here because it's the main trauma center for western Michigan. The doctor says he's in some kind of hemorrhage shock right now."

"He was shot," I said. "Randy was ... Who did this? What happened?"

"We don't know at this point," he said. "We have no witnesses, and of course Mr. Wilkins can't tell us anything. I should probably tell you there's a good chance he's not going to live."

"My God. I can't believe it."

"I'll see you at ten, Mr. McKnight. I'll have some questions."

"What are you talking about? What kind of questions?"

"Just be here," he said. And then he hung up.

Chapter Eleven

It was still dark when I left. It was dark and it was cold, and instead of being in my bed, I was awake somehow, unshaven and unshowered, my stomach burning as I drove south down I-75 to the Mackinac Bridge. I kept catching myself driving too fast, pushing the truck until it went into its death rattle at eighty miles an hour. Then I'd let out my breath and tell myself to slow down and watch where the hell I was going, stop thinking about it, stop asking myself why he was lying half-dead in a Michigan hospital instead of being on a beach in California.

I stopped for gas just south of Mackinac. I stood there shivering as a wind came in hard off Lake Michigan. The sun was just coming up.

Before I left the station, I grabbed a coffee and unfolded my map across the steering wheel. Taking I-75 down to Grayling, then a little jog over to US-131, and I'd be in Grand Rapids by ten o'clock.

Orcus Beach, he'd said. I tried to find it on the map. It wasn't there. I turned the map over and went through the index. No Orcus Beach.

I hit the road again as the sky started to lighten. When I got off I-75, the little jog I thought I had to make turned into a slow parade through the woods behind a flatbed truck carrying a mobile home. A couple cars tried to pass it, but the truck was swinging all over the place whenever the wind picked up. By the time we got to US-131, I had lost a good half hour.

It was ten o'clock when I hit the Grand Rapids city limits. It took another twenty minutes to get to the hospital on Michigan Street. Whoever this Chief Rudiger was, if he was like most other police chiefs I'd known, he didn't like people being late. So I was already off to a great start with the man.

From a couple miles away, I saw the big sign in green neon letters, SPECTRUM HEALTH. When I finally got there, I followed the signs and drove up the ramp, parked on the top level, walked down the stairs and then through a long tunnel enclosed in tinted glass until I came to a lobby. There were a couple people sitting on the blue plastic chairs, watching a television mounted high on the wall. There was a little reception desk, with a guard sitting in front of a clipboard. He might have been twenty-one years old, maybe not. I would have carded him if he were buying liquor.

"I'm looking for Chief Rudiger," I said to the kid.

"He went to get some coffee," he said. "He told me to have you wait in room one nineteen. Just down the hall to the left."

"Can you tell me what room Randy Wilkins is in?"

"The chief said you need to wait for him, sir. Room one nineteen, down the hall on the left." He tried to put a hard edge in his voice, like he had on a real badge instead of a tin security guard's shield.

"Look," I said, "I've got a friend here. I need to see him. He's gotta be in the Intensive Care Unit. Can you tell me where that is?"

"You need to wait in room one nineteen," he said.

"Down the hall to the left. I got it."

"Would you like me to escort you there, sir?"

"I'll manage," I said. "Don't leave your post."

I went down the hall and poked my head in room 119. A table, more blue plastic chairs. A little sink with a coffeemaker next to it. A basket with packets of sugar and artificial sweeteners, a box of that nondairy creamer stuff. Everything you need to make coffee except the coffee itself. Which is why my man was out looking for it instead of sitting here, waiting for me. Brilliant detective work on my part.

I looked back down the hall at the security guy. He was watching me. I gave him a little wave and kept walking, right into an open elevator.

The elevator had a list on the wall. Surgical ICU, Fifth Floor. That sounded like the right place. I hit five. As the doors closed, I heard the security man yell, "Hey!" and then a couple other things I couldn't make out.

When the door opened, I followed the arrows to Intensive Care and opened the double doors. A nurse looked up at me, a telephone pressed to her ear. She raised her hand at me and held it there while she kept listening to someone on the other end. I stood in front of her desk, looking around the place. There were two hallways forming an ell, with the nurse's station at the intersection. Most of the doors were closed in either direction, with gurneys and IV stands littering the hallways.

Then I saw a man in a uniform sitting in a chair outside one of the rooms, halfway down the hall to my right. He was looking straight ahead at nothing, his hands folded in his lap.

I heard the nurse making some kind of noise behind me as I went down the hall. I wasn't listening. As I got closer to the man, I saw that he was a Kent County deputy.

He looked at me for a long moment. "Can I help you, sir?" he finally said.

"Who's in that room?" I said.

"Who's asking?"

"I'm a friend," I said. I knew Randy was in there. In my gut, I knew he was in that room.

The deputy stood up. "Nobody is allowed in this room," he said.

"Do you know Chief Rudiger? I'm supposed to meet him here."

"He's not going to be happy that you came up here."

"Just let me see him," I said. "One minute."

"Nobody goes in this room," the deputy said.

As if to prove him wrong, the door opened and a doctor stepped out. While the door was open, I got a quick look inside. One bed, a man with bandages all over his neck. A tube in his mouth. It was Randy.

"Doctor," I said. "That's my friend. What's happening?"

"You know this man?" the doctor said. He was wearing green scrubs, a stethoscope hanging from his neck. "Can you tell me anything about him?"

"He can't go in there," the deputy said.

The doctor looked at him and back at me. "Do you know anything about his medical history? We can't get anything from his family."

"I don't think anybody's even supposed to know who's in here," the deputy said.

"Too late," the doctor said. "If you'll excuse us." He took me by the arm and led me down the hall a few yards. The deputy looked unhappy for a moment and then just sat back down on the chair.

"Why is there a county man outside his door?" I said. "What's going on?"

"I don't know anything about that," he said. "I'm just trying to keep him alive. Do you know if he has any drug allergies?"

"No," I said. "I'm not going to be of much help to you. Until a few days ago, I hadn't even seen him for nearly thirty years. Wait a minute—what did you say about his family? Why can't you get the information from them?"

"I don't know," he said. "I can't get through to anybody."

"I don't understand," I said.

The doctor shook his head. "He came in yesterday afternoon with a gunshot wound to the neck. He lost about forty percent of his blood and was in hemorrhagic shock. It's been"—he looked down at his watch—"almost twelve hours. His blood volume is almost back to normal, but he's still not conscious. In fact, he's showing signs of paralysis, even though none of the buckshot hit the spinal cord."

"Buckshot? Somebody shot him with a shotgun?"

"They didn't get a clean shot," he said. "Most of it went right over his shoulder. A few inches to the right and he wouldn't have a head on his body. He *should* be conscious right now, feeling lucky."

I thought about it. He'd stayed in Michigan, or else he'd come back. And then he got shot. By a shotgun.

"When will you know?" I said. "When will you know if he's going to live?"

"That's hard to say right now. Do you have a card or something? I can give you a call if anything changes."

I gave him one of my cards. "Thank you," I said. "I appreciate this."

We both heard the footsteps and looked up at the same time.

A man was coming down the hallway toward us, moving fast enough to rattle the papers on the bulletin board.

"Have you met the pride of Orcus Beach yet?" the doctor asked.

"Is he a tough customer?"

"No, but he plays one on TV."

Before I could ask him about that, Chief Howard Rudiger stopped in front of us, his hands hanging down at his sides like a gunslinger. He was breathing heavily, and there was enough mileage on his face to put him in his late fifties, maybe early sixties. But he still had movie-star looks and more hair on his head than any man his age had a right to have. It was black and oiled up into a wave, and it looked so impeccable it could have been a wig. But of course it wasn't. Police chiefs don't wear wigs.

He looked at the doctor and then at me. His eyes stayed on me. "You," he said, pointing his finger at me and then curling it in a come-hither. "Follow me."

Five minutes later, I was back down on the first floor, sitting in room 119 while Chief Rudiger made the coffee. He stood with his back to me the whole time while he loaded the coffeemaker and then watched it make two cups' worth. For another five minutes, there was no sound in the room but the steady dripping. I sat there and looked at all the little flowers and seashells on the wallpaper. It was obviously trying to be a cheerful room, in a place where the news is not always good. When I got tired of doing that, I looked at his police hat sitting on the table. ORCUS BEACH, MICHIGAN, it said, with a picture of a cannon sitting on a mound of sand.

He's making me wait, I thought. I'm supposed to be sitting here wondering what he's going to ask me, and *when* he's going to ask me. An old cop game, but with a twist.

"How do you take it?" he finally said.

"Black," I said.

He poured out two cups and put them on the table. Then he sat down facing me and took a long sip, looking at me over the rim of his mug. I returned the favor.

"Thank you," I said. "I needed this."

He nodded.

"So are you gonna tell me what's going on?" I said. "Why is there a county man outside his door?"

"We'll talk about that," he said. "After I ask you a few questions. We'd be done by now if you hadn't gone up there on your own."

"Chief, please," I said. "Don't run the hard-ass cop game on me, okay? I was an officer in Detroit for eight years, and I've seen it done by the best. Hell, there's a chief up in the Soo who could show you a few tricks, believe me."

"I don't know what you're talking about," he said.

"You can't do it in a room like this, first of all," I said. "You need a dingy little interview room. In your station. You know, on your home turf. And you should be smoking, so you can blow it in my face. And for God's sake, you shouldn't be making me coffee."

"We don't have a police station," he said. "We have one room in back of the town hall. I'm the only full-time officer, with four part-timers. I don't smoke, and even if I did, I wouldn't do it in a hospital. And I made you coffee because I was already making some for myself. I'm not playing a 'hard-ass cop game,' as you call it, Mr. McKnight. If I decide it's time to be a hard-ass, believe me, you'll know it. Now if you're done with your critique, may I ask you some questions?"

"Yes, Chief. Ask your questions."

He took another sip of coffee and then pulled a card out of his shirt pocket. His uniform was perfectly pressed, his tie perfectly knotted. "Is this your card?" he asked, putting it down on the table.

"Yes."

"Prudell-McKnight Investigations," he said.

"Yes."

"It was found in Mr. Wilkins's coat pocket. I take it he hired you?"

"Not really," I said. "He was a friend of mine, a long time ago. I was helping him find somebody."

"Go back to that 'not really' part," he said. "Because it's important. If he hired you, you know you don't have to tell me anything about what you were doing for him."

"He gave my partner some money," I said. "But not me." I thought about it for a moment. "I mean, he did give me some money, but just for gas. For driving him around."

He frowned. "If he gave your partner money, he hired both of you. If you're both in business together."

"Look, it doesn't matter," I said. "I have nothing to hide from you. I was helping him find a girl he met a long time ago. In Detroit. We didn't find her, so he went back home. Or so I thought."

"A girl," he said.

"She was a girl in 1971," I said. "Now she's in her forties."

"He was looking for a girl he knew in Detroit, in 1971," he said. He took out a pad of paper and wrote down 'Detroit, 1971.' "What's her name?"

"Maria something."

He looked up at me.

"We don't know her real last name," I said. "It could be Valeska or Valenescu or Muller."

He made me spell all three of the names. He shook his head slowly as he wrote them down.

"When did you last see Mr. Wilkins?" he said.

"Three days ago. I took him to the airport."

"Where was he going?"

"Back to Los Angeles."

"Did you actually see him get on the plane?"

"No," I said. "I dropped him off at the terminal."

"Okay," he said. "Did he ever mention anything about Orcus Beach?"

"No."

"You have no idea why he might have come up here?"

I hesitated, deciding how to play this one. "I have an idea," I said.

"Care to share it with me?"

"He may have had some reason to believe that Maria was in Orcus Beach."

"The two of you were looking for her in Detroit," he said. "Then you gave up and took him to the airport. Why would he suddenly think she was way up here in my tiny little town?"

I took a long breath and dived into it. "We talked to her family," I said. "They told us that Maria was hiding from somebody. They wouldn't tell us where. Randy may have gone back to their house and found out somehow. In fact, that's where you should start looking, Chief. If Randy was hit with a shotgun."

"Who said anything about a shotgun?"

"The doctor," I said. "When we were at her family's house in Farmington Hills, her brother threatened us with a shotgun."

"What does a shotgun in Farmington Hills have to do with a shooting in my town?"

"A shotgun gets pointed at his head, and then a few days later he gets blasted by one."

"Even if it's not just a coincidence, you can't trace buckshot, Mr. McKnight. There's no rifling to match up like on a bullet. You know that."

"So just ask him about it," I said. "I'll give you his address."

"Write it down."

"She's in your town, isn't she?" I said as I wrote. "She's in Orcus Beach."

"Who, Maria? The woman with three last names?"

"If it's such a small place, you've got to know about her. Hell, if she's got an order of protection on this guy she's hiding from, you'd *have* to know about it."

"Do you know anything else about your friend?" he said. "Do you know what he does for a living these days?"

"You didn't answer my question."

"What does Randy Wilkins do to make money, Mr. McKnight? Do you know?"

"He said something about commercial real estate."

"Is that what he told you?"

"Yes," I said. "Why are you asking me that?"

"I'm trying to figure out what he was doing in Orcus Beach," he said.

"I would think," I said, "that your top priority should be finding out who shot him once he *got* to Orcus Beach."

"Again with the critiques," he said. "I should be grateful for all the free advice."

"What's going on?" I said. "Don't you care who shot him?"

"That would be nice to know," he said. "But there are a lot

146

of private residences on the street where he was found. It could have been anyone, just trying to protect himself from the criminal element. You could almost say Mr. Wilkins got what he deserved."

I looked him dead in the eyes. I said the words slowly. "What are you talking about?"

He looked at his pad, then flipped the page over and began reading, squinting like a man who needs glasses but won't wear them. "Randall Wilkins, born 1951, convicted on multiple federal counts of embezzlement, check forgery, and mail fraud in 1979, did six years at Lompoc. Got out in 1985, then in 1990 was convicted again, this time on state embezzlement charges. Did two years at Avenal, was released, convicted again in 1994, did four years at Folsom. Currently wanted by the state of California on new charges, not to mention violation of parole and flight from prosecution."

"Are you telling me—" I said.

"Your friend's a con artist," he said. "He preys on wealthy women. Gets them to invest in bogus real estate deals, then takes off with the money. That's the commercial real estate he was talking about, I guess."

"No way," I said.

"You had no idea," he said. "You're totally shocked."

"Yes," I said. "Of course I am."

"If you were helping him in any way to set up a scam here in Michigan, you'd be an accessory."

"No," I said. "He was just . . . No. It can't be." I thought about it for a few seconds. "The family, they do live in a nice house, I suppose. Her brother paints houses, so he can't have that much money. But Maria . . . Oh goddamn it, who knows? I can't believe this."

He snapped his pad shut. "Believe it," he said.

"Why?" I said. "Why would he come all the way out here?"

"Doesn't sound like California's too cozy a place right now," he said. "Maybe you're the last friend left who didn't know what he's been up to." He paused a beat. "Now that we've established you had no idea, I mean."

I looked at him. "Why is that county man standing guard?" I said. "Randy's not going anywhere."

"That's what I tried to tell them," he said. "But the state of California insisted on it. I told them I didn't have a man from my force to do it, so they told me to get a county deputy. Now I've just got to make sure they're paying for it."

"And if Randy lives?"

"He goes back to stand trial. And he's out of my hair."

"Never mind who shot him."

"I'm on the case," he said, picking up his cup. "Don't worry about it."

I pushed my chair back and stood up. I took one step out of the room and then went back. "What about his family?"

"What about them?"

"I want to talk to them."

"They don't want to hear anything about it," he said.

"He could be dead by tomorrow," I said.

"The way his ex-wife said it, they all gave up on him a long time ago. To them, he's been dead for years."

"I want to talk to them anyway," I said. "I have to."

The chief just looked at me.

"I'm the last man he talked to," I said. "He told me all about them. If it's the last thing he ever says about them, they need to hear it. No matter what he's done."

He let out a tired sigh and reopened his pad. He flipped

148

through the pages and then copied down the names and phone numbers. "You call them once," he said. "You tell them who you are, you tell them what he said. That's it."

I took the paper from him and looked at it. Four names, four numbers. His ex-wife and three children. "One more thing," I said. "Where is Orcus Beach, anyway?"

"Why do you want to know that?"

"It's not on my map," I said. "I'm wondering where it is."

"You've got no reason to know that," he said.

"It's not a secret, is it? All I have to do is go buy a better map."

"McKnight, let me be clear on this." He stood up and looked me in the eye. "You have no reason to go to Orcus Beach. Go home and make your phone calls. If I need you again, I know where to find you."

I don't know how long I stood leaning over the railing. Thirty minutes at least. Maybe an hour. I looked down from the top floor of the parking garage at the outpatient entrance. I watched patients come and go. A woman came rolling out in a wheelchair, a bundle in her arms. A man took the bundle from her and strapped it into the special car seat, moving in slow motion. Some orderlies came out and smoked with their backs to the wall, then went back inside. There were no emergencies. No ambulances racing to the doors. No accident victims holding bloody towels to their foreheads. It was a quiet day at the hospital.

My stomach made a noise. I looked at my watch. It was just past noon. I had been awake for eight hours, going on nothing more than coffee. I took the stairs down to the street level, walked east down Michigan Street, found a fast-food place, and ate a hamburger without tasting it. Then I found a bar with nobody in it but a bartender washing glasses and a woman watching a soap opera on the television. The bartender set me up and then went back to his glasses. The woman never even looked at me.

I watched the soap opera for a while, because there was nothing else to draw my attention. A woman in an expensive dress kept pacing back and forth in an expensive office, going at some guy in an expensive suit. I gave up on the soap opera and went into the bathroom to splash some cold water on my face. I dried myself off without looking at my face in the mirror. Then I threw some bills on the bar on my way out.

I walked back to the hospital. The security guard jutted his chin at me as I passed him. I pushed the elevator button, waited for the car, got in and pressed five. The Intensive Care nurse wasn't at her station when I walked by it.

The county man was still sitting on his chair outside Randy's door. He folded his arms when he saw me.

"You again," he said.

"I'm sorry," I said. "About before. You're just doing your job here."

"And having so much fun," he said. "I can't believe I'm getting paid for this."

"I was a police officer," I said. "For eight years."

"That so."

"I had to do this kind of stuff," I said. "I know how it is."

He just nodded at that.

"What do you make of this Rudiger guy, anyway?"

"The chief with the big hair?" he said. "What a horse's ass. You ever been to Orcus Beach?"

"Never have," I said.

"One stoplight," he said. "They used to have a furniture factory there, but that closed. So it's a ghost town now. Chief Rudiger's the only full-time officer left."

"So he said."

"Anywhere else, they'd disband the force and contract with the county sheriff. But not Orcus Beach. Rudiger must have everybody hypnotized or something."

"Gotta be the hair," I said.

The man laughed at that. "He's got enough oil on his head, they better not let him go in the lake. What was that ship? In Alaska?"

"The *Exxon Valdez*?"

"Yeah, that one. That's what you'd get in Lake Michigan."

"That's good," I said. "Hey, any chance of me seeing my friend for a minute?"

He stuck his tongue in his cheek and looked down the hall. "Make it quick."

"I appreciate it."

I stepped into the room. The heart monitor was beeping. The ventilator was contracting, blowing air, releasing, again and again. I moved closer to him. His eyes were closed. There were bruises on his face. The breathing tube was taped into his mouth.

And then the bandages, all over his neck, his shoulders. He was wrapped up like a mummy, and looked just as still. Like he'd never move again.

"Don't die yet," I said out loud. "I want some answers first."

The monitor kept beeping. The machine filled his lungs with air and then released.

"Besides," I said, "I want to kill you myself."

Chapter Twelve

I looked at the piece of paper the chief had given me. Randy's ex-wife, Sandra Van Buren. Randy and Sandy. They must have heard that a lot. Van Buren was either her maiden name or else she'd remarried. Either way, I wondered how she'd react to me calling her. I was about to find out.

I was back in my truck, in the parking garage. I dialed Sandra's number on the cell phone I keep in the truck, an old analog piece of crap that I don't use very often. The call didn't go through. I tried again. The connection crackled and gave out. I threw the phone on the seat.

I got out of the truck and went down to the street, then back to the same bar. The bartender had finished washing a few more glasses. The woman was still watching her soap opera. She didn't look up at me this time, either, even when I walked right past her. I had noticed a pay phone in the hallway by the bathroom, with a battered phone book sitting on a wooden chair. I put the phone book on the floor and sat on the chair. It creaked like it was going to give out and then decided not to.

After I keyed in my calling card, I dialed Sandra's number. Over two thousand miles from where I was sitting, her phone rang. After four rings, she picked up.

"Ms. Van Buren," I said. Up to that moment, I hadn't even thought about what to say to her. "My name is Alex McKnight. I'm a friend of Randy's."

There was a long silence; then she cleared her throat and spoke. "Yes?"

"I'm just outside the hospital," I said. "I saw him in the Intensive Care Unit."

"What do you want?" she said.

There was a low humming on the line, riding back and forth across the country. "I just wanted to tell you," I said, "that I spent a few days with Randy last week. He came all the way out here . . . well, partly just to see me, I guess. That's what he said. And we . . ."

We what? What did we do? What could I say to her?

"It was the first time I had seen him in almost thirty years," I said. "We played ball together back in 1971."

She didn't say anything.

"I didn't know anything about what had happened to him since then," I said.

"What do you mean, happened *to him*?" she said. "Nothing happened *to him*. He happened to us, Mr. McKnight. He destroyed everybody around him."

"I understand that," I said. "Now that I know, I mean . . . I just wanted to tell you one thing, because I have to. When I was with him last week, all he kept talking about were your children."

"Stop right there," she said. "Don't even say that."

"It's true," I said.

"If he said that, he was feeding you a line. Why do you think he came out there, anyway? You think he came out there just to hang out with his old baseball buddy?"

"I obviously don't know Randy as well as I thought I did," I said. "But I swear to God, he talked like a man who was very proud of his kids. You can't fake that. Nobody can."

"The policeman told me he was looking for a woman," she said. "What do you think he was going to do when he found her? Tell *her* how proud he was of his kids?"

"I didn't know why he was trying to find her," I said. "I mean I thought I did, but . . ."

"It figures," she said. "He had to go back thirty years to find somebody who'd still believe him."

"Ms. Van Buren . . ."

"It's Mrs. Van Buren," she said. "I'm married to somebody else now. I try not to think about the past, okay? I didn't need that policeman calling me up today, and frankly, I didn't need this call, either."

"I'm sorry," I said. "I just had to call you."

"Okay, you called me. You did what you thought you had to do."

"Yes," I said. "And I was thinking maybe I'd call your children, too."

"I can't stop you," she said.

"If there's a change in his condition . . ."

"Don't bother," she said. "I don't care what happens to him. I really don't."

"All right," I said. "All right, then. I guess that's it."

"I guess so," she said.

"Good-bye."

She hung up.

I sat there on the chair with the receiver in my lap, staring at the wall. The paneling was loose. One good pull and I'd bring the whole thing down on top of me.

The next name was Annette Wilkins. I dialed the number and got a recording telling me that the Turtle Café would open at 11:00 A.M. for lunch. I looked at my watch. It was 2:15 Michigan time, 11:15 California time. Somebody was late opening up the place.

I tried Jonathan Wilkins's number next. I got a secretary telling me I had reached the law offices of about six names I couldn't catch. When I asked for Mr. Wilkins, I was put on hold.

There was classical music for a while, and then a voice. "This is John."

"Mr. Wilkins, my name is Alex McKnight. I'm calling about your father."

"My father the embezzler and con artist? How much did he take you for?"

"I imagine you've heard about what's happened to him here in Michigan."

"Yes," he said. "The police chief from Orcus Beach called last night. Wherever that is. Are you connected with the hospital?"

"No, I'm an old friend of his," I said. "I just talked to your mother."

"I don't imagine that was a pleasant conversation," he said.

"Not really," I said. "But I had to call her, and I had to call you. Your father said some things about you when I saw him last week. I thought you should know."

"What did he say?"

"He said that you had just passed the bar and that you were working as a lawyer in San Francisco. And that you're going to have a baby soon."

"That's amazing," he said. "Not one piece of that is a lie. It's a new record for him."

"He also said that he was very proud of you."

"Ah, well, there you go. The streak is broken."

"I may be out of line, but I think he really meant it."

"Mr. McKnight, what did he tell you about his baseball career? Did he tell you about all the games he won for the Tigers back in the seventies?"

"No, I know he only pitched in one game."

"Aha, that's story B. He shut out the Orioles in his one major-league appearance. Then he hurt his arm breaking up a mugging and never pitched again."

"No, I know what happened. I know he got shelled and then never made it back up."

"Oh, so he couldn't lie to you about that. What a cruel twist of fate. That must have driven him crazy."

"Mr. Wilkins . . ."

"I'm sorry, sir. I shouldn't be taking this out on you. It's just that you don't know what he did to us. Did he tell you about his father's company?"

"He mentioned something about his father being in commercial real estate, and him taking over the business."

"That's rich," he said. "I love that. He took over the business all right. He took it over and drove it right into the Pacific Ocean. Which is basically what he got caught trying to sell. He did time in a federal prison for what he did to his father's company. Did he tell you that?"

"No," I said. "But the chief told me about the prison time."

"And then when he got out? His new hobby? Charming wealthy women and then draining their bank accounts? I don't imagine my father mentioned that, either."

"No."

"I didn't think so," he said. "He's funny that way."

"Well, I don't think there's anything else to say, then."

"No, although you know what?" he said. "Out of all his kids, I'm probably the only one who really owes him something."

"How's that?"

"I became a lawyer just so I can take guys like my father to court and make them pay back everything they steal from people. It's the only way I can make up for being related to him."

I didn't have anything to say to that. Not that he would have heard it. He gave me a "Good day" and hung up.

"Well, this is going beautifully," I said to the wall. "It was such a brilliant idea. If I had a brain in my head, I'd stop right now."

I looked at the youngest son's name on the list. If I was going to keep doing this, I wanted to save him for last. I dialed the daughter's number at the restaurant again. This time, I got a real voice.

"Can I speak to Annette Wilkins?" I said.

"This is she."

"My name is Alex McKnight," I said. "I'm calling about your father."

Click. And then a dial tone.

Okay, so much for the daughter, I thought. This is getting better and better. I'll go for the last one while I'm hot.

There was nothing on the sheet but his name and number, but I remembered Randy telling me that Terry was a freshman at UC–Santa Barbara. I didn't know what to believe anymore, but I assumed that's where I was calling him. When the phone was picked up, I heard a lot of noise and music in the background. It certainly sounded like a college dorm to me.

"Hello," I said. "I'm looking for Terry Wilkins."

"Hold on."

There was just the music for a while; then finally the phone was picked up again.

"Hello?"

"Terry, my name is Alex McKnight," I said. "I'm calling about your father."

A long pause. "What about him?"

"Look, I've already talked to your mother and your brother," I said. "And your sister just hung up on me. I know nobody wants to hear about him. But I'm an old friend of his from the minor leagues."

"You played baseball with my father?"

"Yes," I said. "I was his catcher. He told me that you're a catcher, too. He said you can really hit the ball."

"I don't know how he'd know that," he said. "He hasn't seen me play in like seven years."

"Wait a minute—"

"Yeah, the last time was before he went to Folsom. Gotta be seven years ago, back when I was in Little League. I haven't even seen him since then."

"He talked about watching you play ball there on the college team," I said. "He said you were good behind the plate, like I used to be. That you could really drive the ball. For God's sake, Terry, are you sure he hasn't seen you play at all?"

"If he saw me, he did it without me knowing about it."

I didn't know what to say. Was he lying about that even? About his own kids?

"I'm sorry, Terry. I just felt like I should call you and talk to you. All I've done is make your whole family unhappy today."

"It's all right," he said. "I don't mind. Did you see him today?"

"Yeah, I saw him. He's not conscious now, so . . . I don't know what's gonna happen, Terry."

He didn't say anything.

"Wait a minute," I said. "UCLA. You were playing a game against UCLA, he told me. When I dropped him off at the airport, he mentioned the game. That would have been . . ." I thought about it. "Saturday. The game would have been Saturday."

"Yeah, we did have a game against UCLA on Saturday," he said. "But I didn't end up playing myself."

"But you did have a game," I said. "He was right about that."

"Yeah, I guess he was. Whatever that means."

"Well, for what it's worth, he kept talking about how proud he is that you're his son and you're a catcher like I was."

A long silence.

"Terry? Are you still there?"

"Yeah, I'm here. I just, um . . . Thanks for calling, okay? I gotta go."

"Okay, Terry. Good-bye."

I sat there tapping the receiver against my hand a few times; then I banged it back in place and stood up. When I went back out into the bar, the woman finally looked at me. She was close enough to the hallway to have been listening to my end of the phone calls, and apparently I was more interesting than her soap opera.

I sat at the bar and had one more beer while I thought about what to do next. There was no point in seeing Randy again. I had nothing to say to Chief Rudiger. He was probably back home in Orcus Beach already, investigating the shooting.

Hell, like he was going to lose any sleep over it. A California con man comes to his little town to make a score and gets a shotgun necktie instead. The chief will work hard on that case until he finds the shooter or until dinner time, whichever comes first.

Which leaves what? Me trying to figure out what happened? The chief was right. He got what he deserved.

And yet...

Something. I don't know what.

Was he really just using me to find her? So he could run a scam on her? After all these years?

You heard about his record, Alex. You heard what his family said. His own family. Randy looked you in the eye and lied to you. It's that simple.

So why don't I believe it? Why does my gut tell me it wasn't all lies?

Because your gut is wrong. You think you know him better than his own family? Just because you caught him for one season in 1971?

You can't lie to me, Randy. That's what I said to him. Before I knew better. *I can see right through you.*

It's crazy. It's completely insane. Just leave it alone.

"Hey, barkeep," I said. "You got a good map of the county?"

"Somewhere I do," he said, looking up from the sink. "Where you looking to go?"

"Little town called Orcus Beach. You know it?"

"Not much up there," he said. "But I'll tell you how to get there if you want."

"I'd appreciate it."

"Here, I'll draw you a map. You going up there right now?"

"In a little while," I said. "First I gotta go have my fortune told."

160

Chapter Thirteen

It's a little over two hours from Grand Rapids to Farmington. On a day when you've been up since before dawn, it feels like a hard two hours. I found the house on Romney Street, the same house where Randy and I had been handcuffed in the basement and shown both barrels of a shotgun. It didn't look any different than the first time I had seen it. It was still the same brand-new split-level ranch in a neighborhood of brand-new split-level ranches. But I knew I would never forget it.

It was after four o'clock when I got there. The driveway was empty. No little red car, and no truck with ladders on it, which meant no Delilah and no Leopold. I didn't know if Anthony had a car, or if he drove around in his father's truck, or if he just stayed home all day lifting weights. No matter what, I was sure that Madame Valeska, or whatever the hell her real name was, probably didn't get out much, not if she had to lug around that tank of oxygen.

When I knocked on the door, I got none of the above. An old man wrestled the door open, trying very hard to get out of its way without falling over. He had a wooden cane in his left hand, but he wasn't leaning on it. When he finally had the inside door open, he stood there and looked at me. He must have been a tall man at one time, maybe twenty years ago. Now he was stooped over and a good six inches shorter.

"Hello!" I said. "Is anyone else here?"

He just stood there behind the storm door.

"Anybody?" I said. "I need to speak to somebody. I'm a friend of the family."

He cocked his head. The man couldn't hear a word I was saying through the glass. So I opened it.

"Hello!" I said.

He tried to grab the door handle. "What are you doing?"

"I need to speak to somebody," I said. "Is Leopold here? Or his mother?"

"Close that door!" he said.

"Excuse me, sir," I said, stepping into the house. I had just enough room to edge by him without knocking him over.

"You can't come in here!" he said. "Who are you?"

"Sir, please take it easy. My name is Alex. I need to know who's home right now."

"Nobody!" he said. "It's just me! And you have to get out!"

"Where's Leopold?" I said. "Is he out on a painting job?"

"You can't be in here!" he said. "Out with you! Out!"

"Sir, where is Leopold?"

"I'm going to call him right now!" he said. "I'm going to tell him you're in his house!"

"Good. Please do that. I need to talk to him."

"You can't just walk into his house like this!"

"Sir, will you please relax and go call him?"

"I'm going to call him right now!"

"Listen, I'll wait right here," I said. "You go call him."

"You get outside!" he said. "You can wait outside for him!"

"This will be much more comfortable in here," I said. "Now please, go call Leopold."

"I will," he said. And then he finally started moving away from the door. He shuffled through the living room, into the dining room, where Randy and I had sat a few days before. The old man grabbed a hold of the wall when he reached it and took a hard right toward the kitchen. "Just walking right into the house," he said to himself. "Like he owns the place. Walking right in."

When he was around the corner, I opened up the hall closet and looked inside. There were coats and umbrellas and everything else you'd expect to see in a hall closet, but no shotgun.

I took a few more steps into the living room, looking for a gun cabinet. I could hear the old man still talking to himself in the kitchen. The way he was racing to the phone, he'd get there within the hour.

I took a peek in the dining room. Nobody keeps a shotgun in the dining room, but I had to look anyway. The old man caught sight of me from the kitchen and let me have it. "What the hell is wrong with you? Where are you going?"

"Don't mind me," I said. "Just making myself at home."

"You get out of here right now!" he said. "I'm warning you!" He was holding the phone and shaking it at me.

"Did you call Leopold yet?" I said.

"I'm going to! Right now! You just wait until he gets here! What that man is going to do to you!"

I shook my head and looked down the hallway to my left. There were four doors in the hallway. One of them was closed. As I walked toward it, I started to hear a hissing sound.

"Don't you dare go down there!" the old man said behind me. "Do you hear me? That's her room, goddamn you!"

"Make the call," I said.

"Do not disturb that woman! I swear to God, you'll be sorry! She'll give you the evil eye and you'll have festering boils all over your body!"

That one stopped me long enough to roll my eyes. Then I gently knocked on the door.

"Festering boils!" he said. "I'm warning you!"

I knocked again, a little louder.

"Come in," she said. When I opened the door, I saw Madame Valeska sitting in a rocking chair next to her bed. The clear tube ran from the hissing oxygen tank to her nose, just as it had when I saw her the week before. The same smell of medicine and menthol hung in the air around her. There was a lace blanket wrapped around her legs, and a book resting on her lap.

"You're not going to give me festering boils, are you?" I said.

"I had a feeling I'd be seeing you again," she said.

"I'm sorry to intrude."

"It sounds like you've got poor William in a state," she said. "I hope he doesn't have a heart attack out there."

"He's calling your son," I said.

"William comes over to sit with me during the day," she said. "He's very protective."

"I'd just like to ask you a couple questions," I said. "If you don't mind."

"Come closer," she said. "Let me see your hands."

I stepped into the room. It felt twenty degrees hotter than the rest of the house. The other chair, the chair William must have used when he was sitting with her, was a big old recliner on the other side of the room. I didn't feel like dragging it over to her, so I went to her and stood in front of her with my hands out. It felt awkward looking down at her, so I went down into a

164

catcher's crouch. My legs didn't like that one bit, never mind that I had spent a few years of my life doing this a couple hundred times a day.

When I was at eye level, she took my hands in her own. They were the hands of an old woman, made crooked by ninety years of use, but I could feel in them a surprising strength. "Now what is so important that you have to come into my house and make William so upset?"

"You remember Randy, the man who was here with me?"

"The baseball player," she said. "Are you right-handed?"

"Yes," I said.

"Your left hand shows your ancestry," she said. "It's what's given to you at birth. Your right hand shows your present nature, and what the future may hold." She took my right hand and traced the lines with a bent finger.

"He was shot last night," I said.

"I am sorry to hear that," she said. "He is alive, no? I would hear it in your voice if he had been killed."

"Yes, he's alive."

She nodded her head. She still did not look up from my hands. "You have lived a very hard life," she said.

"I was a catcher," I said. "That's why my hands are so beat-up."

She looked up at me for an instant. "That's not what I'm looking at," she said. "Your fate line is ragged. It shows much misfortune."

"He was shot in a small town called Orcus Beach," I said. "Does the name mean anything to you?"

"No," she said. "Your fingers are well separated. You are a very independent person. But your last finger is set very low, which means you've had to work very hard."

I watched her white head as she held my hand. The oxygen tank hissed in the corner.

"Do you see how your first finger is bending toward your middle finger? That means you are a very persistent man. Very stubborn. And this separation between your head line and your life line, it means you need to work very hard on controlling your temper."

"Orcus Beach," I said. "That's where Maria is, isn't she?"

She looked up at me. "If that's true, it's news to me." She looked me right in the eye as she said it. If she was lying, she was damned good at it.

"Ma'am, there's a shotgun in this house," I said. "Do you know where it is?"

A step behind me, and then a voice from the doorway. "You mean *this* shotgun?" It was William, back from his phone call, pointing the shotgun directly at my head.

"What are you doing?" I said, trying to keep my voice level. "Put the gun down."

"William, dear," she said. "Do as the man says. You're going to hurt somebody."

Hurt somebody, she says. If he unloads both barrels of that thing, he'll do more than hurt somebody.

"William," I said. "If you fire that weapon, you'll kill both of us. Do you understand?"

"You can't just barge in here without me doing something about it," he said. The gun started to waver in his hands. His face was turning red.

"Put it down," I said.

"You think I'm just an old man who can't protect anybody?"

"Obviously, you can," I said. "Now put it down."

He looked at the gun. His face kept getting redder.

Goddamn it, I thought. The gun's too heavy. He's gonna slip and blow both our heads off.

"William!" I said. I could feel the sweat running down my back. "I swear to God, if you fire a shotgun from there, you'll kill both of us! Do you understand me?"

"I'm sorry, Arabella," he said. "I didn't know what else to do."

And then he lowered the gun. I got up out of my crouch, nearly falling over when my legs cramped up. The movement surprised him, and he started to bring the gun back up at me. I took it away from him. For a single moment, I felt like bashing his old fool head in with the butt of the gun. Instead, I made myself take a deep breath.

I had the shotgun barrel in both hands now. This is not what I had been planning on doing. Now with my fingerprints all over the thing, I'd have some explaining to do.

"Ah hell, as long as I'm touching it," I said. It was a classic breach-action Parker, the kind of shotgun some of the older hunters still liked to use. I broke it open slowly so the shells wouldn't eject across the room. They weren't the buckshot shells I was expecting. They were slugs, which made sense if the owner was going after big game, like deer or bear.

"Well, the good news," I said, "is that you wouldn't have killed both of us after all. Assuming you didn't miss."

"I wouldn't have missed," he said. He was holding on to the doorframe with both hands, catching his breath.

"That's great," I said. "And of course blowing two slugs through my head wouldn't have bothered the woman sitting right next to me."

"William, dear," she said. "You really need to think about things before you do them. You've always been too impulsive. You know that."

"Go sit in the chair," I said. "You've had a busy day."

I looked at the gun again. If Leopold had used this gun to shoot Randy, I thought, then he didn't hide it. He cleaned it and put in slugs. It was possible, but it didn't seem likely.

"Where was your son last night?" I asked her.

"Ask him yourself," William said as he slowly lowered himself into the chair. "He's on his way."

"Good man," I said. "How long until he gets here?"

"Not long," he said. "And he won't be happy."

I was waiting outside for him when he finally pulled up in his truck. He hit the brakes with such a jolt it sent one of his ladders flying off the rack. When he came charging out of the truck, I moved out onto the cold, hard ground of his front lawn, my hands in the air, about shoulder height. With your hands up, you look like you want peace, but at the same time you've got them ready for anything else.

He didn't say a word. He came right at me and started swinging. He was the same little fireplug I remembered from our first meeting, built like a bantamweight boxer. Today, he was wearing his white painting overalls, complete with the little white hat.

I blocked a few of his punches and then slipped one into the ribs. I shouldn't have enjoyed seeing the wind go out of him, but I couldn't help myself. When you get thrown down a flight of stairs, handcuffed to the wall, and then threatened with a shotgun, it's not something you can let go of too easily. Even if the guy admits he made a mistake.

"Little different story, isn't it," I said, ducking a big overhand haymaker. "When you don't have a shotgun or your muscle-head son hiding behind the door."

"What the hell are you doing here anyway?" he said as he backed up to regroup. "You got no business here."

"Randy got shot yesterday," I said.

He stopped moving. "What does that have to do with us?" he said.

"Did you shoot him?" I said.

He shook his head. "No, I didn't shoot him," he said.

His little white hat had come off. It was blowing away. I looked him in the eye.

He was telling the truth.

"Why would you even think that?" he said. "What reason would I have to shoot him?"

"Because he found your sister," I said.

"What are you talking about?"

"I know where she is," I said.

His eyes narrowed.

Here it comes, I thought. This will tell me something.

"I know she's in Orcus Beach," I said.

The eyes. If he doesn't know what I'm talking about, I'll see the confusion in his eyes. If it's the truth, he'll look away.

He looked away.

"I don't know what you're talking about," he said. But it was too late.

"How did Randy find out?" I said. "Did he come back here? Did you tell him where she is?"

"Of course not," he said.

"Your mother? Your son? How about . . ." I stopped.

"Nobody told him anything," he said.

"Maria's daughter," I said. "What was her name, Delilah?"

"No," he said.

"He's smooth," I said. "He has a way of making you trust him. Especially women."

"That's impossible."

"Think about it," I said. "He came back here when you were at work. When your son was out doing whatever it is he does. He's got a job or something, right? Let me guess; he works at a gym."

"Yes, he does."

"Delilah was here alone," I said. "He came back. He talked to her. He told her about how he remembered her mother after all these years, how he just wanted to see her again, how he was going to try to help her...."

Leopold didn't say anything. He stood there on the front lawn, shaking his head slowly. "No," he said, so softly I could barely hear him. "No."

He was still standing there on the lawn when I left. The image of him looking down at the dead April grass, shaking his head, it stayed in my mind all the way back to the expressway, all the way west across the state, with the map the bartender had made to get me to Orcus Beach.

When Delilah got home from school that day, she'd find her uncle Leopold waiting for her with some tough questions. Maybe it would be a relief to tell him her secret, that yes, the man had come back and asked her about Maria. She thought she was doing the right thing. She thought she could trust him.

You charmed another one, Randy. Maybe for the last time.

Chapter Fourteen

It felt as if I had already logged a thousand miles that day, but back I went across the state as the sun went down, right through Grand Rapids, until I hit Lake Michigan. I turned north in Muskegon, running up M-31 to the outer edges of the Manistee National Forest. I passed a couple towns called Whitehall and Montague, the last real towns I'd see before heading to the shoreline. There was a sign inviting me to come see the world's largest weather vane, but a man can only take so much excitement in one day. I took a little road called B-5 to a tiny place called Stony Lake, and then the road started calling itself Scenic Drive. It didn't matter what they called the road, because you wouldn't even be on it unless you knew where you were going. There were a few summer houses looking out over the water, then long stretches of road with nothing but pine trees. I had the bartender's hand-drawn map on the seat next to me. I knew I was on the right road, and I was just starting to wonder if he had led me into the middle of nowhere as a joke, when I finally came to an intersection and the only traffic light I'd seen since leaving Montague. WELCOME TO ORCUS BEACH, the sign said. Below those words was the same picture I had seen on Chief Rudiger's hat, with the cannon sitting on the mound of sand.

I drove through the town. It was dark. The only streetlights on the main road were mounted on wooden poles in front of the businesses—a gas station, an IGA market, a little video store. There were neighborhoods spreading out into the darkness on either side of the road, behind the businesses. From what little I could see, it looked like the bigger houses were on the west side of town, facing the water, or facing away from the town, depending on how you thought about it.

The town hall was on the west side of the street, attached to the fire department. I pulled into the lot and drove all around the place, thinking maybe I'd see a squad car. I didn't. I stopped the truck and got out, went to the door in the back marked ORCUS BEACH POLICE DEPARTMENT. Looking through the glass door, I could see one desk with a police radio on it, a map on the wall, a bulletin board with a calendar stuck to it. There was nobody there. Maybe Chief Rudiger is on his way to Farmington, I thought. Maybe he's following the hot lead I gave him about the shotgun.

Or maybe he was home reading the paper.

I got back in the truck and completed my tour of the place. The last streetlight in town burned high on its pole in the middle of an empty parking lot grown over with weeds. To the north, there was nothing but empty road leading into the night.

I turned around in the parking lot, my headlights sweeping across the building. It was a simple two-story rectangle, gray and silent, with thick glass block windows high on the walls overlooking the road. I remembered the county deputy saying something about a furniture factory closing. This must have been it.

I circled back into the center of town, back to the one gas station on the corner with the traffic light. It looked like there had been another station across the street, but that place was as empty as the factory. Even the pumps were gone.

I pulled in and gassed up for the second time that day. It was the old style of gas station, no roof over the pumps, no minimart to sell you beef jerky. Just a cash register inside, a shelfful of motor oil, and a rack of maps. The man came out and watched me as I pumped the gas. He was wearing overalls with STU written over the breast pocket in red script.

"Nice town you got here," I said.

He looked out at the street like he needed to see for himself. "This town?"

"Have you seen Chief Rudiger?" I said.

"You looking for him?"

I gave myself a few seconds before answering him. The kind of day I was having, I didn't want to start taking it out on innocent bystanders.

"Yeah," I said. "I'm looking for him."

"Haven't seen him," he said.

"Okay," I said. I watched the numbers race by on the pump. I was about to set a new record for the most expensive tank of gas I'd ever put in the truck, thanks to the jacked-up price this guy was charging. I guess he had a corner on the market.

"Everybody in town gas up here?" I said.

"Of course," he said, leaning on the pump. "Why not?"

Because you could buy a gallon of beer for less than what you're charging for a gallon of gasoline. "Oh, I just figure you know everybody in town," I said. I gave him a smile.

"Yeah, most of 'em," he said. "I suppose."

"I'm looking for a woman named Maria," I said. "You know anybody in town named Maria?"

"Not off the top of my head," he said.

"Okay, no problem."

"In fact," he said, "I'm pretty certain that there's nobody in this entire town with that name."

I finished up the gas, squeezing it up to the next dollar. "Fair enough," I said, pulling out some cash for the man.

When he took it, he gave me a long look in the eye. "You said you were looking for the chief?" he said.

"I'm sure I'll see him," I said. "Eventually."

"I could give him a message," he said. "I mean, if you don't want to wait around. He might not be back for a while. He goes away for days on end sometimes."

"He should be back," I said. "He's working on a case. I understand you had a shooting here yesterday."

"Oh, yeah," he said. "Yeah, we did."

"Must have everybody in town pretty shaken up," I said. "I don't imagine you get many shootings."

"Not too often," he said. He looked at the ground.

"Where can I get something to eat around here?" I said.

"There's a real good place down in Whitehall."

"That's twenty miles away. There's no place here in town?"

"Not really," he said. "There's no place to speak of here. Not for eating."

"What about that place down there?" I said, nodding my head toward the only two-story building on the block. The sign over the door said ROCKY'S.

"Oh, Rocky's," he said. "That's more of a bar really. If you want something to eat, you should go down to Whitehall."

"Actually, I could use a bar right now." I gave him a slap on the back. I couldn't resist. "Thanks for the recommendation, Stu."

He didn't say anything else. He just watched me get into my

174

truck. I drove half a block south and parked out on the street because the lot was so full. This was the place to be on a night in Orcus Beach, I guessed. Of course, like the gas station, you didn't have much choice.

When I got out, I looked back up the street. Stu was still standing there by the pump, watching me. I gave him a wave. He didn't wave back.

Rocky's was a big wooden place, made up like a mountain chalet, though the nearest mountains were the Porcupines, a good three hundred miles away. There was a big plastic deer mounted right over the door, looking down at me. I stepped into the place, saw a lot of men in plaid flannel. Most of the women were in blue denim. I took a seat by the window. I could see the parking lot and the street, all the way down to the gas station. Stu wasn't standing there anymore.

A waitress came over and gave me the first genuine smile I had seen all day. I ordered a beer and hoped she would move with all speed to get it. While she was doing that, I looked the place over. There was a big horseshoe-shaped bar attached to the far wall, and tables spread out haphazardly until you hit the pool table and dartboards in one corner and the big screen TV in the other. A Tiger game was on, but I couldn't hear it over some horrible crap music coming from the jukebox. A kid who looked maybe fifteen years old was standing over the jukebox, picking out more horrible crap music to entertain everybody. One good reason to miss Jackie's place.

The waitress brought over the beer and a glass. I ordered a cheeseburger and then poured the beer in the glass and drank half of it. It wasn't bad, and Lord knows, I needed it, but it wasn't Canadian. Another good reason to miss Jackie's place.

I sat there for a while, waiting for the food to show up. I watched the game and tried to ignore the music. A heavy cloud of smoke hung in the air. It seemed like half the people in the place had cigarettes going. If there was a nonsmoking section, it must have been out in the parking lot.

The music stopped. For a few blissful seconds, there was nothing but the sound of people talking and laughing, and Ernie Harwell's voice on the television set, calling the game. The Tigers were actually winning.

And then I saw her. She was sitting at the bar, on the farthest side of the horseshoe. She was alone, an empty bar stool on either side of her. She was smoking a cigarette and reading something on the bar in front of her.

I had seen Maria's daughter. Randy was right. There was no mistaking the bloodlines. But even if I hadn't . . .

Would I have known? Would I have taken one look at her and known that this was the woman Randy was looking for?

She looked up as the jukebox started again. I saw her face, the same face that Randy had seen thirty years before. Her hair was dark and pulled back over both ears. Her eyes were dark, as Randy had said, but there was something else about them—something slow and deliberate, something that Randy hadn't been able to describe. You had to see it for yourself. The bartender said something to her and she smiled and then went back to her reading.

I watched her for a while. The door opened and a man came into the place. Stu, from the gas station. He looked around the room and spotted me, then looked away. He went and grabbed a man who was sitting at the bar. I would have bet anything this man was Rocky, the owner of the place. With his hand on Rocky's back, Stu bent his head down and said something to him.

Rocky looked up at him and then did a professional job of looking back at me without really looking.

I watched Rocky lean over the bar and say something to the bartender. Then I watched the bartender go over to the cash register, which happened to be a few feet away from Maria. He didn't face her, but the way she looked up at him told me he was talking to her. She listened to him for a few seconds; then she looked over at my side of the room. When she caught my eye, she didn't look away. She stared right at me for a long moment. I stared right back at her.

We didn't get the chance to see who would blink first, because Rocky appeared in front of me. He was about my size and around my age, but he obviously spent a lot more time taking care of himself. There was an anchor tattooed on his left arm, faded with age. "You the one who ordered a cheeseburger?" he said.

"Nice place you got here," I said.

"We're out of cheese," he said.

"Not a problem."

"We're out of hamburger, too."

"What about the bun?" I said. "Are you out of buns?"

"We've got buns," he said. "You can have a bun with catsup on it. Or maybe you'd better just hit the road and find another place to eat."

"A place that isn't out of cheese and hamburger," I said.

"Exactly. That's what I'd do if I were you." The man folded his big arms and looked down at me. Over at the bar, I could see the bartender watching me. Stu kept watching me from the front door.

"I appreciate the information," I said. "Let me finish my beer and I'll be on my way."

He held his ground like he was making up his mind about it, then slowly backed away from my table and went back to the bar. He sat himself on a bar stool, turning around so he could keep an eye on me. Stu gave me one last look, then went out the front door.

Five minutes passed. Maria sat on the far side of the bar, an odd little smile on her face. The bartender stayed right next to her. He wasn't moving, no matter how many people wanted to order a drink. Rocky kept watching me. I kept sitting there, looking out the window into the night, wondering what the hell I was doing there and what I would do next. Getting in my truck and never coming back was beginning to feel like the right answer.

Before I could make up my mind, Rocky got up and went over to Maria. He bent down and said something to her. When she stood up, he offered her his arm. He walked her to the door and took her coat off a rack by the front register. As he helped her into it, she looked at me and gave me another little smile.

I watched them through the window. In the dim light of the parking lot, I saw them walking to her car, a red Mustang convertible with the top up. Rocky held the door open for her. She got in and he closed the door. As she was pulling away, I took my little pad of paper out of my coat and wrote down the number on her license plate.

She drove out of the parking lot and turned left on the main road. Then I saw another car pull out behind her. It was a white Cadillac.

A white Cadillac.

Bells went off in my head. Where had I just heard about a white Cadillac?

I stood up and looked out the window. The license number.

Could I see it from here? I read it to myself. SBV . . . Is that a *V* or a *Y*? Goddamn it all.

I wrote down the number, as best as I could make it out. I put a question mark over the *V*.

A white Cadillac. In the basement, Leopold had said something about a white Cadillac outside their house.

I threw a couple bills on the table and went to the front door. Rocky was just coming in. "What's the hurry?" he said. "I thought you were going to finish your beer?"

"I'm all set, thanks," I said.

"Let me take your check," he said. He was blocking the door, and doing a damned good job of it.

"The money's on the table," I said.

"Let me get you your change, then."

"Keep the change," I said. "The service here is first-rate."

"Very well," he said. "Have a pleasant trip. Wherever you're going." He gave me one last look, like he wanted to make sure he'd remember my face. Then he stepped away and let me out the door.

When I got to my truck, something didn't look right. I stood there looking at it from top to bottom. When I got to ground level, I saw my problem. Both tires were flat. I went over to the other side of the car. The other two tires were flat, too. I wasn't going anywhere. I slammed my fist down on the hood.

When I was done counting to ten, I knelt down and looked at the tires. There didn't seem to be any damage. Somebody had just let all the air out.

I got in the truck and rode it on the rims back to the gas station. When I got there, my man Stu was sitting there at his counter, reading the *Grand Rapids Press*. He was leaning back in his chair as if he had been sitting there for the last two hours. I stood in front of his counter, waiting for him to look up at me. He didn't.

"I've got a little problem," I said.

"Is that so?" he said, turning the page.

"I have four flat tires."

"That *is* a problem," he said.

"I guess I should be thankful he didn't slash them," I said. "He just let the air out."

"It's your lucky day," he said.

I stood there watching him read his paper. I counted to ten again. "Where's your air pump? I didn't see one outside."

"We're out of air," he said.

"Come again?"

"No air," he said. "We're fresh out."

I started counting to ten again. I got to three and then tore the newspaper out of his hands. I balled it up and threw it away, and then I put both hands on the counter and leaned over him. "Listen, *Stu,*" I said, looking him in the eye. "I don't know what's going on here. Or who you think I am. Or what you think I'm doing here. Or why the hell you think you need to let the air out of my tires. Which is something a little twelve-year-old punk would do, by the way. I'd expect something more creative from somebody who works in a gas station."

He didn't say anything. He just looked at me.

"What's next, Stu? You gonna soap my windows?"

A voice from behind me: "No, we'll skip that one." And then I heard the unmistakable sound of somebody racking a shotgun. "We'll go right to this."

I turned around. Rocky was standing in the doorway, leveling a shotgun at my gut. His bartender was right behind him.

I swallowed. It was the second time that day somebody had

pointed a shotgun at me. This time, it was a pump-action Remington with a short barrel, exactly like the riot gun I used to carry in the trunk of my squad car. And the man holding it obviously knew what he was doing.

This is what happened to Randy, I thought. This is what happens to any stranger in this town. They pull some kind of stunt to get you trapped into a corner like this, and then they shoot you.

"Will you please put the gun down," I said. I watched his hands. I waited for the muscles to tense just before squeezing the trigger. It would be the last thing I'd ever see.

"Give me your pad of paper," he said.

"What?"

"Harry saw you writing something on a pad when she drove away," he said. "Give it to me."

I slipped the pad out of my coat pocket and threw it to him. He caught it with one hand and gave it to Harry the bartender, who then thumbed through the pages. It didn't take him long to get to the last page.

"It's her plate number," he said. "And another number."

"Who's that?" Rocky said. "Who's the other number?"

"The guy who's been following her," I said. "In a white Cadillac. He's the one you should be pointing the gun at."

"Who are you?" he said. "What are you doing here?"

"I'm looking for Maria," I said. "I just want to talk to her. About the man who was shot here yesterday."

Rocky and Harry exchanged a quick look over that one. I was thinking of my next brilliant line when the squad car pulled up outside. There was no siren, no lights. Just Chief Rudiger opening the door and getting out slowly. Like he was just there to pump some gas.

"What's going on, Rock?" he said.

Rocky pointed the gun down. "We've got a man threatening Stu here," he said. "He was just about to physically assault him."

Rudiger raised his eyebrows when he saw me. "Well, look who it is," he said. "Why am I not surprised?"

"You know this man?" Rocky said.

"I do," the chief said. "I'm gonna have a talk with him. Go on back to your place."

"He's all yours," Rocky said.

When the two men had left, Stu started uncrumpling his newspaper. "Let's go, McKnight," Rudiger said. "Get in the car."

"Where are we going?"

"You wanted to see my hard-ass cop routine, didn't you?" he said. "I'm gonna show it to you."

It was a short trip, maybe a quarter mile north on the main road to the town hall. I sat in the back of his squad car. It was one of the newer cars, with hard plastic seats in the back so a suspect had no place to hide anything. When we were parked behind the building, he opened the door for me and led me to the back door, the same door I'd looked through when I first got to town. He turned the light on, pulled a chair over in front of his desk, hard plastic like the backseat of the squad car. Then he went over to the other side of the desk and sat down. He took his hat off and put it on the desk. ORCUS BEACH, MICHIGAN, with the cannon in the sand.

He waited for me to sit down in front of him. When I did, he looked at me for a good minute without saying anything. I was amazed once again by how much hair the man had. Say what you want about this town, the chief had good hair.

"You're not making me coffee this time," I finally said.

"Why are you here?" he said.

"I came to see Maria."

"Why were you threatening Stu?"

"I wasn't threatening Stu," I said. "And you can stop lying to me about Maria. I know she's here. I saw her."

He gave me a little smile. "If you say so, McKnight."

"Where did it happen?"

"The shooting?" he said.

"Yes, the shooting."

"Why do you want to know that?"

"Why didn't you turn this over to the county?" I said. "Or the state? This is a major crime."

"I don't need to turn it over to anybody," he said. "This is my jurisdiction."

"You're the only full-time officer," I said. "You told me that yourself. How many part-timers did you say you have?"

"Four," he said. "You just met two of them."

That stopped me. "Who?"

"Rocky and Harry," he said.

"The men who were going to cut me in half with a shotgun."

"Everybody's a little jumpy around here today," he said. "Don't forget, we had a shooting yesterday."

"Yeah? And where was Rocky at the time?"

"He didn't shoot the man, McKnight. He was in his bar. Like every other night. Until he got the call..."

"What call?"

"Rocky was the one who answered the 'shots fired' call. He found Wilkins."

"This keeps getting better and better," I said.

"Let me ask you something," he said. "You said you were a Detroit cop."

"Yes."

183

"How long?"

"Eight years."

"Then what? You quit?"

"I got shot."

"I've been shot," he said. "I didn't quit."

"Some people never learn," I said. "What's your point?"

"My point is, I've been a cop my whole life," he said. "I started out as a deputy down in Oakland County. Then I was a state trooper for over twenty years. And then I retired and came back home to Orcus Beach. They asked me to take over as chief of police. Even when the furniture plant closed and we lost half our population, the town council kept the police force. And me."

"Don't tell me," I said. "Rocky and Harry are the town council, too."

He let that one go. "My grandfather practically built this town himself," he said. "I grew up here. I've lived all around the state, but I keep coming back. I know every single person who lives here right now. I'm sure they'll bury me here someday."

"Why are you telling me all this?" I said.

"Because I want you to understand, Mr. McKnight. I'm a lifetime cop, not somebody who wrote tickets for eight years and then became a private eye. This shooting happened in my town. It's my case. I don't want the county guys here. I don't want the state guys here. And most of all, I don't want *you* here. Am I making myself clear?"

"What if I have information you need?"

"Like what?"

"Like a white Cadillac," I said. "The license plate is on the pad your . . . your officer took from me. I'm not sure if one of the letters is a *V* or a *Y*. You'll have to run it both ways."

"And what will this tell me?"

"The name of the guy who's following her," I said. "The same guy who was casing out her family's house in Farmington. You did talk to her family, right?"

"We've been in contact," he said. "I told you that at the hospital."

"So you know about this man named Harwood?"

He tapped his fingers on his desk. "You say Rocky has this number?"

"Yes," I said. "I'm not even going to ask you if I can have my pad back."

"You've had a long day, Mr. McKnight. We should let you go home now."

"I can't go anywhere," I said. "My tires are flat and the gas station is out of air."

"We'll see if we can find you some," he said. "Then you can be on your way."

"It's a long drive home," I said. "And I've been up since four this morning. I think I'll grab a room for the night."

"Won't find one here," he said. "Closest motel is in Whitehall. They're probably full, though. Your best bet would be Grand Rapids."

"So you're all out of rooms, too," I said. "April is your peak tourist season."

He just looked at me. He almost smiled. "You're a funny man," he said. "Let's go pump up your tires."

He let me sit in the front seat this time on the ride back to the gas station. We passed a small motel called the Orcus Arms. It was a little six-room affair facing Lake Michigan. The chief caught me looking at it, and the empty parking lot in front. "It's closed," he said. "Doesn't open until June."

The sign in front of the motel was decorated with a big can-

185

non in a mound of sand, just like on the chief's hat. "What's with this cannon, anyway?" I said.

"Goes back to the turn of the century," he said. "When a ship got caught in a storm, it would try to get as close to the shore as it could. There'd be a crew of men here who would use the cannon to fire a rope out to the ship. They could fire that thing a good half mile if they aimed it right."

I tried to picture it. It would take a hell of a shot to hit a boat that far away.

"Just goes to show you," he said. "A gun doesn't always kill you. Sometimes it saves you."

With that thought ringing in my head, we pulled into the gas station. Stu managed to find some air to put in my tires. He pumped up my tires himself and then he stood next to the chief while I climbed into the cab. When I closed the door, the chief stepped closer and rapped a knuckle on my window. I rolled it down.

"Sleep well tonight, Mr. McKnight," the chief said, "and then have a safe trip back home tomorrow morning. I hope you enjoyed your visit to Orcus Beach."

There were a couple things I could have said to him, but I decided to keep my mouth shut. I turned the key and gunned the engine.

"Seriously, Mr. McKnight," he said. "I know we've got some pretty extreme characters around here. You gotta understand— people in this town, they just have a habit of acting very protectively. You know what I mean? As a matter of fact, I'd say overall, you caught us on a good day. The next time, we might not be so friendly."

I pulled away and left him standing there in the light of the gas station. He got smaller and smaller in my rearview mirror as I headed south, away from Orcus Beach and everyone who lived there.

"Good night, Chief," I said as he faded out of sight. "I'll be seeing you." In my mind's eye, I pictured the pad of paper and the license numbers I had written down. I recited the numbers to myself, just to make sure I remembered them. One for Maria. And the other for whoever was driving that white Cadillac.

Chapter Fifteen

I woke up the next morning in a strange bed, in a motel room in Whitehall, Michigan, twenty miles south of Orcus Beach. I had pulled in around eleven o'clock, my eyes burning from driving all day, my stomach empty. The motel was called the Whitehall Courtyard, and each room had a bright green light above the door that made you think you were in an aquarium. I asked the man at the front desk if there was a restaurant open at that hour. He just looked at me and laughed. "In Whitehall?" he said. "That's the best one I've heard all day."

So I settled for cheese and crackers and Oreo cookies from the vending machine, and then I closed the blinds against the green light and went to sleep. I had disjointed dreams about shotguns and woke up suddenly in the middle of the night, dead certain that I was about to feel the hot blast of buckshot in my chest. It took a few seconds to remember where I was, and what I was doing there. I went back to sleep for a few hours. When the morning came, I sat up in the bed and reached for the telephone. Leon picked up on the second ring.

"Alex!" he said. "Where are you?"

"I'm in a motel in a town called Whitehall," I said. "I need you to run a couple plates for me."

"Whitehall? Where's that? What's going on, Alex?"

I gave him the five-minute version. Seeing Randy in the hospital, going back to Leopold's house, then my adventures in Orcus Beach.

"How can you be sure it's Maria?" he said. "You didn't even talk to her."

"I know it's her," I said. "It has to be. Let me give you those plate numbers."

"All you gotta do is call the secretary of state," he said, "and give them your PI number."

"That's right," I said. "I remember you telling me that now."

"I'll do it," he said. "You've got another call to make."

"What's that?"

"A Dr. Havlin called here looking for you," he said. "Early this morning. He had one of our cards, so he tried both numbers."

"What did he say?"

"They're going to operate."

"Is it . . . I mean . . ."

"He didn't say, Alex. He just said you should call him."

"Okay," I said. "Thanks. I'll do that."

"So give me those plate numbers."

"Here's Maria's plate," I said. I closed my eyes and called up the three letters and three numbers.

"This could get us her current address," he said.

"It might," I said. "And whatever name she's using now."

"Okay, give me the other one."

I gave him the three letters and three numbers from the white Cadillac, then told him he'd have to run it two ways, with a *Y* and a *V.*

"This white Cadillac," he said. "You really think it's the same

189

guy who was staking out her family's house? There are lots of white Cadillacs in the world."

"Maybe it's the same guy," I said. "Maybe it isn't. If it is, then somehow he found Maria."

"Maybe Randy went to Leopold's house," he said, "and then to Orcus Beach, and this guy followed him."

"If that's true," I said, "then I helped make it happen."

Leon didn't say anything for a while. "I'll run these plates," he finally said. "And I'll call you right back."

"No, let me call you," I said. "As soon as I call the doctor, I'm gonna get something to eat. Or I'll need a doctor myself."

I said good-bye, then punched in the doctor's number. A woman at the hospital in Grand Rapids answered. She told me that Dr. Havlin was in surgery.

"Do you know the name of the person he's operating on?" I said. "It may be the man I'm calling about."

"You're going to have to speak to the doctor directly," she said. "I can't discuss it over the phone."

I told her I'd try later. Then I got dressed and went out to see if the town of Whitehall had a place where you could get a decent breakfast. I ended up finding a restaurant with a seven-dollar all-you-can-eat buffet, and I ate enough scrambled eggs and bacon and hash browns to make it the best seven dollars I ever spent. The man who showed me to my table, the woman who took my money, the boy who kept taking my empty plates away—they all looked genuinely happy that I had chosen to visit their little town. It restored my faith in the people who live in Michigan, and it made me wonder why Orcus Beach was so different. I had a few minutes to think about it as I drove back up that lonely two-lane road.

I pulled out my cell phone on the way and tried to call Leon.

The call didn't go through. I barely overcame the temptation to open my window and throw the phone into the lake.

I got to see Orcus Beach in the daylight this time. It was a sleepy little shoreline town that had seen better days. You wouldn't have thought it was much different from a thousand other towns, until you happened to stop in and sample the local hospitality.

I drove past Rocky's place. The parking lot was full again. Either they did a good breakfast or they did the only breakfast in town. I kept going north, through the traffic light and past the gas station. I could see Stu sitting at his counter, but I didn't think he noticed me driving by.

I went past the town hall and the fire station. I didn't drive around back to see if Chief Rudiger was there. I didn't figure he'd be too happy to see me.

I kept going, past the old furniture plant. The road opened up again into a long stretch of nothing but pine trees and glimpses of the lake to the west. I drove another ten miles, just to confirm to myself that Orcus Beach really was in the middle of nowhere. I pulled over and tried the phone again. The signal teased me for a few seconds and then disappeared.

I went back to town. This time when I got to the traffic light, I took a left and went east, away from the lake. I crossed over some railroad tracks and drove through a neighborhood of small houses set closely together. Everything looked heavy and wet, like the snow had just melted. There was an empty ball field at the next corner, with wooden bleachers down the first-base line. I watched for white Cadillacs as I drove. I saw one parked in front of a little bait shop at the edge of town, but the license plate didn't match the one I had seen the day before.

As I drove, I couldn't help wondering exactly where Randy

191

had been shot. It had been only two days since the shooting, and it was such a small town. I kept expecting to see yellow crime-scene tape, but I didn't.

The road leading east went over a small bridge, then turned north. After another few houses, the pavement gave way to gravel. I stopped and turned around. When I got back to the middle of town, I kept going west, right through the traffic light, toward the shoreline. I figured I might as well see the whole town.

The road led directly to a public boat launch. The place was empty. I pulled in and looked out at the water for a minute. I could hear the sand ticking against the truck, driven by the wind off the lake. I tried the phone again. The planets must have been aligned just right this time, because I got a signal and it stayed strong enough for me to make two calls. The first was to Leon. It was busy. He's probably calling about the license plates right now, I thought. The second call was to the hospital. I got through to Dr. Havlin this time. The signal wavered for a few seconds and his voice started to break up, but then the line cleared and I heard him telling me what he had just done to Randy.

"Mr. Wilkins had what we call a pellet embolism," he said. "A piece of buckshot entered the bloodstream and then migrated away from the wound, all the way to the brain. Which is why we didn't see it when we were working on his neck."

"How serious is that?" I said. "It goes right into the brain?"

"Well, actually, it stopped where the cerebral artery enters the brain. The end result was a stroke, which explains why he didn't regain consciousness. It must have knocked out both hemispheres."

"So now what?" I said. "Is he conscious now? Is there going to be permanent damage?"

"He's not conscious, no," he said. "As far as permanent damage goes, we just don't know right now. We're doing a neuro check every hour. Meanwhile, we've still got a county deputy outside his door every minute, day and night. I don't know what they think Mr. Wilkins is going to do. Anyway, I've got your number, Mr. McKnight. I'll call you if anything changes."

"I appreciate it," I said.

I hung up and pulled back out onto the secondary road, taking it south until it came to a dead end, then headed north. The homes on the lake side of the road had mailboxes next to long driveways. Some of the houses were bigger than others, but they all looked a little beaten up by the long winters and the storms on the lake. I saw a lot of NO TRESPASSING signs. Like most of the lower Great Lakes, the shoreline here was strictly private property.

I didn't see any white Cadillacs. I didn't see Maria's red Mustang. The road ended abruptly where a little inlet cut in from the shoreline. There was a guardrail there to keep you from driving right into it, and behind that a chain-link fence with four seasons' worth of litter pasted to it. I turned the truck around and headed back to the center of town.

So now what, Alex? Either you go to the hospital and wait to see what happens to Randy. Or you stay here in town and do something stupid.

When I got back to Rocky's place, I saw Maria's car in the parking lot. I tried the phone and somehow it worked again. A day filled with miracles already. Leon picked up on the first ring.

"Alex, I've got some names for you," he said. I could hear the enthusiasm in his voice. This kind of stuff was what he lived for. "Are you ready?"

I didn't have my little pad of paper anymore, so I grabbed a deposit envelope out of the glove compartment. "Go ahead," I said.

"I'll give you the white Caddy first," he said. "If that was a *V* you saw on the plate, then it was a woman named Ethel Birmingham from Center Line, Michigan. And it wasn't really a white Cadillac; it was a brown Buick."

"I'm guessing it wasn't really a *V*," I said.

"Good man," he said. "If it was a *Y*, then you've got a Mr. Miles Whitley, who just so happens to own a white 1983 Cadillac, and just so happens to be a private investigator out of Detroit."

"A private investigator?"

"Are you surprised?"

"I don't know," I said. "I guess not. Not if he's been following her. Maybe this Harwood guy hired him."

"My thought exactly," he said. "I've got his number here if you want it. I don't know if we should just call the guy or not. What do you think?"

"Good question," I said. "Let's think about that one."

"Okay, so you want the other plate now? It gets better."

"How can it get better?" I said. "We know it's Maria, right?"

"The plate is registered to Maria Zambelli," he said. "The address given is on Romney Street in Farmington."

"Leopold's house," I said.

"Right."

"So now we know the last name she's using these days. Where's the 'better' part?"

"That name, Alex. Zambelli. It sounded familiar to me. I was sitting here for a half hour trying to remember where I've heard it before."

"And?"

"You remember when you came back up here after you were done running around with Randy? What did you tell me?"

"Hell, I don't know. I told you what happened. About how we ended up at Leopold's house."

"And about how you were kidnapped and held hostage in the basement."

"All right, Leon, I don't have to relive the whole thing now. What's your point?"

"You told me that they thought you were working for this guy named Harwood, right? That's why they did that to you?"

"Yeah?"

"And when you told me that, what did I say?"

"I don't honestly remember. I'm sorry."

"I told you we should try to find out about Harwood, so we could help them, right?"

"Okay, I remember now. And I said forget about it."

"Exactly. And do you think I just forgot about it?"

"Knowing you, no," I said. "Now that you mention it."

"I just poked around a little bit, Alex. On the Internet, looking up the name Harwood."

"Okay, what did you find, Leon?"

"Nothing," he said. "At least it seemed like nothing at the time. I was searching through a database of old newspaper articles, looking for any hits on Harwood. You know, like if I found an article about a man named Harwood being arrested for stalking somebody. Something like that. But I came up empty. So I let it go. But then I remembered, somewhere when I was looking, I saw those two names together. Harwood and Zambelli."

"Where did you see them together, Leon? Were you able to go back and find it?"

"Sure, all I had to do was go back and look for any articles that had both of those names," he said. "I've got it right here. Harwood-Zambelli, Incorporated. A real estate development company, formed in 1969. They were mentioned in a state investigation in 1977 after purchasing an acreage lot from the state. There was some suspicion of bid tampering, but no charges were ever filed."

"Harwood-Zambelli," I said. "Any first names in the article?"

"No, but I'm gonna keep looking."

"Real estate, huh? Just out of curiosity, where's the land they bought?"

"It's up near Traverse City," he said.

"A couple hours north of here," I said. "Do you have anything else on that?"

"That's all I have right now," he said. "I just thought you'd like to know. Assuming there's a connection."

"Be a hell of a coincidence if there isn't," I said. "Damn it, Leon, you do good work, even when you're sitting on your ass all day."

"So what are you going to do now?" he said.

I looked out at Maria's car, less than thirty feet away. "I'm feeling a little dry," I said. "I'm gonna go have a drink." I hung up, got out of the truck, and walked right through the front door.

Nothing happened. It wasn't at all like the scene in the saloon, when the gunslinger pushes open the swinging doors and the piano stops playing and everybody looks up. Nobody even noticed me. They all went on eating their breakfasts or brunches or drinking their early beers.

Maria was in the same spot as the night before. She sat reading a newspaper, with an empty plate on the bar in front of her. I went right over and sat down next to her.

"Ms. Zambelli," I said. "Good morning."

She put her paper down and looked at me. It was my first chance to see her up close, and for the love of God, she had eyes that could make a man write poetry.

Or hell, even sing Romeo's song. In French.

The last woman I had known with eyes like that was Sylvia Fulton, and those eyes had owned me for a year and a half before she finally went away. Maria's eyes were darker, but they had that same way of making you feel like you were losing your balance when you looked into them.

"Do I know you?" she said.

The bartender stepped in before I could say anything. He leaned over the bar until his face was about twelve inches from mine, and he said, "What the hell are you doing here?"

When I had first hit this town the night before, it seemed a little strange that I'd found Maria so quickly. Just walked into the only bar, and there she was. But then it hadn't taken long to see why she could hide in plain sight like this. There were certainly enough well-armed men around to come to her rescue.

"Your name's Harry, if I recall," I said. "Where's Rocky? I wanted to say hello to him when I came in."

"You've got ten seconds to get out of here," he said.

"Yeah, count to ten," I said. "That always works for me." I threw a couple bills on the bar. "And then get me a beer."

He didn't look down at the bills. He didn't get me a beer. Instead, he took exactly one step backward and then, without taking his eyes off me for a second, grabbed the phone off the wall.

"Hold on, Harry," she said. "Before you arrest him, let's hear what the man has to say. It might be good for a laugh."

"Now why on earth would you arrest me?" I said to him. "I'm just sitting here trying to buy a beer."

He didn't say anything. I could see his knuckles whiten as he gripped the phone.

"Never mind," I said. "I'm sure you guys would think of something."

"We're waiting to hear your story," she said. She picked up her pack of cigarettes and pulled one out. "Do you have a light?"

"I don't smoke," I said.

Harry put the phone down and produced a lighter. As he held it to the tip of her cigarette, once again he never took his eyes off me for a second. The man was talented.

"You like having big men around to look after you, don't you," I said.

"You're not exactly a lightweight yourself," she said. "I have to admit, you're put together better than any of those other men Charles has sent after me."

"By Charles, I assume you mean Mr. Harwood?"

"Aren't you the guy who's been following me around in the white Cadillac the last couple days?"

"No, ma'am," I said. "I drive a truck."

"Well, who the hell are you, then?" she said. "No, wait. Let me guess." She took a long drag on her cigarette and then blew the smoke straight upward. "I bet you I know. My brother told me a couple men came by his house last week looking for me. Mother told him that Charles didn't send them, but Leo's still not convinced."

"I thought your brother hates being called Leo," I said.

"Aha, so you *were* one of those men," she said. "I thought he sent you on your way without telling you where I was."

"Ms. Zambelli," I said. "Maria." Harry bristled when I said her name, like I had taken an indecent liberty. "Didn't your brother tell you who we were?"

"I think he mentioned a couple names," she said, taking a drag on her cigarette. "I don't remember them."

"My name is Alex McKnight," I said. "Which shouldn't mean anything to you. But the man I was with was Randy Wilkins."

She looked at me without saying anything. After a long moment, she looked away.

"Do you remember him?" I said.

"He's the man who was shot here a couple days ago," she said. "That's where I've heard that name. The chief told me." She looked up at Harry, but he didn't notice. He was too busy watching me.

"Yes," I said. "Randy was looking for you. Do you remember him? From thirty years ago?"

"No," she said. "That was a long time ago."

I hesitated. "You don't remember him? Your mother did. As soon as she saw him."

"My mother has a good memory," she said. "It's one of her many gifts. Unfortunately, I didn't inherit most of them."

"My God," I said. "I don't believe this. You're telling me you don't remember him. And he didn't find you here? I mean, before he got shot? He didn't talk to you at all?"

"Harry," she said. "You've got some customers waiting on you." She nodded her head toward two men on the other side of the bar. They were standing over two empty glasses and looking like their patience was about used up.

Harry didn't move. He kept watching me.

"Go ahead," she said. "I think he's harmless. You can go ahead and frisk him if it'll make you feel better."

He backed away slowly and went over to the two men. He kept watching me as he poured out a couple drafts.

Maria put her hands together in front of her face. Without looking at me, she whispered something.

"I can't hear you," I said.

"Shhhhh," she said in a low voice. She kept her hands in front of her face. "Just act natural. Tell me you made a mistake and then leave. In twenty minutes, I'll go out to my car. Just follow me."

She brought her hands down and put out her cigarette. She jabbed it in the ashtray like she was punishing it. "I'm sorry," she said out loud as Harry came back to us. "I don't remember a Randy Wilkins. The name means nothing to me."

Chapter Sixteen

Twenty minutes later, I was sitting in my truck, watching the front door, wondering if my new friend Harry would be coming out to ask me why I was still on the premises. The sun had just come out, a rare event on any of Michigan's shorelines in mid-April. Maria stepped out into the sunlight and stood there blinking for a moment. She was short and compact, like her brother, Leopold. But where Leopold had muscles, Maria had curves. She looked around the parking lot and saw me sitting there in my truck. She stared right at me for a long time, her head tilted a little to the side. Then she went over to her red Mustang and got in.

She pulled out of the parking lot. I followed her as she took a left toward the center of town. At the intersection, I saw Stu outside pumping gas, but he didn't look up at either one of us. Maria took a left at the traffic light and went west, toward the shoreline. I lost sight of her for a few seconds; then when I saw her car again, it was stopped in front of the boat launch. I pulled in next to her.

She jumped out of her car, opened my passenger door, slid into the cab, and then closed the door behind her. "Tell me everything you know," she said. She opened up a black leather bag and left her right hand inside it.

"You don't waste time," I said. "And do you mind telling me what kind of gun you have in that bag?"

"Somebody will see us," she said. "Just tell me. Is he going to live?"

"I don't know," I said. "The doctor says they're going to operate on him. A fragment went up into his brain."

"I can't believe this is happening." Her right hand stayed in the bag. I imagined a little revolver with a pearl handle. At least it wasn't a shotgun.

"I'm supposed to call the hospital later," I said. "The doctor may have a better idea then."

"How do you know Randy?" she said. "You're a friend of his?"

"I was an old teammate of his. He came to me last week and asked me to help him find you. He told me all about how he met you in Detroit, back in 1971."

"You were his teammate then? In Detroit? I'm sorry, I'm trying to remember you . . ."

"No, we played ball together in Toledo. He got called up in September, but I didn't. So I wasn't around when he met you."

"Why did he say he was trying to find me?"

"Maria, I don't blame you for being careful, but I've had too many guns pointed at me this week. It's starting to get to me."

"It's not pointed at you," she said. "I'm just holding it."

"Either you trust me or you don't," I said. "If you don't, then get out of the truck and I'll be on my way."

She pulled her right hand out of the bag. For one frozen instant, I saw a flash of something white in her hand.

It was a hairbrush.

I took a breath. "Remind me to never play poker with you," I said.

"I'm sorry," she said. "After all I've been through . . . Well, never mind. Just tell me what he said. Why was Randy trying to find me?"

"He said some pretty crazy things. About running out on you back then, and still thinking about you all these years later. And then suddenly deciding that he had to find you again."

"My God," she said.

"Of course, now I know he was probably trying to scam you."

She looked at me. She didn't say anything.

"We ended up at your brother's house," I said. "You know about that. I thought it was all over. I thought he went back to California. Then I found out he came here and got himself shot."

She looked out the window. The sun went behind a cloud, turning the lake a different shade of green.

"Maria," I said. "I swear, I had no idea he was a criminal. Not until the chief told me."

"You hadn't seen him at all in what, thirty years?" she said. "You had no contact with him?"

"No," I said.

"And then he just comes back and asks you to help him? Why did he do that?"

"I don't know," I said. "Because I live in Michigan. Because I know Detroit."

"And why did you help him?"

"I don't know that, either," I said. "Because he asked me to. Because I thought he was looking for you for a good reason. Or at least a harmless reason. I had no idea he was trying to scam you. Although I suppose it makes sense now. His racket is real estate, and I assume this has something to do with Zambelli-Harwood. . . ."

She looked me in the eyes. "How do you know about that?"

"My partner," I said. "He found an old news article. He just told me about it. The Zambelli in the name, is that you, or . . ."

"My husband," she said. "My late husband. Harwood killed him."

I didn't say anything. The words hung in the air.

A car drove by on the road behind us. Maria slid down in her seat.

"When we were in the bar," I said, "why didn't you want Harry to know you recognized Randy's name?"

"It's a long story," she said. "Can you come to my house?"

"I can do that," I said. "Are you sure you want me to? Your friends in the bar wouldn't like it if they found out."

"I showed you my gun, didn't I?" She put the hairbrush back in her bag. "I'm not as good as my mother, but I think I have some sense of what's inside a person, as soon as I meet them. I think you're telling the truth."

"I'll follow you," I said. "Lead the way."

She got out of the truck and went to her own car, got in and pulled back out onto the road. I followed her for a half mile, until she turned left into a gravel driveway that was heavily rutted. There was an old wooden fence running along the front of the property, so I couldn't see the house from the road. As soon as I did see it, I knew it was the biggest house in town.

The driveway snaked around to the front door, but she didn't stop there. She kept going until the driveway stopped at the side of the house. I pulled in behind her, next to a small boat on a trailer. The plastic tarp that covered it was tied down with enough rope to withstand a hurricane.

She took me in the side door. There was a low concrete porch, and then a path that led down to a small boathouse. A late-morning wind was coming in off the lake.

"Nice house," I said as I stepped inside. There was a little room to take your coat off in, and then a large living room done up in white pine, with big rough-hewn beams running across the ceiling. I saw a few nautical maps framed on the walls, and a mariner's barometer set inside a gold wheel. Somehow, I knew she hadn't decorated the place herself.

"I'm renting it," she said. "You'll never guess who from."

"Captain Nemo," I said.

"Chief Rudiger," she said.

"That's wonderful," I said. "He'll be so happy if he finds out I was here."

"For what he's charging me, I should be able to entertain anybody I want. Can I get you a drink?"

"A beer?" I said. "I didn't get much service at Rocky's."

When she left, I looked out the big picture window at Lake Michigan. It was calm now, but I knew that could change without much warning. A pair of binoculars sat on the windowsill—one of those Leica models that cost at least five hundred dollars. I picked them up and looked out at the lake, spotted a freighter in the distance. It was heading north, probably from Chicago. It would go under the Mackinac Bridge, sneak around Drummond Island, and then head through the Soo locks. If I go home right now, I thought, I'll be able to see it again, coming through White-fish Bay.

Maria came back into the room with two beers and two

glasses. She was one of those women who always surprise you with how good they look, even if they've only been away for thirty seconds. The beers in her hands didn't hurt the effect.

"He's got good taste in binoculars," I said. "Why's he renting this place, anyway? Where does he live now?"

"He's got a little place in town," she said, putting the bottles down on a coffee table. "He says he doesn't need this big place now that his wife is dead and his kids are moved out. So he rented it to me. Not that I need this big a place, either. It's just temporary."

"Until what?" I said.

She looked at me. "Until I move someplace for real," she said. "Now sit down here and tell me more about Randy."

I obeyed her. I sat down and poured myself a beer. She sat down on the couch next to me.

"So, you do remember him," I said, "from 1971?"

"Yes," she said. "Of course I remember him."

"It was almost thirty years ago."

"It could be eighty years," she said. "I'd still remember."

"He certainly is one of a kind, but—"

"Alex, I know I already asked you this," she said, "but why did he come here, really? Do you really think he was—what did you say? Trying to scam me?"

I looked at her. "I told you before. At first, I thought it was because he wanted to find you again. Because he thought you were the one who got away."

"You believed him."

"Yes," I said. "If I had seen you in person, it would have been easy to believe."

"I appreciate the flattery," she said. "But even so, Alex, most people wouldn't have come all the way down here to help him."

"I'm a complete idiot," I said. "I think I've established that pretty well."

"No," she said. "You believed him because that's the kind of man you are."

"The idiot kind."

She smiled. "What do you believe now? Do you really think he came here to steal money from me?"

"It seems to be his calling," I said. "I think his record speaks for itself."

She looked out the big window at the lake. "I do have money to steal," she said. "My husband's business was very successful, before . . . before he died."

"You said Harwood killed him."

"Yes."

"Can you tell me about it?"

She took a deep breath. "Alex, when I met Randy, I was very young. But he was the first, if you know what I mean. When he left without saying a word, it hit me very hard. I didn't think I would love another man ever again. But then a man came to see my mother. A man named Harwood. Charles Harwood. He kept coming back, and he always paid her a hundred dollars for each reading. That was a great deal of money in those days. He drove a big convertible, too. My father was very interested in this man. And this man, this Charles Harwood, he was obviously very interested in me. He asked me many times to go driving with him in his big convertible, but I always turned him down. My father was angry with me. Eventually, he persuaded me to go with Harwood. 'Just a little trip around town,' my father said. 'What is the harm, a short trip in the car? With this man who pays your mother a hundred dollars every time he sees her.' So I went with this man, and he drove around Detroit with the top down.

He asked me all these questions, but I didn't feel like talking to him. So he finally shut up and just drove me back home. I thought that would be the end of it, but the next week he was back, asking me to go driving with him again. I went with him, and this time I did not say one single word the entire time. But he kept coming back, and he kept giving my mother a hundred dollars every time, and he kept asking me to ride in his car. And I would go and not say a word. Until finally one day he drove right out of the city and through all the suburbs and right out into the countryside. I was scared. But I didn't say anything. I didn't want him to know how scared I was. He drove all the way out to a farm in Oakland County, right down this little dirt road in the middle of nowhere, and when he finally stopped, I was sure he would do something terrible to me. But he didn't. He just sat there and looked out at the farm, and then he told me that he and his partner had just bought the place and that they were going to build a golf course. And then they'd find more land and build another one, and then another one. And they would both become very rich. He asked me if I had ever thought what it would be like to have lots of money, but before I could answer him, his partner showed up. He drove right up behind us in his beat-up little car, and he came up to see who this young girl was sitting in Harwood's convertible. His name was Arthur Zambelli."

She paused to take a long drink; then she looked out the window at the lake again and continued.

"Arthur Zambelli was everything that Harwood wasn't. He was kind and gentle. And he didn't care about money, even though he would end up having a lot of it. He just didn't think about it. All he wanted to do was build things. And eat. And drink good wine. And champagne. The man loved champagne.

He told me that every single day of your life should be special enough to celebrate with champagne. Which sounds kind of corny, but he made you believe it. We were married for ten years, Alex. Almost ten years. Our ten-year anniversary would have been . . ."

She stopped again, a small smile coming across her face, then disappearing.

"Harwood was not happy when I chose Arthur over him. He tried not to show it. He would have left the partnership in a second, but he wasn't about to walk away from the golf course deal. And then after that, there was another deal, and then another deal. There was always another property to buy. Another hotel or golf course or resort to build. They were very successful. I married Arthur, and eventually Harwood married another woman. We spent a lot of time together, all four of us. We had to. But the way Harwood looked at me, and the way he talked to me whenever we were alone, I knew he hadn't forgotten.

"Harwood's marriage didn't last. I wasn't surprised. The more I got to know him—I mean, with all the time we had to spend with him . . . My God, Alex, he is the most horrible man. He had Arthur fooled so badly. For years, I tried to warn him. I tried to convince him to dissolve their partnership. I think he would have, too, if Harwood hadn't . . ."

She stopped.

"What did he do?" I said.

"Arthur was out on one of the properties one night. He liked to do that—just walk around for a couple days to get a feel for the land. They found him the next morning at the bottom of a drainage ditch. His neck was broken. They said he walking alone and he must have fallen, but I knew better. Harwood killed him. I know he did."

"When was that?"

"It was just six months before Delilah was born," she said. "We had been trying for so long to have children. Can you believe it? He never even saw his own baby. I've been a widow for eighteen years now, and I've been running from Harwood the whole time."

"How can you run that long?" I said. "Eighteen years."

"Not all the time," she said. "I move; he finds me. I move again, and a few years later, he finds me again. . . ."

"Maria, what does he want from you? Does he hate you that much just because you married his partner instead of him?"

"It's not that," she said. "There's more to this than just a personal vendetta. A few years before Arthur died, they bought about seven hundred acres up near Traverse City. There was nothing up there then, but now the whole county is booming. There are so many new resorts up there right now, and this land they bought, it's right next to one of the big golf courses, with a little ski mountain even. We could sell that land for twenty million, easy."

"So why don't you?"

"Alex, the old partnership still owns that land. Harwood-Zambelli. And there's a provision in the partnership that both partners have to agree before selling any jointly owned property."

"And you can't agree? Why wouldn't you both want to sell it?"

"It's not so simple," she said. "The terms are very specific about what happens if either partner dies. A surviving spouse takes over the partner's vote and is entitled to half of the profits. A divorced spouse only gets twenty percent, and no vote. Harwood's ex-wife is fighting that one, even though she signed the prenuptial agreement. Michigan's a pretty strong common-property state, so she has a shot at it."

"So what does that have to do with you?" I said. "You're a surviving spouse. He can't change that. Unless—"

"Unless I'm no longer surviving," she said. "There's a provision for that, too. Just like the divorce clause. Twenty percent to my estate, and no vote. Arthur didn't realize what he was doing when he signed that agreement, Alex. He didn't know he was signing my death warrant."

"So twenty percent instead of fifty percent," I said. "Out of twenty million. He'd kill you for the difference of what, six million dollars?"

"I think it's safe to say that he would do that for six million dollars, yes."

I took a hit off my beer and thought about that one.

"I can't see your brother running away," I said. "Ever. How come he hasn't killed this guy by now?"

"He almost did," she said. "When Arthur died, I told Leopold what I suspected. He went after Harwood, tried to kill him. Thank God he didn't. He would have gone to jail. Since then, Leopold has always wanted to make a stand, to stay in one place and dare Harwood to come get me. That house in Farmington, that's the first house that any of us have owned outright. Delilah's in high school now. I want her to finish there. Leopold promised me that she'd be safe. They watch her every minute."

"I know," I said. "I saw that firsthand."

"So you did," she said. "So you did. And I'm close enough, I can see her sometimes. We're very careful about it. We meet on weekends. We make sure nobody follows her."

"Randy wasn't careful," I said. "That white Cadillac, it belongs to a private investigator."

"How do you know?"

"My partner ran the plate," I said. "His name is Whitley. He works out of Detroit."

"Harwood must've hired him," she said. "He's done that before."

"Well, we could contact him ourselves," I said. "Tell him to lay off."

"He'd send somebody else," she said. "Now that he's found me again. Or he'd come himself. . . ."

"Maria, why don't you just sign away the full partnership money? Tell him you'll take the twenty percent and forfeit the rest?"

She looked at me.

"You could stop running," I said.

"I don't know," she said. "Maybe you're right. Maybe that's what I should do."

"You already have money. You said so yourself. The money your husband left you, right?"

She looked out at the lake. "It may be too late," she said. "I should have done that eighteen years ago. Maybe even ten years ago. It's an obsession with him now. After all this time, I don't think he'd settle for less than everything. Every dollar, Alex."

When she faced me again, I saw tears in her eyes. God help me, all I could think about was how lovely she was. That was the only word for her. Not beautiful, not pretty. Maria was lovely.

"Every dollar," she said. "And my life, Alex. He wants me to die."

I wanted to reach out and take her hand. But I didn't. "Okay," I said. "Okay. I'm sorry. I'm sure I can't imagine what it's been like."

"And now Randy shows up," she said. "It's unbelievable."

"Maria, you still haven't told me why you said that stuff in the bar, about not remembering him."

She looked down at the glass in her hand. It was empty.

"Maria?"

She didn't say anything.

"Maria, what's the matter?"

"It was me," she said, her voice so low now, I could barely hear her.

"What do you mean?"

"It was me," she said. "I shot him."

Chapter Seventeen

She opened the front door. She didn't follow me out onto the landing, just stood leaning against the door frame, her arms folded across her chest. The landing was made of flat bluestone, with tall plants on either side that were nothing more than tangled bare branches at this time of year. The air was cold. I'd left my coat behind, somewhere in the living room. But I didn't care. I stood there looking down at the landing while she told me what had happened.

"I came home three days ago," she said. "As soon as I walked in, I knew somebody had been here. Everything was where it was supposed to be, and yet not *exactly*. Something was just . . . wrong. I could feel it. I called Chief Rudiger, but he swore he hadn't come here. Even though he has a key, he doesn't do that. Not without asking me. Then when I started seeing the white Cadillac around town, it didn't take me long to figure it out. Harwood had found me again. Somehow. And the man in the Cadillac, he broke in here. He had touched everything in the house, Alex. Everything that belonged to me, he had put his hands on it. I called the chief again. He told me he'd keep an eye out for him but that he could only do so much. He's the only full-time officer in town."

"So I've learned," I said. "One professional and a lot of amateurs with guns. So what happened next? Did the car come back?"

"Yes," she said. "I saw it the next day. There's a room up on the second floor; you can see out onto the road, through the trees. The car was just sitting there. I called the chief, but by the time he got over here, the car was gone. It came back later, just after dark. I was upstairs, watching for it. He pulled up there in the same spot on the road, just through the trees there where the fence starts. I was just about to call the chief again, when I heard somebody coming up the walkway."

She stopped. She stood there with her arms still folded in front of her, staring out at nothing.

"What happened?" I said.

"I had a gun," she said. "One of Leopold's shotguns. He keeps one at the house, and he made me take the other one. I was sure it was Harwood, or somebody Harwood had hired to kill me. I got the gun, and when I looked out the little window by the door here, I saw something in his hand. It was dark, but I could see he was holding something. It's a gun, I thought. It has to be a gun. He was coming to kill me, Alex. It didn't matter if the door was locked. He had already gotten into the place before. Nothing could stop him. There was nothing I could do, except . . . open the door and shoot. I shot him, Alex. I threw the door open and shot him. Then I ran past him, got in my car, and drove away. As I was driving, I started seeing the man's face. Like I looked at him but I didn't really *see* him until later, when I had time to think about what had happened, you know what I mean? I could still see his face, just before the gun went off. And I *knew* him. I knew that face. He has a beard and mustache now, doesn't he? He looks different. Yet he's still the same. All these years later, he's still the same. And I shot him."

"Did he have a gun?"

"What?" She looked up at me.

"In his hand. You said you thought he had a gun. Did he?"

"No," she said. "It was a flower. A lilac. That's what he was holding. It's supposed to mean something, isn't it? When you give somebody a lilac? Something about the innocence of youth. If it did mean something, he never got the chance to tell me."

I looked down at the stones. There were no lilac petals there now. There was no blood, no trace of what had happened.

"He was the first man I ever loved," she said. "And I shot him."

She didn't cry. I didn't know if she wanted me to hold her or if she wanted me to go away and never come back. I just stood there.

"You have to tell them, don't you," she said.

"Tell them what?"

"That I shot him. You have to tell the chief, and I'll go to jail."

I thought about it for exactly two seconds. "Not necessarily," I said. "It was an accident. You panicked. What did you do with the shotgun, anyway?"

"I threw it in the woods."

"Where?"

"Down the highway," she said. "A couple miles outside of town."

"Probably not the best place," I said. "But there's no sense trying to move it now."

"Will you help me, Alex?"

"What do you want me to do?"

"Find out why he came here. If he found out I had money, or if Harwood was using him somehow. And then help me find

216

Harwood. Somehow, I have to make him stop. Will you help me?"

"I don't know if I can, Maria. How are we going to find him? What do we have to go on?"

"We have this man," she said. "The man in the white Cadillac. I'm sure Harwood hired him."

"We can't prove he broke into your house," I said. "Aside from that, he's just following you around. The police can give him a warning, but I doubt they could charge him with anything. And they certainly can't make him talk about who hired him. There are laws that protect that information."

"Like a doctor and a patient," she said. "Or a lawyer and a client."

"Exactly."

"Or a private investigator," she said. "If I hire you, you don't have to say anything, either. About any of this."

I could see where she was going. I guess I didn't blame her for wanting to protect herself, now that she had made her confession to me. And I didn't blame her for wanting to find Harwood so she could put an end to it. I didn't blame her for anything, not even for the shooting itself.

I was the man who'd helped Randy find her. If I was going to blame anybody, I would start with myself.

"Maria, I'll talk to my partner. Maybe he'll have some ideas. He's good at this stuff."

"And what are *you* good at?" she said.

"Well, the police can't make that PI tell them who his client is, or *where* he is. But maybe I can. That's the advantage of not being a police officer anymore. I don't always have to follow the rules."

"Do you think you can catch him?"

"I may not have to," I said. "I'll try calling him, see if he'll meet me. One private eye to another."

"Does that mean you're on the case?"

"If I can help you, I will," I said. "But you should know that I'm not really a private eye. It just sort of happened. I was a cop once, but—"

"Does that mean you're on the case, Alex?"

I looked at her. I couldn't think of a good reason to say no.

We went back inside the house, our faces red from the cold air. She told me more about Harwood, about the ways he had tried to find her in the past. After her husband's death, she had moved to Florida, had her baby there. She'd spent four years in Tampa, without the slightest contact from him. She let herself believe that he had given up, until the day she went home and stopped to talk to her neighbor before going inside. The neighbor told her that two men had come that day to repair her refrigerator. The landlord had given them the key, or so they said. Maria knew better. She called her brother, Leopold, who was living in Seattle with their mother, and then drove right to the airport. She left everything behind.

She spent three years in Seattle with Leopold and their mother. Leopold was married. His son, Anthony, was a couple years older than Delilah. Harwood found them. They moved to Cincinnati. Leopold's wife left him, moved back to Seattle. She couldn't take it anymore. Harwood found them in Cincinnati, so they all went back to Seattle. Leopold tried to reunite with his ex-wife. It didn't work. Harwood found them again. They finally moved back here to Michigan, where it had all started. As Leopold put it, they were making their stand, once and for all.

It was late afternoon by the time I left. I told her I needed to make some calls. She offered me her phone, but I told her I wanted to check for messages back at the motel in Whitehall, and that I had left my list of numbers there anyway. The truth was, I wanted to be by myself for a while, to think about what I was doing and why I was doing it. I gave her the number for my cell phone and made her promise to call me if she saw the white Cadillac.

"You're on the case," I said out loud, just to hear how it sounded. "You are on the case." I shook my head and kept driving.

As soon as I made my right turn onto the main road, I saw the flashers in my rearview mirror. I pulled over to the side of the road, closed my eyes, and waited for Chief Rudiger to stick his face in my window.

The door opened. "Out of the truck," he said.

I looked at him.

"I said out of the truck, McKnight."

As soon as my feet hit the ground, he spun me around and pushed me against the side of the truck.

"Chief, what the hell do you think you're doing?"

"Hands on the top of the vehicle," he said.

"You've got to be kidding me."

"Hands on top, McKnight."

I put my hands up. He kicked my legs apart and patted me down. Then he pulled my arms behind me and put the hand-cuffs on.

"Rudiger, are you going to tell me what the hell is going on here?"

He pushed me toward his patrol car. When he opened the back door, he tried to push my head down. It was an old cop

219

trick. You push the perp's head down like you're trying to help him clear the top edge of the door. Accidents will happen, though, and if you happen to misjudge the clearance, you end up bashing his face right against the door frame. Which is a damned shame, especially if the man whose nose you just broke happens to be a rapist or child molester.

I thought about kicking him right in the *cojones,* then thought better of it. No sense making the situation any worse. I just sat there in the back of the patrol car and counted to ten. I had been doing a lot of counting to ten in the last few days, not to mention all the time I had spent in handcuffs. Along with the number of shotgun barrels I had looked into, it had been quite a week.

"You need to tell me what's going on, Chief," I said as he got in and closed the door. "You can't cuff me without telling me why."

He swung the car around, did a U-turn, and headed north.

"We're going to the station," I said. "Am I under arrest?"

He didn't say anything.

I sat back, getting as comfortable as I could on the hard plastic seat. There was nothing I could do except play out the hand.

Two minutes later, he pulled in behind the town hall. He got out, his boots crunching on the gravel in the parking lot, and opened my door. "Out," he said.

I got out. He pushed me toward the building. I walked. He opened the door and held it for me, then followed me into the office. "Sit," he said.

"I'm not sitting down until you take off these cuffs," I said.

"Suit yourself," he said. "You can keep standing. I'm gonna sit down." He pulled out the chair behind his desk.

"Chief Rudiger, you are way over the line here. Do you want me to start naming all the rights violations?"

"Ms. Zambelli filed a complaint," he said, leaning back in his chair. "I just brought you in for questioning. You are handcuffed because we are alone in this office and because in the brief time I have known you, you have proven yourself to be hostile and uncooperative."

"What complaint? What are you talking about?"

"For the past few days, Ms. Zambelli has been aware that she is being followed by an unknown party. Today, one of my part-time officers observed you waiting for her in the parking lot, then following her to her residence."

"The man who has been following her drives a white Cadillac," I said. "I've already given you that license number. If you bother to run it, you'll see that it belongs to a private investigator out of Detroit. His name is Whitley."

"Ah, so she's got two investigators following her? I don't suppose the two of you are working together."

"I've never met him," I said. "I presume he's working for Charles Harwood, the man who's been trying to find Maria for the last eighteen years."

"You seem to know a lot about the situation," he said. "I mean, for a man who supposedly has no involvement."

"You know my story, Chief. I came here to see Maria because my friend was looking for her."

"Your friend the con man."

"So it turns out."

"And today, you were following her because . . ."

I hesitated.

"You waited in the parking lot for twenty minutes," he said. "After she told you in the company of my officer that she had no recollection of this friend of yours, the friend who was supposedly looking for her."

"She did say that, yes. I wasn't satisfied. I wanted to ask her some more questions."

"So you waited in the parking lot. For twenty minutes."

"Thereabouts."

"And then you followed her home."

I felt stuck. I couldn't tell him that she wanted to know about Randy. More than anything, I couldn't tell him about what she had confessed to me.

It was time to play my trump card.

"I can't tell you anything more," I said. "It's between me and my client."

He looked at me for a long moment. "Well now," he finally said. "Your client."

"Yes."

"Isn't that convenient."

"It was her idea," I said. "She asked me to help her."

"You don't say."

"You can call her and ask her."

"I might just do that," he said. "Maybe later. For now, I'd better get those handcuffs off you. I mean, seeing as how I've made such a terrible mistake."

He stood up and took the key out of his pocket. I turned around. He unlocked the cuffs and took them off, dropping them on his desk. I stood there rubbing my wrists as he went back to his chair. He didn't sit down this time. He put his hands on the back of the chair and leaned over his desk.

"What's your game, McKnight?"

I shook my head. "No game, Chief."

"I think you're as dirty as your friend. I think you're trying to take advantage of a very frightened woman who happens to have a little money. Which makes you what? I don't think the scale goes that low."

"I'll have to muddle through despite your opinion of me," I said. "Is there anything else you want to say to me? Or am I free to go?"

"That's all you're gonna do? Just walk out of here? After I dragged you down here like this?"

"I've had worse, Chief. Believe me."

"Nobody's here, McKnight. Maybe you want to take a swing at me."

"If you're going to shoot me," I said, "you're gonna have to do it in cold blood. I'm not gonna give you an excuse."

"Shoot you? My, you do have an active imagination."

"Sure," I said. "And that's why you're making a point of standing across the room from me, with your hands free."

I didn't really think he'd shoot me. I was just trying to rattle him. The day before, I'd been wishing he'd get off his ass and find out what had happened with Randy. Today, I was hoping he'd spend all of his time thinking about me instead. I was on the case, and this was just part of the service.

Perhaps the man *would* have shot me if he'd thought he could have gotten away with it. Or if I *had* given him a good excuse. Or if he'd simply had enough guts to do it.

Hell, maybe he would have worked up the courage to do it, if he had a few more minutes alone with me. He would have shot me and then watched me die on the floor, and my last thought would have been how familiar the feeling was, to be looking up at a ceiling and feeling all of my blood flow out of my body. But one of his part-time men showed up at the door just then, breaking the spell. It was Rocky.

The chief offered me a ride back to my car. I declined.

"It's two miles," he said.

"It's a nice day for a walk," I said. "It'll give me the chance to get to know the place a little better. Now that I'm going to be working here."

A half mile down the road, I heard him behind me. I turned and watched his patrol car. He sped past me without the slightest glance in my direction.

Damn it all, I said to myself. I forgot to compliment the man on his house.

Chapter Eighteen

When I got back to the motel in Whitehall, I called Leon.

"I don't have anything new on this PI, Whitley," he said. "I've called his number a few times, but nobody's answering."

"He's been hanging around in Orcus Beach," I said.

"A good PI would have an answering service," he said. "Or he'd automatically forward his calls to his cell phone."

"I don't know if Whitley would make the 'good' list," I said. "If he's working for Harwood, he doesn't have very good taste in clients. We've got reason to believe that he broke into Maria's house, too."

"He broke into her house? That's offensive, Alex. The man is giving private investigation a bad name."

"I seem to recall the two of us doing the same thing," I said. "Twice, in fact."

"That was different," he said. "We were wearing the white hats on both occasions."

"Whatever you say."

"So why did he break into her house?" he said. "Did he take anything?"

"No, he probably just went through her mail and whatever else he could find. You know, gathering information."

"He could have planted a bug," he said.

"That would explain some things," I said. "Every time she spots him and calls the police, the guy disappears. I'll check her phone when I go back over there."

"Don't be surprised if you don't find anything," he said. "It's too obvious. The guy would be better off using a couple UHF receivers. They make them to look just like pens, or those little outlet adapters—you know, the kind where you plug it in and you've got three outlets instead of one? They put the receiver right in there. That way, you can hear everything that's going on in the room. All the time, not just on the phone."

"That's gotta be against the law, right? I know they can't prove he broke into her house, but if they catch him sitting there in his car, listening to her?"

"I'll bet you he's got a nice metal box in the front seat," he said. "With a lock. He sees them coming, he just throws it all in there. They can't open it without a warrant."

"Leon, how do you know all this stuff?" I said. "Never mind. I've seen all the catalogs you get. I'll look around her house and see if I can find anything."

"Good man."

"By the way," I said, "we're officially hired."

"I'll come down right away."

"Leon, you have two broken ankles."

"My wife will drive me."

"Leon, you're not coming down here. I'll call you if I need anything."

When I hung up, I pictured him sitting in his bed, banging the telephone on his head. I was sure he'd be driving his wife crazy for the next few hours.

I called Whitley's number next. I got the same monotone recording asking me to leave my name and number. The guy had no future as a telemarketer.

"This is Alex McKnight," I said. "I'm a private investigator working for Maria Zambelli. We know you're following her, Whitley. And we know some other things, too. I'd like to meet with you and talk about it. She's prepared to make your client a very generous offer, so let's all be adults, eh? No more slinking around like juvenile delinquents. My partner says you're making us all look bad." I left my number and hung up.

Almost immediately, the cell phone in my coat pocket rang. I dug it out and hit the button.

"Alex, it's Maria."

"Maria, listen very carefully. Don't say a word. Okay? Just say yes or no, I mean. You got that?"

"Yes."

"Okay, look at your phone, very carefully. Try taking the receiver apart if you can. If it's one of those old-fashioned models, I mean. With the mouthpiece that comes off. Is it that kind of phone?"

"Yes."

"Okay, try unscrewing it, see if there's anything in there besides the transmitter."

I heard the scraping of the plastic as she unscrewed it. A few moments later, she screwed it back on.

"No," she said.

"Okay," I said. "My partner thinks it's more likely that he put a receiver in the room, anyway. Is there someplace you can go, like a closet?"

"Yes."

"Okay. Say a couple things and then say good-bye. Then go in the closet."

"That's sounds good," she said. "I'll see you tomorrow. I'm looking forward to it. Good-bye."

A minute passed. Then her voice came back in a whisper.

"Do you really think he bugged the place?" she said.

"It's a good possibility. Why else would he break in?"

"I don't like this, Alex."

"Don't worry, I'll look around when I get there."

"Chief Rudiger stopped by," she said. "What did you do to him?"

"We just had a friendly chat," I said. "No big deal."

"He wanted to know why I hired you. I told him I was scared and I wanted you to find Harwood for me. He didn't seem to like that too much. I don't think he's real happy about me living in his house right now."

"So why even stay?" I said.

"Let's just finish this, Alex. Then I'll get out of here."

"No sign of our man in the Cadillac?"

"No, but it'll be dark soon. I don't like being here alone. I want to go out and get some dinner. I don't suppose you'd want to join me."

"Go do your usual thing at Rocky's," I said. "I don't think I'd be welcome there. I'm gonna make one more call and then I'll go out to your house. I mean, if that's the way you want to do this. . . ."

"Yes," she said. The woman knew how to whisper a yes. I felt it go right through me. I tried to picture her face.

Bad idea, Alex. Exactly what you don't need right now.

"I'll see you at the house," I said. "Be careful."

I hung up the phone and sat there for a long moment with her voice buzzing in my head. Then I called the hospital.

228

"Dr. Havlin, please," I said. "I'm calling to find out about Randy Wilkins."

I was on hold for a few minutes. Then the doctor came on the line.

"Mr. McKnight," he said. "Mr. Wilkins is in recovery."

"How does it look?"

"I removed the fragment," he said. "Now we just have to wait. If he's going to regain consciousness, it should be in the next forty-eight hours."

I thanked the doctor and hung up.

Forty-eight hours, Randy. If I didn't have other things to do, I'd go there and wait. I want to be the first person you see when you wake up.

It was dark when I left the motel. You shouldn't have let it get so late, I thought. You should be at her house now.

Relax. She's not even there. She's at the bar, having dinner.

The cell phone rang. I picked it up and hit the button.

"Alex," she said. "Where are you?" Her voice was low again.

"I'm on my way."

"He's here."

"He's where?" I said. "Where are you?"

"I'm at home," she said. "It was just too weird being at Rocky's. The way he was looking at me when he found out about me hiring you."

"Are you in the closet again?" I gunned the accelerator. I was still a good twelve miles from Orcus Beach.

"Yes," she said. "I just went upstairs and looked out the window at him. I used the binoculars this time. He turned the light

229

on in his car for a second. I could see he was wearing earphones."

"Okay, just relax," I said. "I'm on my way."

"He looked kind of big, Alex. And ugly."

"Just sit tight," I said. "I'll be there soon."

"What if he comes to the house again? What if he breaks in here?"

"He won't," I said. "He knows you're there."

"Maybe he *wants* me to be here this time," she said. "Alex, I'm scared."

The signal wavered. Goddamned stupid piece of crap. "Maria, are you still there?"

"I'm here."

"Do you want to call the police? If you do it from the closet, he won't hear you. They'll be able to catch him this time."

"I thought they can't do anything to him. You said that yourself."

"They can put him through the wringer," I said. "But ultimately, no, they probably can't charge him. My partner thinks he probably has a lockbox in his car to hide everything."

"Even if they could," she said, "we still couldn't find Harwood."

"Probably not."

"Unless you think there's a way," she said.

"There may be," I said. "I could talk to him. I could ask him real nice."

"I probably don't want to know what 'real nice' means."

The signal went out, came back, went out.

"Maria?"

"I'm still here."

"Which way is his car facing?"

"It's facing . . . south, I think. I'm terrible with directions, Alex.

If you're coming up the street to my house, he's facing so that he'll see you coming."

"That figures," I said. "All right, just make sure the doors are locked. I'm gonna try something here." I had just left M-31 and was racing up B-15 along the shoreline. I caught up to a station wagon pulling a boat on a trailer. The driver was taking it nice and slow, so I blew by him.

"I'm gonna go back to the window and take a look," she said. "I'll keep talking like nothing is happening. In fact—"

"What? What is it?"

"I'm going to keep him occupied, Alex."

"What do you mean?"

"I'm gonna make sure he keeps listening."

I heard a door open. Moments passed. "Is that you?" she said. Her voice was normal now.

"Maria, what are you doing?"

"I've been thinking about you," she said. "I know we haven't spent much time together yet. But I can't help wondering."

I didn't say anything. I let her talk. The road curved suddenly. Two wheels slipped over into the sand. I touched the brakes, swerved hard to the right, and then snapped it back to the left.

"Can I make a confession?" she said. "I was thinking about you while I was taking a bath today. Which reminds me of a story. Do you want to hear it? It happened when I was a lot younger."

I was pushing eighty miles an hour now. Two lanes running along the edge of the world, water on one side, pine trees racing by in a blur on the other side.

"When I was eighteen years old, my whole family came out here to the lake for the summer. The water was always so cold, even in the middle of July, but at night it didn't seem so cold. It felt warmer than the air. So some nights when everybody else had gone to bed, I would sneak out onto the beach in just my bathrobe. If I was brave enough and I was sure nobody was around, I'd take my robe off and jump into the water."

I kept driving.

"One night, after I had been swimming for a little while, I got out and ran back to where I had left my robe. But it wasn't there."

There was a long pause.

"Maria?"

Nothing.

I looked at the phone. The signal was gone.

"Oh no, you worthless piece of shit." I picked it up and shook it, as if that would really make it start working again. "Come on, don't do this now."

I tried calling her number, but it wouldn't send. The stupid little display kept saying the same thing: LOOKING FOR SERVICE.

"I'll give you service," I said. I was about to smash it against the dashboard, then stopped myself and tossed it onto the passenger's seat.

I concentrated on driving the truck, on getting there as quickly as I could. I saw the sign welcoming me to Orcus Beach, passed Rocky's place, turned left at the corner, gunned it down the access road, across the little bridge to Maria's street.

I didn't turn. I stopped the truck at the boat launch and got out. The sudden quiet was unnerving. Just the thin sound of the waves lapping and the lingering hum of the road in my whole body.

Okay, Alex. Let's be smart. If you walk down the road, he's

gonna see you. It's a dead end, so there's no way to come from behind. Unless . . .

The beach.

I stepped down over the boat launch onto the sand and rocks. It was rough going, especially in the dark. The only light came from a half-moon hidden behind clouds and the even dimmer light from the houses along the shore.

I made my way north, behind the line of houses. I knew Maria's was almost at the very end. The next to last, if I remembered right. I had to go all the way down, at least a half mile.

I thought of Maria on the beach. In her bathrobe.

I tripped over something and landed hard. I picked myself up and kept going.

I got to Maria's house. The chief's house. If he could only see me now, sneaking up on it from behind. I remembered the fence that ran all the way down the roadway. I needed to be even farther down the road, to be sure he couldn't see me climbing over the damned thing. I passed her house and went to the very last house on the block. There was a cyclone fence around three sides of the property, stopping a few feet from the shoreline.

I grabbed the fence and caught my breath. What kind of paranoid bastard puts a fence like this around his property, totally open to the water? He obviously wasn't considering the possibility of a sea invasion. The house was completely dark. Either nobody was home or they'd all gone to bed early.

I remembered the dead end, and the lower fence that ran along the guardrail. If I could make it all the way around the place . . .

I walked across the man's beachfront, waiting for the motion detectors to trigger the spotlights and then the running guard dogs. Nothing happened. When I got to the other side, I saw a narrow strip of land running along the far fence line. It sloped down sharply to the little inlet I had seen from the road.

It was time for a little tightrope walk. I held on to the fence as I made my way down the strip of land. In some spots, the erosion had eaten all the way under the fence. I had to climb my way over the gaps until I could walk again. Finally, I came to the concrete embankment and the low fence that ran behind the guardrail. I could see the dim shape of the Cadillac up the road.

I climbed over the fence, trying for silence and failing. I caught my pants on the top of the fence and nearly tumbled over onto my head. Another brilliant display of agility by the former athlete. I made it to the ground and dropped into a crouch, rubbing my right shoulder.

I watched the car for a while. There were no signs of movement. I figured it was about two hundred feet away, with not much cover between us. I had to move fast and quiet.

The wind kicked up, the sand swirling in my face. I closed my eyes, waited for it to pass. Then I moved.

I kept low, hoping he wouldn't see me in the rearview mirror. I pictured him sitting there with his eyes closed, listening through the earphones. That's it, just keep listening. No reason to look back here. It feels so good to just sit there and rest your eyes . . .

The light went on inside his car.

I dove to the ground, breathing hard. Had he seen me?

I looked up. I was still a good thirty feet away. Why was his light on?

I waited. The door didn't open. Nothing.

Okay, start moving again. Slowly. Very quiet. Why the hell did he turn his light on?

This will actually help me. He won't be able to see outside very well with that light on. I came up to the rear of his car. Okay, now which side? Driver's side or passenger's side?

On the driver's side, I can open the door and pull him out. If the door is unlocked. And if he doesn't see me in the side mirror.

On the passenger's side, I can open the door and jump in beside him. If the door is unlocked. I peeked around on that side of the car. No mirror there. I thought Cadillacs always had mirrors on both sides. Maybe it fell off. Maybe it doesn't matter and I should just do something before the night is over.

And you know what, Alex? This would be a really good time to have your gun with you. Too bad it's in a shoe box in the bottom of your closet, five hours away in the Upper Peninsula.

Never mind. Let's go.

I picked the passenger's side. I inched my way around to the back window, took a peek. One man. He had earphones on, which was good. Less chance of hearing me. He was looking down at something. Maybe reading? Also good.

Is this door open? Yes. It was an older car, with the good old-fashioned metal lock sticking up a good two inches in the air. God bless old Cadillacs.

Here goes nothing.

I yanked the door open.

A gun. Right there on the passenger's seat. I grabbed it, just before he could reach for it himself. The man screamed his way through a few syllables until he could finally put words together. "Oh my God, you son of a bitch, I'm dying, for the love of . . . What the hell are you doing? Who are you?"

"Good evening," I said, sitting down next to him. "You must be Miles Whitley."

"Oh goddamn it," he said, holding onto the steering wheel. "I'm dying here."

"Calm down," I said. "Get a hold of yourself."

"That's easy for you to say, you son of a bitch. Oh my God."

I looked him over. He was big, like Maria had said. A solid 250 pounds, easy. He was even bigger than Leon. His hair was thin, and he'd combed it over, in a losing battle to cover his head. His face was rounded and gray, the kind of face you see with a cigar in it down at the racetrack. The earphones had slipped off his ears and were now around his neck. As I looked down, I saw the stain all over his pants. In his left hand, he held a mason jar filled halfway with what could only be urine. I made every effort not to look at anything else.

"God, my back," he said through gritted teeth. "My whole back is locked up now. Goddamn it all."

"Looks like I caught you in the middle of something," I said. "I do apologize."

"Goddamn it all, who are you?" he said. He found the lid to the mason jar and screwed it on. Then he started waving his hands around like a man who desperately needs a paper towel.

"My name is Alex McKnight," I said. "I left you a message today."

"So what?" he said. He started to arch his back. "Goddamn it all."

"You didn't call me back," I said. "I was worried about you."

He looked at me, really looked me in the eye for the first time. "What, is that some kind of a joke?"

"I got a million of 'em," I said. I looked down at all the stuff he had piled around him: newspapers, some candy bar wrappers, a bottle of Vernors ginger ale. I picked up one of the newspapers and saw the UHF receiver, which was plugged into the cigarette lighter. On the floor, there was a metal box with a lock, just as Leon had predicted. "You obviously get all the right catalogs," I said. "Didn't you see the special surveillance pants you can buy, with the little pissing tube? Just like the astronauts use in outer space?"

"Are you gonna tell me what the hell you want? Jesus, my back."

"I want to know where Harwood is," I said.

"Who's that?"

"The man who's paying you to sit here listening to a woman who's scared half to death," I said. "The man who paid you to break into her house."

"I don't know what you're talking about."

"I got an idea," I said. I flipped open the revolver, saw the back ends of six bullets. "You should learn to clean your gun, Miles."

"You should learn to blow it out your ass."

"Here's my idea," I said. "The other day, somebody held a gun against my knee and asked me what it would feel like if he pulled the trigger. Sort of like this." I put the barrel of the gun against his right knee.

He looked down at the gun. He didn't say anything.

"Of course, this man had a shotgun," I said. "So you can imagine what I was thinking. One blast and my knee would have been gone. Nothing but knee soup all over the walls."

I saw him swallow.

"Now, a little revolver like this," I said. "It's not going to cause nearly as much damage. Of course, you've got six bullets in here."

"You're not going to shoot me," he said.

"The first bullet would probably penetrate right under the kneecap. Do you think it would come out the other side?"

"You're not going to shoot me," he said again.

"How do you know that?" I said.

"Because you can't."

"The second bullet would probably shatter the kneecap itself," I said. "I think you'd forget all about your bad back at least."

"I'm just working here," he said. "You know that. You're a private dick yourself. You said so in your message."

"Private dick? You actually call it that?"

"What do you want?" he said.

"Harwood, the man who hired you," I said. "Do you know why he's been looking for that woman all these years?"

He looked down at the gun. "I don't need to know that."

"Of course not. Not if he's paying you enough."

"I'm just keeping things together," he said. "You know how it is. It's a tough business."

"Do you have a cell phone in here?"

"Under your seat."

"I hope I don't accidentally pull the trigger," I said as I reached for it. "There it is." I flipped it open and turned it on. It scanned for two seconds and then locked right in. "You've got a better phone than I do, I'll say that much for you."

"Who are you calling?"

"My client," I said. "You know how it is. You've got to check in now and then, keep the customer happy."

Maria picked up on the first ring.

"It's me," I said.

"Alex! My God! What happened? Where are you?"

"I'm right outside," I said. "On the street. I'm hanging out with Mr. Whitley."

"The man in the car? Alex, how did you . . . I mean, I was so worried when you hung up the phone before. I was afraid you—"

"Everything's okay," I said. "You can relax now. Mr. Whitley has a much better cell phone. He was kind enough to let me use it."

I could hear her take a deep breath. "Thank God," she said. "I didn't know what to think."

"It sounds like I missed a good story."

"You did," she said. "Too bad."

I didn't know what to say to that, so I didn't even try.

"What are you going to do now?" she asked. "If you're right outside, why are we talking on the phone? Do you want me to go out there?"

"No, that would be embarrassing for Mr. Whitley, I'm afraid." I took the gun away from his knee and leaned back in the seat. Something brushed the top of my head. It was the fabric on the car's ceiling, hanging down like some kind of harem tent. The smell of the car, a mixture of sweat and urine and God knows what else, was starting to get to me.

This was not going to be pleasant, but it was the only way. I had no idea how long it would take. Maybe thirty minutes. Maybe all night.

"You stay there," I said. "We've got a little trip to make."

"What do you mean? Where are you going?"

I gave Whitley a little wave with the gun. "As soon as he zips up his pants," I said, "we're both going to go say hello to his client."

Chapter Nineteen

Whitley surprised me. I figured he'd work his way east, back to one of the interstates. Instead, he drove north, right up M-31, the little two-lane highway that runs all the way up the shore of Lake Michigan.

"Where are we going?" I said finally.

"North," he said.

"Can you be a little more specific?"

"Will you put the gun away, for God's sake? Why do you have to turn this into a kidnapping?"

"I'm not pointing it at you," I said. "Just relax and drive. And slow down, eh? If you're thinking about trying to get pulled over, think again. I'm sure the police would be very interested to hear what you were doing back there."

"I was doing my job, friend."

"You broke into her house and planted a bug," I said. "You were eavesdropping on her."

"It sounds like such an ugly thing when you say it that way."

"Why were you doing it?" I said. "I don't get it. I know Harwood was looking for her, so okay, you found her. Good for you. Why were you following her around and listening to her conversations?"

He let out a long breath, then rubbed his face. "The client wants you to follow the mark around, you follow the mark. You know how it is. He wants you to spy on her, you spy on her. You sit there and you listen and you tell him what she's saying. I'd have the phone right there with me. She's talking to her brother; she's talking to her kid. It didn't mean anything to me. It's just her talking, you know. But the client wants to know this stuff. As long as he's interested, and he's paying, you go along with it."

I shook my head. I didn't know what to say.

"Don't tell me you don't do crap like that," he said. "What's the worst thing you ever did as a private eye?"

"I'm the wrong guy to ask," I said.

"I'm just reaching for my pills here. Don't get excited." He went down between his legs and pulled a plastic pill bottle off the floor. "Here, open this," he said, tossing it to me.

I read the prescription as I opened it: Miles Whitley, one pill four times daily, as needed. A red sticker warned against driving or operating heavy machinery.

I took out one of the pills. It looked familiar. It was a Vicodin, the same pill I'd once had a little problem with. After the shooting, I'd use them on the bad nights. For a while there, they were all bad nights.

"Hell of a job to have with a bad back," he said as he took it from me and popped it in his mouth. "Sitting around for hours. And then having people jump in my car and scare the piss out of me."

I thought about taking one of the pills myself. Instead, I put the cap back on and threw the bottle in the backseat.

"How long have you been a private eye?" he asked.

"I'm not a private eye," I said.

"You said you were, on your message."

"I was just pretending."

"Pretending, my ass," he said. "I've been doing this for a lot of years. More than I care to admit. The business has changed, let me tell you. They got guys who do nothing but look at computers all day now. Christ, they got women private eyes now. There aren't many of us old-timers left. It was a tough business back then. It took a special kind of man."

"For God's sake, Whitley . . ."

"Are you a private eye or aren't you?" he said. "Do you have a license?"

"Yes," I said. "But it was an accident."

"What the hell does that mean? You're working for this lady, aren't you?"

"She asked me to help her," I said. "So I am."

"A private eye by accident," he said, looking out his window at the lake. "And he gets clients that look like that. While I get—"

"Harwood," I said. "I know who hired you."

"I cannot divulge the identity of my client."

"Give it up," I said. "We'll see him soon enough. How long do we have to drive, anyway?"

"Little over an hour," he said.

"That's it? Where is he?"

"This way."

"This way, where? Are we going to his house?"

"Nope. Don't know where he lives."

"What, he's staying in a motel up here? So he can be close to her?"

"Not a motel," he said.

"Stop jerking me around. Where are we going?"

"He owns some land up here," he said. "That's all I know."

"The partnership land. That's where he's staying? How long has he been up there?"

"Not long," he said. "Just since he found out where she was."

"The name Randy Wilkins mean anything to you? Or to Harwood?"

"Who would that be?"

"He's the man you followed." I said. "From her brother's house."

"Is that his name?"

"Yes," I said. "You followed him, and now Harwood knows where she is." It helps to be mad at somebody when you're making them do something at gunpoint. The thought of this clown staking out the house in Farmington, and then tailing Randy all the way out here so he could find Maria. It helped me build up steam again.

"It's what he paid me to do."

"Yeah, I know. Just doing your job."

"Look, I don't get to 'accidentally' dabble in being a private investigator, okay? This isn't my hobby."

"Just drive," I said.

He shook his head and kept driving. We stayed on M-31 all the way up to the outskirts of the Sleeping Bear Sand Dunes. They were calling this whole area the "Gold Coast" now, or the "Michigan Riviera." With all the new resorts going up, it was a good time to own land.

Unless somebody wanted to kill you over it.

"What are you going to do, anyway?" he said. We hit the little town of Beulah; then the highway turned east into the heart of the state forest.

"I'm going to talk to him," I said.

"While holding a gun to his head."

"Hey," I said. "I'm just doing my job. Just like you."

The woods opened up and we saw a golf flag in the middle of a green, and then, soon after, the lights of a ski lift running upward. By Michigan's standards, it was a long slope. Golf in the summer, skiing in the winter. The place didn't look too busy now, but in another month, I knew it would be booked solid.

As we drove past the place, the pine trees reclaimed the land, thick enough to deepen the night into total darkness. Whitley slowed the car. I couldn't see why. There was nowhere to turn. Just trees as far as we could see.

He swung the car through a gap in the trees. I didn't even see it until the headlights swung around. The trees towered over us on either side.

"Is this the place?" I said.

"No," he said. "I just thought I'd drive down this deer trail here, see where it goes."

"There's no reason for anybody to get hurt, Whitley. So don't do anything stupid when you get there, okay? Don't try to tip him off or anything. All I want to do is talk to the man and then leave."

"How do you plan on leaving?"

"You're gonna drive me back," I said. "It's not far."

"Now I'm a chauffeur. My life is improving by the minute."

He drove down through the trees for a good mile. There was nothing but the shaggy bark of pine trees on either side of us, and the sound of the weeds whipping at the bottom of his car. Finally, he came to a clearing and swung his car hard to the right. The headlights passed over something large and white.

They used to call them campers. My father had one for a couple years, back when he was heading up to the Upper Peninsula every weekend to work on his first cabin. Now they call them RVs, and they've got kitchens, bathrooms, color televisions, you name it. The better ones run well over $100,000. The only difference between a small house and an RV is that the RV gets about three miles to the gallon.

As we got out, I told Whitley to leave his keys in the ignition. "I'll drive back," I said. "It's only fair."

"Not sure you want to do that. There's still piss all over the seat."

"Leave the keys in anyway."

"Suit yourself," he said. As he got out, he reached down and pulled out a wooden cane.

"What's that for?"

"I need it," he said. "For my back." He winced with every step, making slow progress over the rough ground. There were lights on inside the vehicle, and one good exterior spotlight that lighted up the entire clearing. I walked behind Whitley, told him to knock on the door. He did.

No answer.

"Where is he?" I said.

"It takes him a while," he said.

"What do you mean?"

"He's coming. Just give him a minute."

I started imagining the worst. Harwood had spotted me through the window, or else they had some kind of secret code. Two knocks means everything is okay, three means trouble. I pictured him inside, loading his gun. Probably another shotgun, the way my life had been going.

"Whitley, what the hell is going on?"

Finally, the door opened. The sudden light from the interior blinded me. Then I saw a metal grate. There was a sound like the bolt of a rifle. It made my heart race for a moment, until I realized what was happening. The sound was a gear being engaged. Then a platform slowly extended itself from the doorway.

The man who must have been Harwood rolled his wheelchair out onto the platform. This was the demon Maria had been running from for so long.

There was a console mounted on one of the arms of the wheelchair. He pressed a button and the platform lowered itself with an electric hum. When it hit the ground, he rolled off. Then he turned the wheelchair to face me. He appeared to be about sixty years old, with eyes the color of ashes. His body had the top-heavy look of a man who had spent many years rolling himself around. His forearms could have belonged to a lumberjack.

"Who's your friend?" he said. He was looking at me, but he could only be talking to Whitley.

"This would be Mr. McKnight," Whitley said. "He's another private investigator. Sort of, anyway. He works for Ms. Zambelli."

"Is that right," Harwood said. "And this gun in his hand?"

"Would be mine," Whitley said. "Fully loaded, I'm afraid."

"Very unfortunate," Harwood said.

"I just want to ask you a couple questions," I said. "I have no desire to shoot anybody."

"That's very reassuring."

"First of all, do you know a man named Randy Wilkins?"

He thought about it, or at least made a show of thinking about it. "Randy Wilkins. Not offhand. Randy Wilkins. It might be ringing a very faint bell, but I can't remember where I've heard the name."

"Any chance that bell can get a little louder? He was running some real estate scams out in California. All of a sudden, he decided to come back to Michigan to look for Maria. The fact that you're in real estate, more or less, and also looking for Maria, it seems like too much of a coincidence."

"I'm sorry. I still can't place him."

"All right," I said. "Now do you feel like telling me why you're doing all this?"

"Doing what, exactly?"

"Don't play games with me, Harwood. You killed her husband, and you tried to kill her. You've been hounding her for what, eighteen years?"

Harwood just sat there. Whitley stood behind him, looking useless. The wind kicked up and rocked the trees above us, but it was just background noise. We couldn't even feel it in the shelter of the clearing. It was April, so there weren't any mosquitoes out yet. In July, it would be hell.

"Are you going to say anything?" I said.

"No," he said. "I don't think I will. Go ahead and shoot me if you want. Shoot Whitley, too. He deserves it."

"That's not funny," Whitley said.

"What would it take to get you to stop?" I said. "To leave her alone. And her whole family."

"That's an interesting question," he said. "You have no idea how interesting."

"What if she signed an agreement to give you complete control of the property, and the eighty percent cut you seem to want so badly?"

"Did she tell you to say that?"

"We talked about it," I said.

"You came all the way out here to try to cut a deal?"

"She wants this to be over. This is a way to end it. What's wrong with that?"

"Mr. McKnight," he said, "can I ask you something? Do you have any idea how ridiculous you look right now?"

I didn't say anything. None of this was going as planned, because Harwood held the ultimate trump card. There was no way I could intimidate him physically. What was I going to do? Hit him in the face? Tip his wheelchair over? Let the air out of his tires?

"Men are amazing," Harwood said. "Don't you agree, Whitley?"

"Sure," Whitley said. "Whatever you say. Men are amazing."

"A man will commit crimes. He'll kidnap somebody, which is what you did, Mr. McKnight. And then threaten somebody else with a gun, which is called menacing, I believe. Also a felony. For what? Just to impress a woman. Maybe get her to go to bed with him. Absolutely amazing. Am I right, Whitley?"

"Incredible," Whitley said. "Although I gotta admit, after seeing this woman . . ."

I should have shot them both right then just to shut them up. "All right," I said. "Can we cut to the chase here? I'm not leaving here until I know you're gonna stop harassing her."

Harwood looked up at the sky for a moment, then back at me. "What do you think of this property, Mr. McKnight?"

I let out a breath. "It's dark, Harwood. All I see are trees."

"You must have seen the resort," he said. "On the other side of the hill."

"I saw it."

"Do you have any idea how much seven hundred acres of forestland are worth right now? Up here on the Gold Coast?"

"She mentioned something about twenty million."

"I bought this land in 1976," he said. "Arthur and I bought it together, I mean. Even then, I knew it would be a jewel someday."

248

"This would be the partner you killed," I said.

He stared at me. The light was coming from behind him, so I couldn't see his face very well.

"Whitley, can you get me a piece of paper?"

Whitley stuck his hand in his pocket. Without even thinking about it, I leveled the gun at him.

"I'm just getting the man a piece of paper," Whitley said, pulling out a pad. "Private eyes always gotta have some paper, am I right? Tell me you at least carry a pad of paper with you."

"Here," Harwood said, taking the pad from him. "Show this to Mr. McKnight. I think this may help solve our problem."

When Harwood was done writing, Whitley took the pad and hobbled over to me. One man in a wheelchair, another man holding himself up with a cane. Me with a gun in my hand, deep in the forest on a cold April night. Life couldn't get any stranger.

But then it did. Just as I was wondering what this piece of paper would say—some kind of dollar figure maybe, some kind of deal he wanted to make for the land—I saw Harwood's right hand move. There was a little console attached to the armrest on his wheelchair. There were buttons on it. He pushed one of them.

Whitley's cane was already whistling through the air when the lights turned off. The pain was instantaneous as he caught me on my right wrist, just above the thumb. My hand went numb. The gun dropped to the ground. As I went down for it, a gunshot ripped through the night. The bullet must have gone right over me. The flash from Harwood's gun was a single frame of light, enough for me to make out Whitley's foot coming my way fast. I got a forearm up just in time to block it. I rolled before the next shot could find me.

You let your guard down, Alex. Harwood wrote it out for him, right there on his little private eye's notepad. When I turn out the lights, hit him! Or something else just as brilliant. And you fell for it.

The cane caught me again, this time on my right shoulder blade. I went to the ground face-first and tasted pine needles.

This is it, Alex. They're gonna kill you right here. They'll dig a grave in the woods and bury you.

"Don't shoot!" Whitley said. "He's right here!"

"Well, get out of the way!" Harwood said.

"Turn the lights on!"

"Damn this thing!" Harwood said. "I can't see what I'm doing!"

I got up on my hands and knees and crawled. Something stopped me. It was Whitley's leg. Before he could kick me with it, I grabbed and pulled. I was already on my feet and running when I heard him screaming something about his back. I didn't stop to help him.

The lights came on just as I was about to run into a tree. A thoughtful gesture on the part of my host. Then a bullet hit the tree and sprayed bark in my face. So much for thoughtful gestures.

I ran for the car. The hell with zigzagging, or whatever you're supposed to do when somebody's shooting at you. I just ran as fast as I could make myself go, a forty-nine-year-old ex-catcher who never had any speed anyway. Not even in his twenties.

I went down behind the car. Harwood fired a couple more shots at me. That's right, use up those bullets. How many does he have left? Did he shoot five times? Six? Clint Eastwood asking the punk if he feels lucky. Hell of a thing to think of at a time like this, but it rang true. It was time to see how lucky I was.

I opened the door and got in. Piss or no piss, I was taking Whitley's Cadillac for a ride. I turned the key and listened to the engine grind.

And grind, and grind. Then it caught. I flipped the lights on, gunned it forward. I had no choice. There was no way I could back it up all the way down that trail. As I swung the car around, I saw Whitley in the glare of the headlights. He was still on the ground, flat on his back.

Then Harwood in his chair. The gun pointed right at me.

I swung hard to the left. The window on the passenger's side exploded. The wheels spun, kicked up dirt, and then I was finally moving in the right direction. I took that big white boat right down the alley through the trees, making myself breathe. In, out. You're in the clear now. Relax and drive.

When I got back to the main road, I took it west and then south, back toward Orcus Beach. And Maria. The cold air rushed in and made my eyes water.

The same damned thing had happened to my truck. Somebody had shot at me and blown out the window on the passenger's side. What are the odds against that happening twice in a lifetime? What a strange and terrifying world this is, I thought, and how glad am I to live to see another night of it?

If I had only known. The night wasn't through with me yet. Not by a long shot.

Chapter Twenty

My right hand was useless. Just a little pressure with the right thumb on the steering wheel, goddamn it all to hell, that hurt. I knew it was swelling and would be every color in the rainbow come morning. I knew this because it had happened before, at least half a dozen times. As a catcher, you try to keep your right hand protected, either behind your back like I used to do or tucked under your right leg. But sooner or later, you're going to get hit in the hand with a foul tip. Or with the bat itself. If you're lucky, you can still pick up a baseball the next day.

I kept driving. I needed ice, a tight bandage, and a drink. And I needed to get out of this filthy, stinking homeless shelter of a car, take a shower, and maybe burn my clothes. Then, with my hand wrapped up, a shot and a beer, four Advil, I'd be a new man.

Come to think of it, my back didn't feel so hot, either. Whitley's second swing had put a nice little knot in my muscles. A back rub would be the only other thing I would need out of life. I imagined Maria doing just that. This time, I didn't tell myself to stop thinking about her that way. I let the movie run in my head, imagining what would happen next. And then after that.

When I got back to Orcus Beach, I dropped the Cadillac off

at the boat ramp. I grabbed his UHF receiver and his cell phone. Then I threw the keys out into the sand as far as I could, and instantly regretted it. There was nothing wrong with the idea, but I should have thrown the keys with my other hand.

I fired up my truck and drove up the road to Maria's house. The clock read 11:15. It was hard to believe so much had happened that night, and it wasn't even midnight yet.

I went to the door and knocked. This is where Randy was standing when she accidentally shot him, I thought. "Maria, it's Alex!" I said. I didn't want her to make the same mistake. "Let me in! Everything's okay!"

I heard the scrape of the dead bolt and then the door opened slowly. She looked out at me. She didn't say anything.

"Are you okay?" I said.

"Yes."

"They tried to kill me."

"I'm sorry, Alex."

"Don't be sorry," I said. I went past her into the house, into the kitchen. I emptied out a tray of ice cubes into a dish towel and then wrapped it around my hand. Then I started looking around the place, first by the phone, then on the kitchen counter, looking for a pen, or an outlet converter, or whatever the hell else there was in the house that was actually a bug. I didn't need to find it. Not at that moment. But I wanted to be doing something. I wanted to be moving. For some reason, I was suddenly a little nervous about what might happen if I stopped.

"Say something," I said, putting the earphones on. I kept one ear free. "I can run this on battery power, find out where the bug is."

"What happened?" she said.

"He's up by Traverse City," I said. "On the land."

"There's nothing there."

"He has an RV," I said. "He's sort of camping out up there." There was a jarful of pens on a little table in the hallway. I started going through them. "Do any of these pens look strange to you? Or is this all the chief's stuff? If it is, you're not going to know if something's out of place, are you?"

"What did he look like?" she said.

"I don't know," I said. "I mean, I have nothing to compare him to. Except, well, you know he's in a wheelchair."

"Yes."

"How long has he been in that?"

"Ever since Leopold threw him down the stairs."

I stopped going through the pens. "Leopold has a thing about stairs, doesn't he."

She came closer to me.

"He wasn't what I expected," I said. "I've seen killers before, believe me."

"But then he tried to kill you," she said. "You said so yourself."

"You have a point there."

"Where is he now?" she asked. "Is he on his way here? He knows where to find me."

"I don't know," I said. "Don't worry, I'm not going anywhere. We'll get you out of here tomorrow."

"Can you find the place again? Where he's staying?"

"I'm sure he's moved the RV by now," I said. "I didn't think to get the plate number."

She closed her eyes. "This will never end."

"Hold on," I said. "I have Whitley's cell phone."

"What good will that do?"

I pulled out the phone and turned it on. "It's gotta have a call history on it." I turned the dial on the side. A number came up.

It was Maria's. "No, wait," I said. "That was me. When I called you from his car." I turned the dial again. Another number came up. I recognized it. "This is his office number," I said. "He must have called to get his messages."

One more turn. Another number, with a 313 area code. Detroit. "This could be it," I said. "One way to find out."

I pushed the send button. The signal went out into the air, to a tower somewhere, miles away. Then down the regular phone lines to Detroit, where it was received by the cellular service, sent back out on different lines, to a different tower, searching for the matching signal from one particular cell phone. Somewhere to the north of us, in an RV either sitting in the woods or already out on the road, that phone rang five times. Then somebody picked it up.

Silence. Then finally, "Who is this?"

"It's him," I said.

Maria's face went white, as if I had summoned the man himself into her kitchen.

"Who is this?" the voice said.

"I just wanted to say good night," I said. "You know it doesn't seem right to beat the hell out of a man in a wheelchair. It's just not fair, you know? But next time, I'll get over it."

He hung up.

"Maybe we should get you out of here now," I said. "Not even wait until morning."

"No," she said. "I told you, I'm not running anymore."

I didn't feel like fighting over it. "I'm dripping all over Rudiger's carpet here," I said, wrapping the ice tighter around my wrist.

"What did you do to your hand?"

"It's just a bruise."

255

"Like hell it is. Let me see."

I put the ice down on the table and showed her my hand. "This must hurt," she said.

"A little bit."

She took my other hand and looked at it. Then back to my right hand.

"Your mother did that, too," I said.

"She tried to teach me," she said. She was close to me. There was a delicate scent of something in her hair, something exotic and wise and Gypsy-like. All she had to do was look up at me and I'd be a goner.

She looked up at me. "Did my mother do this?" she said. She kissed my hand.

"No," I said. "I don't recall her doing that."

She kissed my hand again, right where it hurt the most. Then she took my hand in her own and led me up the stairs to her bedroom. She sat me down on her bed and undressed in front of me. The slightest moonlight came through her window, but it was enough to see her. She took my shirt off and laid me on my back. She unbuttoned my pants. When she pulled them off, I twisted my sore back in just the wrong way and let out a little yell.

"You're just a wreck, aren't you," she said. "You're a great big wounded bear."

I watched her climb on top of me. She kissed me and then she put her hand on my chest. "You have something inside here," she said.

"It's a bullet," I said.

"No, that's not what I mean. Although I can see the scars." She ran her fingers down the seams on my chest. "I mean in your heart. You are a good man. Maybe too good."

She kissed me. "You're too good, Alex," she said. "You're too good."

"Kiss me again," I said. "We'll see how good I am."

She did. She kissed me and started moving on top of me, with her hair falling down in my face and the smell of her filling me up until I couldn't help myself. I slid my hands down along her body, along every inch of her skin as she kept kissing me and punishing me, until her legs were spread open wide and I was about to enter her.

She stopped.

"Alex," she said.

"What is it?"

"Tell me."

"Tell you what, Maria?"

"Tell me he won't kill me."

"He won't," I said. She slid down over me. I was inside her.

"Tell me again," she said.

"He won't," I said. "I won't let him."

She moved again.

"How are you going to stop him?"

"Maria . . ."

"Tell me, Alex."

"I won't let him kill you, I promise."

She slid down on me, and then again, and then again.

"Tell me," she said. "Tell me that you'll kill him."

"Maria . . ."

She stopped. "Say it," she said.

I looked into her eyes.

"Tell me," she said. "Tell me you'll find him and you'll kill him."

I kept looking at her. I didn't say anything.

She slid off me and sat on the edge of the bed. I watched her for a long time, waiting for her to say something.

She didn't.

I finally got up and put my clothes back on. I looked at her as I left the room. She hadn't moved. She sat there naked and silent, looking at the floor.

I went downstairs and picked up the towel. The ice was mostly gone, melted into a puddle on the table. I got some more ice from the freezer and wrapped up my hand. I went to the big window and looked out at the lake for a while. Then I went to the back door and opened it. The cold air hit me in the face, but it was just what I wanted right then.

I stepped outside and walked down to the shoreline. Lake Michigan was calm on this April night. Lake Superior would have looked different. It would have looked wilder, more violent. It would have *sounded* different. But this was another kind of night, on another shore, a long way from home.

I stood there by the water for a while, until I started to shiver. I went back to the house, opened the door into the kitchen.

Maria was there. She had put on a long black robe. She stood with her back to me. I could see cigarette smoke curling around her head.

"How does it feel?" she said. But she wasn't talking to me. She had Whitley's cell phone pressed to her ear. "You tried to kill him, and you failed. Again. Like always. And then he came right back down here to me, and you wanna know what I did to him, Charles? You wanna hear what I did? I took my clothes off in front of him and then I climbed onto his body, his whole, perfect, hard body, Charles, and I fucked him so hard, he won't be able to walk straight for two days. Oh, pardon me, Charles. How insensitive of me, seeing as how you never get to walk anymore. You wanna hear how good it feels to be fucked by a real man who isn't propped up in a wheelchair like some pathetic little worm? God, my nipples are so sore right now. And my legs are still trembling. I came so hard, Charles. Even when you were a whole person, Charles, even on the very best day of your life, you could have never fucked me half as good as Alex just did. How does that make you feel? How does it feel to know that you will never even touch a woman again, Charles? For the rest of your miserable little life, you'll just be a broken little gimp stuck in a wheelchair and you will never, ever, ever feel a woman touching your body, because even if she did, Charles, even if she did, you wouldn't even be able to feel it. I don't know why you don't just kill yourself. You've got nothing to live for. Nothing at all. Unless you think getting back at me is gonna somehow make you feel better. You're welcome to try, Charles. Maybe I'll send Alex back up there so you can try killing him again. And then when he makes you look like a pathetic little dog, I'll fuck him all over again. Would you like that, Charles? Would you like that? . . . Yeah, that's right, go ahead and tell me what you're gonna do to me, I'm really scared. Just keep talking, Charles. You know where to find me. Why don't you come here your-self next time? Are you afraid to face me in person? . . . Yeah, that's right. You're all talk. You've got nothing. I'm gonna hang up now, you little worm. Have a nice night. Try not to dream about me."

She hung up. She took another drag on her cigarette. Then she turned around.

"What are you doing?" I said.

"Just talking to an old friend."

I looked at her. If there was a single word I could have thought of saying, I would have said it.

"Who are you?" she finally said.

"You know who I am."

"No, really," she said. "Why did you come here? You were gonna help Wilkins put the touch on me, right? You were in on his little scam."

"I thought he was looking for you," I said. "For other reasons."

"You wanna know something?" she said. "Randy Wilkins? I barely even remember him. You know how many men we were setting up back then?"

"What do you mean, setting up?"

"God, how dumb are you, Alex? I mean, really? That was our scam back then. My whole family. Wilkins was the pitcher, right? Came from a rich family?"

I stood there for a while, going over the whole thing from beginning to end. I watched her standing there, and she watched me back.

"Everything you told me," I finally said, "since the moment I met you, was a lie."

"Yeah, no kidding," she said. "I was playing you. I wanted see what your angle was."

"I didn't have an angle, Maria."

"Everybody has an angle," she said. "And if you really don't, well"—she took a drag on her cigarette, blew smoke to the ceiling—"then I was right. You *are* too good."

Chapter Twenty-one

My father never said much to me about women. He had opinions about baseball, and hockey, and every other sport he had ever seen. He had opinions about how to take care of an automobile, about how to fix a piece of furniture. God knows, he had opinions about how to build a log cabin. He had opinions about all these things because he believed that there are many wrong ways to do something, and only one right way. With women, there is no right way. At least that's what he told me. "Just try to find the one woman who'll always tell you the truth," he once said, maybe the only time in his life he tried to give me some advice about the opposite sex. "It's hard enough to figure out a woman, even if they're straight with you. If they start lying, you don't have a prayer."

It seemed like some pretty outdated advice the first time I heard it. Now I'm not so sure.

Maria had lied to me about recognizing Randy, about remembering him after all these years. She had lied to me about her past, and about her family. It all made sense now. Her mother did "cold readings," as they call them in the business. It's not so hard. You create the right atmosphere, you suspend disbelief as much as you can, and then you start looking for weaknesses.

Everybody has them. Your parents don't understand you. You have big dreams, but something is holding you back. You're afraid of something. If you don't get a nibble, you quickly move on to something else. When you finally get a hit, it's as obvious as a neon sign over the sucker's head. Yes! That's it! That's my problem! How did you know?

And then you reel them in. If it's a young man on the hook and you need to use your daughter to pull him into the net, so be it. That's how the game works.

The Harwood business was still a little confusing. I didn't know how much of that was a lie. Clearly, they hated each other. But now I didn't know who the victim was, or even if there *was* a victim. Suddenly, it didn't seem to matter anymore. Not to me.

As I thought about it I was pretty sure I knew when the hook had been set, the exact moment when she must have decided I could be very useful to her. When I walked into that bar and sat down next to her, and spoke to her for the first time. Hello, I'm the guy who was with Randy Wilkins. Yeah, the con artist. Although I didn't know it at the time. He asked me to help him find you just because he wanted to see you again after all these years. *And I believed him.*

She must have had me marked for the ultimate sucker right then. Was she right? Maybe she was. Although she didn't get what she wanted, not in the end. Harwood was still alive. And I was backing my truck down her driveway.

When my truck was aimed in the right direction, I punched it. If I could have squealed my tires, I would have. All I did was kick up a little gravel. Good night, Maria. And good luck.

A half mile down the road, my night got even worse. Chief Rudiger's squad car was parked at the boat launch, and the man himself was standing next to Whitley's white Cadillac, looking in through what used to be the window on the passenger's side. When he saw my truck coming, he stepped out into the middle of the road. Running him over would have felt pretty good right about then. I resisted the temptation. He stood motionless until I stopped in front of him, and then he came around to my window. I rolled it down.

"Evening, Mr. McKnight," he said.

"What can I do for you, Chief?"

"Do you know anything about this car?" he said.

"Looks like he needs a new window," I said.

"Do you happen to know where the owner is right now?"

"No," I said. Technically, it was the truth.

"I think we need to discuss this matter," he said.

"Chief," I said. "Please. I have to tell you, I'm no longer working for Ms. Zambelli. I no longer have any interest in anything that ever happened in this town. Or anything that ever *will* happen. In fact, I'm on my way out of here right now. As soon as you let me go, I'm going to leave and never come back. Ever. I should think that would make your night."

"I can't let you leave here," he said. He put both his hands on the top of my truck. "Not without buying you a drink."

"Excuse me?"

"Follow me to Rocky's," he said. "I'm buying."

"Chief, if you don't mind, it's been a long night. . . ."

"You got two choices," he said. "Either we go to my office and talk about what happened to that car over there or we go to Rocky's and I buy you a drink. What's it gonna be, McKnight?"

"Lead the way," I said.

He got into his car and drove back to the main road, then

down a block to Rocky's place. It was just after 2:00 A.M., but the place was still doing a good business. I parked the truck and met Rudiger at the door.

"I never thought I'd be welcome here," I said.

"After you," he said, holding the door open.

I walked in, ready for anything. Surely this was a trap. Rocky and Harry would be waiting to jump me. They'd beat the living hell out of me, and if I was lucky, they'd dump me at the city limits instead of killing me.

Nobody jumped me. Nobody hit me over the head with anything. There were maybe thirty people in the place, mostly men, the late-night crew. The television was off now, the place transformed from a family restaurant to a bar for serious drinkers. Rudiger led me to a place at the horseshoe bar, on Maria's side—in fact, just a few stools down from where she had been sitting when I first saw her. Rocky looked at me, then at Rudiger. If he was surprised to see us there together, he did a good job of hiding it.

"What'll you have, McKnight?" Rudiger said.

"Beer will do," I said.

"Two beers, Rock," he said. "Put a shot next to mine."

Rocky set us up without saying a word, then went back to his business.

"I didn't think you could serve alcohol in this state after two o'clock," I said.

"I think you're right," he said. "Let's call the police."

"Never mind," I said.

He downed his shot and then put the glass down. He didn't slam it. He placed it so gently, you couldn't even hear it touch the bar.

"Are you gonna tell me why I'm here?" I said.

"Why do you think you're here?"

"I can't even imagine," I said. "I was under the impression you didn't care for me too much. I would have put the odds against you buying me a drink around ten thousand to one."

"That's quite a long shot," he said. "What about the odds against me apologizing to you?"

"That would be off the board," I said.

"You were a cop once yourself. You never heard a police chief apologize to somebody?"

"Not that I can recall."

He raised a finger to Rocky. The shot glass got refilled.

"Can I ask you a question, McKnight?"

"Go ahead."

"You ever been in love with somebody?"

I drank my beer. "Chief, why are you asking me that?"

"Just answer it."

"Yes," I said. "Yes, I have."

"You ever do anything stupid because you were in love with somebody?"

I thought about that one. Not so much about the answer but about why the hell he would ask me that. "I'll say yes to that."

"How stupid was it?" he said. "What's the worst thing you ever did just because you were in love with somebody?"

"I'd have to think about that one."

He nodded and then drained his second shot.

"I knew that that private eye was watching her," he said. "I could have stopped him anytime."

"You had no proof he broke into her house," I said. "You couldn't have arrested him for anything."

"I could have made his life a little miserable."

"Like you did to me."

265

"Exactly," he said. "Did I actually apologize for that yet, or did I just talk about apologizing? I forget." He raised his finger again. Another shot.

"We'll say you did," I said. "So why did you leave Whitley alone? Is that the stupid thing you did because you're in love?"

He laughed. "Hell, that doesn't even make the top twenty."

"How long have you been in love with her?" I said.

He drank his third shot. This one went down even faster than the first two. He put the shot glass down again, as gently as possible. He kept looking at it.

"A long time," he said finally. "I met her when I was a state trooper. God, when was it? Nineteen seventy-two? I stopped this big convertible on the expressway, guy was doing eighty-five miles an hour. She was in the car with him. Turns out this man was named Harwood, the same son of a bitch that's been after her all these years. But this was back then, before she married this other guy, Zambelli."

He raised his finger again. I was hoping Rocky would start acting like a friend and cut him off, but he didn't. Rudiger drained his fourth shot and continued.

"I ran his driver's license," he said. "And then I ran Maria's, too. Her name was Valenescu back then. I got a hit on her name. She was wanted for questioning, some case down in Detroit. I found out later there were accusations her whole family was involved in a some kind of ongoing con game. Her mother would read fortunes, find out if the customer had any money. If they did, they'd find some way to get their hooks into them. If it was a woman and if she'd fall for it, they'd tell her her children would suffer bad fortune unless she paid for guidance. Or spells to ward off evil spirits. People believe that shit. If it was a man ..."

He stopped. He was staring at the empty glass.

"Then they'd find some other way," he said. "There's always a way, especially when you have a beautiful daughter. I didn't know all this at the time, though. I just had this little red flag on Maria Valenescu, to bring her in for questioning. The guy tried to stop me. This Harwood guy. I ended up writing him every ticket I could think of. Then I put Maria in the back of my car and took her in. On the way, she started crying, told me that her family had made her do all this, said she was trying to get away from them. She wanted me to stop so she could explain it all to me. She was afraid of what would happen if I took her to the station."

He stopped again.

"You never took her in," I said.

"I was a married man," he said. "I had three kids. I never thought something like that could happen to me. She was just too . . ."

He didn't finish the thought. He just shook his head.

"I kept seeing her," he said. "Even after she got married. This Zambelli guy, he had to be the most oblivious man who ever lived. Or else he knew and didn't do anything about it. I suppose that's possible. Every once in a while, she'd call me, tell me her family was in a jam, needed some help. A couple times I went and got her brother, Leopold, out of jail, convinced whoever it was that put him there to drop the charges, just forget it ever happened. The one time it was another state trooper, that one was easy. The other time, it was a deputy in Oakland County. Right after Zambelli died, Leopold went after Harwood, threw him down some stairs, I think. That one, I had to be real persuasive with. I can be a persuasive man, McKnight."

I let him have that one. I finished my beer.

"She disappeared right after that. Before the baby was born. I was back to being a regular married man with three kids. Two of them were out of the house by then, the other one getting ready to go to college. I used to look at my wife and say to myself, This is what you've got for the rest of your life. I forgot all about Maria. Didn't think I'd ever hear from her again. I retired from the state police and took this job. My wife died. I was all by myself here in this town, the town I grew up in. Figured I'd just spend my last twenty years here and that would be it. Then she showed up. Out of nowhere. 'Hello Howard,' she says. 'Remember me?' I just about died right there on the spot. She was older, of course, but my God, McKnight. I mean, you've seen her. It's not like she doesn't look like she's forty-seven years old, you know what I mean? It's like she's forty-seven years old and *this is what it's supposed to look like.* It's even better than twenty, better than thirty. Hell, I bet she'll look even better when she's sixty. Is that crazy?"

"No," I said. "Not at all."

"You wouldn't be saying that if you hadn't seen her," he said. "Anyway, she tells me she's been thinking about me this whole time. And that she's been running from this man Harwood, the same man I had stopped all those years ago. She wanted me to help her. So I put her up in my house."

She lied about that, too, I thought. All this history with Rudiger. What a surprise.

"I didn't try to take advantage of the situation," he said. "Although I was thinking about what it'd be like to have her in the house every day, see her in the morning, make breakfast for her. I remembered she always had this thing about having breakfast made for her. She didn't seem too hot on that idea, though. It was too much all at once, she said. I told her she'd stay in my house and I'd find a place in town for a while. She liked that idea. But she said she'd be calling me one night. One night she'd call me and ask me to come over. That's what she said. I waited. And waited. When this private eye started watching her, I figured something would happen. Maybe I'd get to be the knight in shining armor."

He looked at me, like he had forgotten I was sitting there next to him. His eyes seemed to have a little trouble focusing on me. "And then something *did* happen," he said.

"What happened?" I said.

He stood up, holding on to the stool for support. "I'll show you."

"What do you mean?"

"Come with me," he said. "I want to show you something."

"Chief, it's getting late here."

"McKnight, either you come with me or I'll arrest you. I swear to God, I'll make something up and arrest you. We're having a good man-to-man conversation here. Don't screw it up."

I followed him outside. He got in his squad car, motioned me to the other side. "Get in," he said.

"Where are we going?"

"Just get in," he said.

I got in the front seat. He started the car and backed it up, right into a lamppost.

"Chief, I don't think you should be driving," I said.

"Don't worry," he said. "Who's gonna pull me over?"

"That's not what I'm worried about."

"It's not far," he said. "We'll be there in one minute."

He pulled out of the parking lot, drove north on the main road, past the little motel with the cannon on the sign. "I told you the story about the cannon," he said.

"You told me."

"I told you. That's good. I told you the story."

It was a dead-straight road, so he managed to keep at least two wheels on it at all times. Those four shots at the bar, they couldn't have been his first of the night. When I noticed the empty bottle rattling around under my feet, it started to make sense. "Chief," I said, "I really don't think you should be driving right now."

"Almost there," he said. He took a hard right turn onto a side street. He didn't hit the stop sign head-on, but the pole scraped the passenger's side of his car with a loud metallic screech. I grabbed the dashboard and held on.

"Ouch," he said. "That one hurt. There goes the police budget."

"Chief, please," I said. "Stop the car."

"We're here," he said. "Home away from home."

He pulled up to a small cottage, slamming on the brakes as he hit the mailbox. When I got out of the car, I saw the long scrape on the side of the car, and in the headlights, the mailbox post bent over at a forty-five-degree angle. Aside from that, no problems.

"Come on in," he said, walking to the front door. I reached into the car and turned off the lights and the ignition, took the keys with me. I figured I'd just see him inside, make him lie down, and then leave. I could walk back to my truck.

"How do you like it?" he said as he turned on the light. It wasn't much of a place, just one tiny living room with a patched-up couch and a coffee table. A small television sat on one of those metal caddies with the plastic wheels, the kind you used to see back in the sixties. There was a table for two in the dining room, with metal chairs covered in vinyl. Also from the sixties. He

270

turned on the dining room light and pushed a pile of papers onto the floor. "Sit down," he said.

I hesitated a moment, then sat. Humor the man, see this through, then get the hell out of this town and never come back.

He brought back a bottle of Wild Turkey and two glasses. "Set us up," he said. "I'll go get Exhibit A."

"I don't think either of us needs any more to drink tonight," I said.

"Just pour," he said. He left the room, going into what had to be the bedroom. I just sat there in the cheap glare of the overhead light, waiting to see what he was talking about.

He came back into the room with a shotgun. Just what I needed to see at that point. Another shotgun.

"You know what this is?" he said, sitting in the chair across from me.

I didn't say anything. I couldn't breathe.

"For God's sake, McKnight, I'm not going to shoot you. Relax."

He laid the gun on the table. It was pointed away from me. I tried to breathe again.

"I bet you don't know what this is," he said.

I shook my head.

"This is the gun Maria shot Wilkins with."

I just looked at it.

"I bet you're wondering why I have it."

I nodded my head.

"After she shot him, she called me. It was about nine o'clock at night. I figured, This is it. This is the call. She wants me to go over there.

"I thought I told you to pour us a drink," he said. He took the bottle and poured himself three fingers, then poured the same for me and put it down in front of me. I didn't touch it.

"She wanted me to come over all right," he said. "Because she had just shot a man on her front porch, and she didn't know what to do. I went over there and saw what had happened, told her to get in her car and get on over to Rocky's place, quick. Act like nothing had happened. I took the gun, looked around outside a little, made sure nobody was around. Then I left. When I got back to the station, the phone was ringing, somebody calling in about the gunshot. I let Rocky go down first. Then I was right behind him, after I stopped in here to hide the gun."

He drank half the glass and looked at me. "You ever do something that stupid?" he said.

"Chief, you made a mistake," I said. "I can understand how it happened. Why don't you put the glass down and go to bed."

He shook his head. "It gets worse," he said. "Once you do something stupid, you gotta do something else. And then something else. It kinda just builds on you, you know? Until you don't have any control over it anymore."

"What else did you do?"

"Oh, not that much," he said. "Besides compromising a crime scene, hiding evidence . . . What else did I do?" He drained the rest of his glass, leaned forward to pour another. He missed the glass with some of it, dribbling whiskey onto the barrel of the shotgun.

"I almost killed you, for one thing," he said. "When I dragged you in for no reason. Took the cuffs off you. I was thinking maybe I could shoot you right then, tell everybody you tried to jump me. Then you wouldn't be trying to find out what'd happened to Wilkins, and wouldn't be . . ." He looked to his right, as if he could see all the way across town. "You wouldn't be in that house. With Maria."

"You didn't do it," I said. "It didn't happen."

"Rocky showed up," he said. "If he hadn't, I think I would have done it. I really do, McKnight. I would have killed you. That's how far it's gone. One mistake, then another. Until you don't even recognize yourself anymore."

"Chief..."

"You know what else?" he said. "Your man Wilkins there. The con artist. I've been talking to the doctor. I know they took that piece of buckshot out of him. He could wake up any minute, you know? I'm sitting here thinking, If he remembers what happened, all hell is gonna break loose. Maybe it would be better for everybody if he didn't wake up. That county man who's watching him, I'm thinking maybe I could go tell him to go home. I'll watch him myself. Nobody's looking, I'll pull the plug on the respirator thing. I'm actually thinking this, McKnight. This is what I've come to."

I sat there and listened to him. He was staring down at the gun.

"I know I'd kill that Harwood in a second," he said. "That much, I'm sure of. I even told Maria that. I told her I'd kill Harwood for her, if that's what it took. She didn't believe me. She said she knew I'd never be able to do that."

"Chief..."

"It gets even better," he said. "There's more to the story. I bet you're wondering why I'm letting her lead me around by the dick this whole time. Aren't you? Doesn't it seem a little strange to you that I'm doing all this?"

"I don't know," I said.

"Delilah."

273

"What about her?"

"What about her?" he said. "You want to know what about her? Maria told me she was my daughter."

I didn't have anything to say to that one.

"She told me it wasn't her husband. They'd been trying for years. It was me, she said. I'm Delilah's father."

"When did she tell you that?"

"When she showed up here in Orcus Beach," he said. "Eighteen years later, she tells me I'm her father. That was all part of the package, McKnight. When everything settled down, it was gonna be me and Maria together for the rest of our lives. With a daughter to come visit us."

I let out a long breath, then sneaked a look at my watch. It was almost three in the morning. My hand was throbbing. I needed more ice.

"I bought it," he said. "I totally bought it."

"You don't think it's true?"

"I wanted to know for sure," he said. "I knew she was born down in Florida, after Maria ran away. I called the vital records office down there, asked them to help me find Delilah's birth certificate. They found it in two minutes, read it to me right over the phone. You know how hard it is to get a birth certificate in Michigan, McKnight? Things are different down there, I guess. Anyway, it said the father was Arthur Zambelli, deceased, but that was no surprise. Who else was she gonna say? But it also had the hospital where she was born, in Tampa. I called over there and got the medical records. This time, I had to tell them I was a police officer, but they didn't even make me fax a letterhead or anything. They just gave me the information."

"What did they tell you?"

"It said that baby Delilah's blood type was B, and mommy Maria's was O."

"And yours is . . ."

"I'm an O," he said. "An O and an O don't make a B."

"Okay, so she lied to you."

"You know what else I did? Just for the hell of it?"

"What's that?"

"I got the forensics report on Arthur Zambelli. From when he fell into that ditch and broke his neck. They did an autopsy. You wanna know what his blood type was?"

"Go ahead."

"He was an A," he said. "An O and an A don't make a B, either."

"Okay," I said. "So what? What does it matter?"

"I think I know who Delilah's real father is," he said.

"Who?"

He just looked at me. He didn't say anything.

"No," I said. "No way."

"They were together," he said. "All that time when she was married to Zambelli. I know it."

"You gotta be kidding me."

"They've always had this sick thing between them," he said. "I can see it now. I can see the whole—"

"For God's sake," I said.

"The whole sick thing," he said.

He looked at his drink. He put it down, picked up the shotgun with one hand. With the other, he fumbled around in his shirt pockets, finally pulled out a piece of paper folded in half. "You want to know what I was seriously thinking about doing this afternoon?" he said. "Here, read this."

I took it from him and unfolded it. It was a piece of official Orcus Beach stationery, with the little cannon insignia on the top. It read, "For Maria, and everything I wanted to believe." That was it.

When I looked up, he had the shotgun barrel in his mouth. I dove over the table and knocked the gun away from him. He grabbed at it. For one horrifying instant, it was pointed right at my face. I knocked it away again, flipping the table right over into his lap. He fell backward in his chair, with the table and me and the gun all flying in different directions. Somehow, the gun landed without firing, without blowing either of us into pieces. He lay there on his back, his knees up in the air over the edge of his chair. I crawled over to him and looked at his face.

"Was that necessary, McKnight?" he said. "I was just seeing if I could reach the trigger. In case I work up the nerve someday."

"Why are you doing this to me, Chief? Why did you bring me here?"

"Are you Catholic?"

"No," I said. "I'm not Catholic."

"So you've never been to confession."

"No."

"Father, forgive me for I have sinned," he said. "It has been forty-five years since my last confession."

"I'm leaving," I said. "You need to sleep this one off."

"I thought you'd understand, McKnight. I thought you'd be the one person in the world who I could tell this to. To whom, I mean. To whom I could tell. All of it."

I got to my feet, turned the table back upright. I was going to leave the gun lying there in the corner, then thought better of it. I broke the gun open and put the shells in my pocket. Then I put the gun, still breached, on the table. I put his car keys next to the gun. I picked up the suicide note and put that next to the gun, too.

"McKnight," he said. He was still on his back. His eyes were still closed.

"Good night, Chief," I said.

"Give me the phone," he said.

"Good night."

"I want to call her," he said. "Give me the phone. I want to call Maria."

"Don't call her," I said. "Go to bed."

"I'll get it myself," he said, not moving. "I'm going to call her. I'm going to wake her up and tell her that I know. She's not my daughter."

"Good night, Chief."

"Don't go," he said. "You can't go. You have to be my witness. I want somebody else to hear this."

"Good night, Chief."

"You can't go," he said. "You're under arrest. I order you to stay here and be my witness."

"Good night, Chief," I said. And then I left. I walked out into the cold air, past the chief's car and the leaning mailbox. I walked back down to the main road, all the way back to Rocky's place. It still looked open, even after three o'clock in the morning.

This is what you do in Orcus Beach, it would seem. You sit around and you drink, and you think about all the mistakes you've made.

I fired up the truck and got myself out of there. At the edge of town, I saw the sign in the rearview mirror, WELCOME TO

ORCUS BEACH, the letters backward, and under that the cannon in the sand.

I rolled down my window and threw out the two shotgun shells. And then I just kept driving.

Chapter Twenty-two

A sound woke me up. A bird chirping at me, then stopping, then chirping again. No, it was a phone. I picked my head up. I was still in my clothes, lying on the motel bed in Whitehall. I hadn't even turned down the covers, just walked in at 4:30 in the morning and fell over. My right hand was still swollen, a little reminder just in case I thought it was all a bad dream.

What time was it now? I couldn't see the clock, but there was daylight in the room, brighter than anything I'd ever seen.

The phone rang again. I pulled myself up. I picked up the phone. Dial tone.

I lay back down and stared at the ceiling. The phone rang again. It wasn't the motel phone. It was my cell phone. Which was impossible, because it was out in the truck.

The phone rang again. Okay, it wasn't my cell phone. My phone doesn't sound like that. My phone isn't nearly as annoying.

Whitley's phone. It was still in my coat pocket, and apparently still on. I got up and grabbed my coat, took the phone out of the pocket. It rang one more time before I could answer it.

"Who is this?" I said.

"Is that you, McKnight?" I knew the voice.

"What is it, Harwood? Why are you calling me?"

"You stole Whitley's phone," he said. "Not to mention his car. He's not happy."

"And yet somehow I'm not overcome with guilt," I said. "Is that all you wanted to say?"

"Sounds like you had quite a night," he said. "I mean, unless she was exaggerating."

"Good-bye," I said.

"Why did you ask me about Randy Wilkins?"

"I thought you said you didn't know him."

"He was the pitcher, right? For the Tigers. The guy who got destroyed in his only game. I was at that game. Did you know that?"

"You don't say."

"His father was a real estate developer out in California. We were going to do some kinda deal, but it fell through. I guess that's why I went to the game. His father couldn't make it, so I said I'd go. Man, did he get shelled, though. What did he give up, like eight runs in the first inning?"

"Harwood, that's the only contact you ever had with him? Just going to his game?" I didn't know what to make of this. It was too much of a coincidence.

"I think I saw him a couple days later, at a restaurant somewhere. I stopped by to pay my respects, you know, offer my condolences. . . . And then—wait a minute."

"What is it?"

"It's coming back to me," he said. "It was the Lindell AC, in downtown Detroit. You know it?"

"Yes."

"I had a quick drink with him, figured it was the least I could do. I was still trying to put together some kind of deal with his father. I was trying to maintain a good rapport with the whole family, you know? And here's this poor kid who made a total fool of himself in front of a whole stadium. Out of the blue, he says I have to go down the street and get my fortune told by this old woman. He didn't say anything about Maria, just Madame whatsherface, whatever the hell she was calling herself. The deal with Wilkins's father fell through right after that. I don't think I've even heard the name again until you asked me about it last night."

"So that's how you met Maria? Randy told you to go have your fortune told?"

"I guess it was, now that I think about it. Goddamn it, I never really put that together. Wilkins was the guy who told me I should go see the fortune-teller. Goddamn it all. Although I don't remember even stopping by there until—what, the next year? That game was in '71. Yeah, I think it was the next season. I was at another game in '72. That was the year they lost to the A's in the play-offs, right? I was walking back to my car from the stadium, saw her sign there on Leverette Street, remembered I was supposed to go see her. I was curious, you know? I never had my fortune told. I went just for the hell of it. Obviously, the biggest mistake I ever made. Boy, did they rope me in. Your little girlfriend had been running con games her whole life. I hope you know that, McKnight. Her whole family. They got me into a pretty tight spot, set me up and then took some pictures. In a hotel room. They blackmailed me for years. Then she got her hooks into my partner, Arthur Zambelli. He never knew what hit him. They were married for what, ten years? I tried to warn the man. I told him what she had done to me. He didn't believe me. Although you know what? When I look back on it now, I think maybe he did believe me, but he didn't care. He must've thought she had changed or something. That's the kind of guy he was."

"What's your blood type?" I said.

"Why do you want to know that?"

"Just tell me."

"This is about her daughter, isn't it?" he said.

"Zambelli wasn't her father."

"No shit," he said. "Why do you think she killed him?"

That one stopped me. "What are you talking about?"

"He had some kind of physical problem. Like no sperm count at all. When she got pregnant, she had three choices. Tell him and risk getting dumped for good, and lose out on some serious money. Or get an abortion, which is what most women would have done. Or just kill him. Hell, she even gets a nice insurance payoff with that choice. There wasn't much to think about."

"Are you Delilah's father?"

"Hell if I know."

"So it's possible?"

"I suppose so. Does it even matter? If she's my daughter, she grew up hating me. She probably went to bed every night hearing about how evil I am."

"So it's possible," I said. "The two of you were together, even then. Just out of curiosity, how does that work? This was the same woman who set you up and blackmailed you, right?"

"She still was," he said. "The whole time. For ten years. I figured I was already paying for it, so why not?"

"And why would Maria have anything to do with you at that point?"

"Don't you get it, McKnight? I'm the best she ever had. It still drives her crazy."

"All right, all right," I said. "Spare me. I'm sorry I asked."

"You want to know what she did after she killed Zambelli?"

"She had her brother throw you down the stairs," I said. "I know the story."

"No, after that," he said. "When she moved down to Florida, she sent my wife a little good-bye present. Those pictures they took of us back in 1972. It wasn't enough that I was fucking crippled, McKnight. She had to ruin my marriage, too."

"Why are you telling me all this?"

"I thought you should know the truth," he said.

"Why didn't you tell me any of this last night?" I said. "Oh yeah, I guess you were too busy trying to shoot me."

I heard something in the background. It sounded like the hum of traffic, and somebody yelling.

"You'll have to excuse Mr. Whitley," Harwood said. "I just drove over some railroad tracks. He's lying down, trying to get his back to loosen up. You really did a number on him."

"You're driving?" I said.

"Yes, I'm driving. I can do anything I want in this thing. Drive with just my hands, even talk on the phone at the same time."

"Well, good for you," I said. "Is that all you wanted to tell me?"

"I just hope you've got some brains left," he said. "Get out now, while you still can."

"Your concern for me is overwhelming," I said. "But I got news for you. I'm already out. I don't care what the hell happens now. The two of you deserve each other. The only thing that bothers me now is Delilah being in the middle of all this. She doesn't deserve either one of you."

"I've got a feeling everything will be changing soon," he said.

"I'm glad you won't have to be around to see it. It's not your problem, after all."

There was a long pause. I heard more traffic noise in the background, and then static.

"Stay away," he said. The words were breaking up. "Stay away." Then the connection was broken.

I turned the phone off for good. It would go into the first public trash can I saw that day.

The sun was shining when I left the motel. It was one of those April days in Michigan where the temperature gets up to seventy and you start to think summer is around the corner. The next day, it'll be thirty degrees again. But you still fall for it, every time.

After breakfast, I hit the road, with serious thoughts about going home. But then I thought, Hell, if Randy is going to open his eyes again, this is probably the day he'll do it. That's what the doctor had said anyway. So instead of driving straight north to a Canadian beer at Jackie's place, I drove southeast to the hospital in Grand Rapids. One more day, I told myself. One more day.

I found the doctor standing at the nurses' station. "He's showing some good signs," he said. "He's responding to light, and to physical stimulation. But he's not conscious yet, so we have to be concerned about some possible neurological damage. Remember, essentially he had a stroke. Which is always a guessing game."

I thanked the man and went down to Randy's room. The same county deputy was sitting outside the door.

"Don't tell me you've been sitting here this whole time," I said.

He laughed at that. "I just got here," he said. "I have the day shift."

"That's what I miss the most about being a cop," I said. "The excitement."

"You're the only guy who's come around to see him. Doesn't he have any family?"

"Not really," I said. "Not anymore. Mind if I poke my head in?"

"Why not? What are they gonna do, fire me and get somebody else to sit in this chair all day? I hear it's seventy-two degrees outside."

I went into the room and just stood there for a while, looking down at him. He didn't look any different from the last time I had seen him. His neck and his shoulders were still covered in bandages. The same machines monitored his heart rate and breathing. His eyes were still very much closed.

"What's it gonna be?" I said to him. "Are you gonna wake up today or not?"

The machines beeped.

There was a chair in the corner. I sat down and closed my eyes for a while. I got up and looked out the window at the beautiful day going on outside, then sat down again.

I thought about Harwood's phone call. I still didn't understand the connection, this business of Randy telling him to go have his fortune told, back in 1971. It didn't make any sense. There had to be more.

Something else was bothering me, something more immediate. The way he sounded when he said everything would be changing soon.

Forget it, Alex. It has nothing to do with you. Not anymore.

I went out of the room and walked around the rest of the

hospital for a while. That got old fast, so I went outside to let the sun shine on me. I killed an hour walking around outside, bought a newspaper, then went back up to the room. The doctor was shining a light into Randy's eyes. "Nothing yet," he said. "I'll be back."

I sat there in the room reading the newspaper for another hour. The Tigers were already pitching themselves out of the season. The Red Wings were getting ready for another run at the Stanley Cup. The Pistons would make the play-offs, but nobody believed for a second that they'd make it past the first round.

I told the deputy I'd bring him up some lunch, went down to the street, and walked to the same bar I had been in the first time around. The bartender recognized me immediately. But then, the place wasn't exactly filled to capacity. The woman who'd been watching the soap opera the first time I was there had been replaced by a man watching SportsCenter.

"Hey, did you ever make it up to Orcus Beach?" the bartender said.

"I stopped in," I said.

"What did I tell you?" he said. "Pretty boring place, huh?"

I didn't remember him saying that, but I wasn't about to correct him. I let him set me up with a Strohs and the sandwich of the day, some kind of pastrami with cheese. I ordered a second one to go for the deputy. While I was sitting there eating, I kept thinking about Harwood's call, and wondering why it was still bothering me. I kept picturing Maria in my mind, whether I really wanted to or not, the way she looked when she took me up to her bedroom.

Forget about it, Alex. Just forget about it.

I took the sandwich back to the deputy. I sat in Randy's

room and waited. I took another walk. The sun kept shining all afternoon.

Before the deputy left for the day, he told his replacement to keep letting me through the extra-tight security. He gave me a wink on his way out, and thanked me again for the sandwich. I figured I'd get off to a good start with the new deputy by offering to bring him back dinner. He liked that idea, so I went back down to the same bar. The same bartender was still there, the same man sitting on his stool watching television. It was the kind of bar that never changed, for better or worse, and when I sat down again, the same thought invaded my mind. Maria. Her face. Her body. Her lies.

Then I thought about the rest of her family. Her mother, her brother. Her daughter. Maybe Harwood's daughter, too. It didn't sound like it mattered to him.

Delilah, standing in the doorway, in the softball uniform.

Everything will be changing soon, Harwood said. I'm glad you won't have to be around to see it.

He was driving his RV. There was traffic in the background.

Lots of traffic.

It hit me. He was going to their house, in Farmington. I knew it.

That's why he'd called me. To see where I was. To make sure I wouldn't be there. Stay away, he said. Stay away.

Goddamn it, I thought. He wouldn't do that.

The hell he wouldn't.

I got up and went to the pay phone. The same wooden chair sat in the narrow hallway. I had used this same phone to call Randy's wife, and his three kids. Now I was going to call somebody I never thought I'd call again.

She answered on the third ring.

"Maria," I said. "Listen very carefully."

"Alex! I'm glad you called."

"What?" I looked at the phone in my hand. "Maria, Harwood called me this morning. He said some things that got me thinking. That's the only reason I'm calling."

"Leopold is here," she said. "He says hello. Everybody says hello, Alex."

"Everybody? Everybody is there?"

"I called them last night," she said. "After you left. Even when everybody else lets you down, your family's going to be there for you."

I let that one go. "Okay, then," I said. "That's good."

"Chief Rudiger came over first," she said. "I called him and asked him to come over. He stayed with me until they got here."

"You called the chief?"

"I know it was late," she said. "But he came right over. That's the kind of man he is."

I let that one go, too. "How did he look?"

"He was just fine. A little tired, I suppose. Why do you ask?"

"Never mind," I said. More lies, just what I needed. "It doesn't matter. Look, I'm sorry I called."

"Don't be," she said. "I'm sorry things happened the way they did. I shouldn't have asked you to help me in the first place. But it's okay, because I have my whole family here now. We had breakfast on the beach, Alex. It was such a beautiful morning. Leopold made pancakes. And the chief said he's going to go take care of things. So I'm fine."

Leopold made pancakes. What the hell was I supposed to do with that? "Okay," I said. "I'm hanging up now."

"Good-bye, Alex. I hope you'll think about me sometime."

"I imagine I will, Maria. Good-bye."

I went back to the bar. What a wonderful idea that was, giving her a call. I am so full of wonderful ideas.

"Leopold made pancakes," I told the bartender. "Give me another beer."

He slid one over.

"And the chief is going to go take care of everything," I said. The chief who supposedly came over to sit with her until her family got there. The same chief I left lying on the floor with a bottle of Wild Turkey on his chest.

I froze, the beer bottle lifted halfway to my mouth. "Oh no," I said.

I put the beer down.

"Oh my God."

Chapter Twenty-three

I have an excuse. It's not much, but here it is.

Have you ever picked up a baseball? Have you ever felt how hard it is? A good pitcher throws it at speeds approaching a hundred miles an hour. Sometimes the batter swings at the ball and just barely makes contact with it. In that case, the ball doesn't slow down, and it doesn't change its direction more than a few inches. But those few inches are enough to make the catcher miss it completely. That's why a catcher wears a mask.

If you've ever worn an old catcher's mask, you know that it's basically just a metal cage with padding around the edges. If a foul tip catches you square in the mask, that metal cage is there to make sure you don't lose half your teeth or break your nose. The problem is, if a fastball hits you right in the middle of your mask and then drops to the ground, all that force has to go *somewhere*. It doesn't matter how much padding you've got on that thing. Your head is still absorbing the blow.

Nowadays, they've got these catcher's masks that look more like the masks hockey goalies wear. They're streamlined, so that anywhere you hit them, it's just a glancing blow. A catcher never has to take a straight-on fastball in the head anymore. Of course, they didn't have those when I played. So how many of those fastballs to the head had I taken? Two thousand? Three thousand? I couldn't even guess. But I do remember what it felt like when I took a couple good ones in the same inning. I'd go back to the dugout feeling like a prizefighter staggering back to his corner.

So maybe I'd taken too many balls off the mask. That's my excuse. Or maybe I was just born this way. Either way, sometimes I just do things without thinking. I usually end up paying for it.

I drove east, back across the state, toward the suburbs of Detroit. I knew the route well, having taken it twice already in the past few days. I didn't think I could change anything. It was almost six o'clock at night. Whatever had been done had been done several hours ago. It was nothing more than curiosity at that point. That, and a sick sense of dread and something almost like fascination. I couldn't believe they'd really done it. And I was sure they had. I just had to see for myself.

All that business about how her family had been there all day, breakfast on the beach, Leopold making pancakes, and about how Chief Rudiger had said he was going to take care of things. She'd told me all that for a reason. She hadn't known I was with the chief the night before, didn't know I would see right through it.

That's what I thought about all the way down I-96, then I-275 to Farmington. I found the subdivision again. Corriedale Street to Romney Street. As soon as I turned the corner, I saw the two vehicles in the driveway.

The chief's patrol car was closest to the garage, the long scrape still fresh on the passenger's side. Harwood's RV was right behind it. There were no other cars in the driveway, because, of course, they were all in Orcus Beach at that point.

I drove past the house, then doubled back and stopped on the street. I sat there and watched the house for a while. Nobody came or went. Nothing happened. As I sat there, it occurred to me that Whitley had done the same thing, maybe sitting in this exact same spot, watching the same house.

I sat there for at least an hour. A couple kids came down the street on their bikes. A few cars passed. Somewhere, a dog barked. Otherwise, it was a quiet, pleasant evening in the suburbs. The two vehicles sat in the driveway. I stared at the scrape on the side of Rudiger's car, hypnotized by the shape of it. It didn't take a fortune-teller to know something was very wrong in that house.

I should have left then. That's what I should have done.

I didn't.

I got out of the truck and walked up to the house. The beautiful April day was all but over, the warmth of the sun long gone. There were no neighbors outside to see me walking down the driveway to the front door. When I got there, I saw that it was ajar. I pushed it open and went inside.

Silence.

I went through the living room, then into the dining room.

No sign of life. Nothing.

The stairs. I knew these stairs. I went to the edge and looked down.

One wheel.

That should have been enough for me. One wheel. That's all I needed to see. But I kept going. I took a step down. The stairway creaked. I stopped. I took another step. Another creak. With each step, I saw more of the wheelchair. It was turned onto its side.

It was empty.

I kept going, step after step. I saw a leg, then another. And then the blood.

Two men against the wall, each with one arm in handcuffs. The handcuffs going through the metal ring in the wall. The same ring in the wall, the same handcuffs. Two men. Whitley and Harwood. What is left of them. Each blown apart by a shotgun. This is what it looks like. Blood everywhere. The smell of death and blood. The pure evil sight of it.

Shotgun casings on the floor. Lying in the blood.

Look to the right. There is more. Chief Rudiger, the man I saw how many hours ago. The head destroyed now. Obliterated. All over the mirror behind him, pink and red. He is lying on the weight bench. The shotgun hanging from him onto the floor, one dead finger still caught in the trigger.

A piece of paper on the floor, one corner soaking up blood.

The chief wanted to call her. Those were his last words to me. He wanted to get up off the floor and call Maria. If he had managed to pull himself off the floor and call her, then what happened next? How long did it take her to see the opportunity? To see the whole scene laid out in front of her? It's airtight. She calls Leopold. He wakes the entire family. They load up Leopold's truck, Delilah's car, Anthony's car. The whole family goes to Orcus Beach in the middle of the night, just like Maria said. Is the chief already at Maria's house when the family arrives? Maybe he is. Maybe Maria asked him to come, and somehow he pulled himself together and drove over there. Or maybe Leopold and Anthony had to go get him. Either way, the piece of paper is with him. Written in his own hand. He brought it with him, or it was there on the table when they picked him up. And the shotgun. Don't forget the shotgun. They put him in the back of his patrol car, drive him back to Farmington. Two cars. Anthony following Leopold, who is driving the patrol car. It's five in the morning then. Maybe six. Leopold has the chief's hat on, just in case somebody sees him in the car. But it's so early, there aren't many cars on the road. When they get to the house in Farmington, they wait. Anthony parks the car down the road, of course. Only the patrol car can be seen in the driveway. Maria calls Harwood. She has his number now. She calls him and tells him to come to Farmington. Time to make a deal. Time to end this once and for all.

Which is exactly what they do.

After it is done, Leopold and Anthony drive back to Orcus Beach. The police will find them, of course. Three dead men in their basement, they'll need to talk to them. An apparent double murder and then a suicide, the chief's finger still in the trigger guard. Will the forensics man find something that doesn't add up? What *can* you find when you're dealing with shotgun blasts? How hard will they even look?

They'll go to her, of course. To the whole family. They'll have to talk to them.

Oh my God, she'll say. It can't be. The chief was such a good man. He told me he'd help me. He told me he wouldn't let those men hurt me. But my God, Officer, I had no idea.

You've got your own story to tell the police, Alex. Your own little theory, with absolutely no proof. And yourself right in the middle of it. First you threatened Whitley and Harwood at gunpoint; then you ended up in Maria's bed. Then you had a nightcap with the chief, at the bar and then back at his house, where you then knocked a shotgun out of his hands. And took the shells out. For all you know, your fingerprints are still on it. Unless you go lift that gun off the chief's chest and wipe it clean.

Think about what you've got, Alex. This is the hand you're holding if you try to make this whole thing come out differently in the end.

I made myself turn around and go back up the stairs. I didn't have to read the note on the floor. I knew what it said. The words scrawled below the official seal, with the cannon in the sand.

"For Maria, and everything I wanted to believe."

Chapter Twenty-four

"Alex."

I opened my eyes.

"Alex."

I sat up straight in the hard wooden chair, feeling a sudden pain run down my neck and into my back.

"Alex." His voice was low, like a whisper.

I looked across the room. Randy's eyes were open.

"Do you need the doctor?" I said. I looked at my watch. It was after 11:00 P.M. I had gotten there at 9:00, just in time to catch the doctor writing out his charts at the nurses' station. Randy had regained consciousness just after I had left that afternoon, the doctor told me. He still had some localized weakness on the left side of his body, but aside from that, he was doing remarkably well. They took the tube out of his throat and hooked up a minidose morphine drip. They had told him he had been shot, and that there was a county deputy stationed outside his door. He had been awake for a couple hours, but by the time I got back there, he was asleep. I sat down in the chair and did the same. Now he was awake again, and I didn't know which question to ask him first.

"They told me what happened," he said. He still had the bandages on, but without the tube running down his throat, he looked human again.

"Yeah," I said. "I talked to the doctor."

He looked toward the window. "What time is it?"

"Just after eleven."

"Were you here the whole time?"

"No, I was up in Orcus Beach."

He looked at me, then closed his eyes.

"The last thing I remember," he said, "was going to her door."

"Her daughter told you where she lives," I said.

He opened his eyes again. "Yes."

"Maria told me she thought you were Harwood," I said. "Or somebody he sent."

"You saw her."

"Yes. I saw her."

"What else did she say?"

"She said a lot of things," I said. "Of course, every single thing she said was a lie."

"I could use something to drink," he said.

"She's a very good liar, isn't she," I said. "Not unlike yourself."

"The doctor said I'm not supposed to talk too much."

"You may have some permanent damage to your vocal cords," I said. "That's gonna affect your technique a little bit."

"Alex..."

"I know the whole story," I said. "Your record in California, the arrest warrant waiting for you when you get back. That deputy's been sitting outside your door the whole time."

"You should have gone home," he said.

"I called your family. I thought they should know."

"Let me guess," he said. "They were not overwhelmed with concern."

297

"Your youngest son came the closest," I said. "He seemed to care a little bit."

Randy closed his eyes again.

"Feel free to tell me why you did all this," I said. "Anytime. I'm all ears."

"I didn't lie to you," he said.

"Excuse me?"

"You heard me," he said. "I didn't lie to you."

"Good-bye," I said, turning toward the door. "I'm gone."

"Alex, wait."

I stopped.

"I didn't lie," he said. "Not exactly. I just didn't tell you everything."

I rubbed my forehead. "Oh God," I said. "Here we go. You should run for office, you know that?"

"Let me explain."

I moved back. I stood over him with my arms folded across my chest. "Give it your best shot. First lie you tell me, I'm out the door. This time, I'll know it. Believe me."

He took a long breath and rested his head back on the pillow. For a moment, there was nothing but the sound of the heart monitor, still attached to his chest. Then be began.

"Everything they told you about me is true," he said. "Everything and then some. I have no excuse for it, Alex. I'm not going to try to defend myself. All I can say is, there was a time, many years ago, when things were different. You knew me then. You knew how much I loved playing ball. It was the only thing I ever wanted to do. When I got my big chance and failed, it was all taken away from me. In one game, *in one inning,* it was all gone. I knew it right then. I knew I'd never get another chance. Even though I ended up getting kicked around in the minors for another six years, deep down I knew it was hopeless. I'd never get another shot."

He paused to catch his breath.

"When I got sent up to Detroit, it was the best month of my life. When I met Maria, it got even better. I figured this was the girl I'd spend the rest of my life with. I'd be a big-league pitcher for twenty years and I'd go to the Hall of Fame one day, and she'd be there in Cooperstown with me, sitting in the front row. With our three kids. I could see my whole life opening up in front of me. I really could. When I got knocked out of that game, I went down into the clubhouse and I just sat there, Alex. I didn't cry. I didn't take a bat and destroy a television set or anything. I just sat there and thought to myself, This is what life is really like. Dreams don't come true. Things don't happen just because you want them to. Nothing is fair. Nothing is really *good*. Are you following me, Alex?"

"Keep going," I said.

"All I'm trying to say is, in that exact moment, I saw things the way they really were. This girl I was spending so much time with, this beautiful, wonderful Maria, she didn't really love me. She was just setting me up. It was all a big scam."

"Giving up seven runs made you realize that."

"The night before the game," he said. "She told me about this debt her father had, going all the way back to the old country. He couldn't repay it. No matter how she begged him, this man was so old-fashioned, he was willing to take his whole family back to Europe just so they could work as servants in some guy's house to repay the debt to him. I told her I'd help her take care of the problem. She was so happy. Then I stopped thinking about it, because I was too preoccupied with the game. When I was sitting there in the locker room, watching my whole life go down the drain, I finally thought about it again, the whole story. A debt from the old country. They needed money. My God, Alex. Can you imagine? I was buying it. The whole thing. All the time we had spent together. It was all coming together. On that day, after what had happened to me, I could finally see it."

"Okay, so you figured out she was a con artist," I said. "And you blew her off. Why come back now? It's a long time to wait for revenge."

"I had already gotten my revenge," he said. "Or so it turns out anyway. There was this man in Detroit named Harwood. He was trying to put together a deal with my father. The minute I met him, I hated him. You ever meet somebody like that?"

"Yes," I said. "Just last night, in fact."

"He was such a fraud. Everything he did, everything he said, it was all such an act. He was the most arrogant, pompous jackass I had ever seen in my life. And here he was, trying to suck up to me just because he wanted something out of my father. He made my skin crawl. He came to the game. Did you know that? He was there. I saw him a couple days afterward at the Lindell. I was getting drunk. Again. With Maria a couple blocks away, with her whole con artist family, probably putting the screws on some other sucker even as I was sitting there. And in walks Harwood, just the man I needed to see that night. He starts telling me how sorry he was I had gotten blown out of the game, how embarrassing it must have been, all this other crap. I could tell he was loving it. If he hadn't still been trying to put the moves on my father, he'd have been standing there laughing at me. So I told him he really needed to go see Madame Valeska down the street to get his fortune told. It would really be an eye-opening experience for him, and he'd really get something out of it. I was hoping he'd go see them. I was really hoping. I knew they'd put him through the wringer. He was such a sleazebag. He was smart about money, but I knew he'd lose his head over Maria. And Maria would actually have to spend time with him. Even...get close to him. So in the end, they'd both get what they deserved."

He stopped. He looked out the window, at nothing but darkness.

"Is that why you came back?" I said. "To see what they'd done to each other all these years?"

"No," he said. "Don't you understand? I had no idea. I didn't even know if Harwood ever went to see them. I was long gone by then. And I never looked back."

"You had no idea?"

"When we found her family's house," he said, "when they told us about Harwood and how they thought he had sent us? That was the first time I had heard his name in nearly thirty years. It was the first time I had even *thought* of him. It was just a drunken, spur-of-the-moment thing when I saw him that last time in Detroit. My little good-bye present to both of them. I never dreamed it would become something like that. It was all my fault, Alex. I made it happen. At that point, I didn't want to drag you into it anymore, so I sent you home. I wanted to see if I could...I don't know. I guess I was thinking I could fix things somehow. I wanted to try to help her."

"Why even bother? After what she did to you?"

"I remember it so well," he said. "How it felt. Back in 1971, when I realized she was just setting me up. All those things she said to me. All those lies. It was so easy to believe, because I wanted it to be true. I wanted it too much. When I was finally done playing out the string in baseball, when I finally went home, I knew I had to start acting like a real grown-up. My father's business was doing well. Everybody was expecting me to take it over someday. I tried to do it the right way, Alex. I tried to work hard, the same way my father did. But then when the real estate market crashed out there...I was afraid I was going to lose everything. Again. The same feeling, everything going down the drain again. There was this woman, one of our clients. She was very rich. She liked me. I could talk her into anything. It was so easy, Alex. It was so easy."

"Okay," I said. "A con man is born. I can fill in the rest. But you still haven't told me why you came back in the first place. Before you knew anything about Harwood, when it was just you deciding to come back here after all these years. You could have made things right with your family. You could have tried at least. Why did you come back here?"

"Think about it," he said. He managed a weak smile. "When was the last time everything was good, Alex? When was the last time I was on top of the world?"

"When, Randy?"

"When I was pitching for Toledo, and Alex McKnight was behind the plate, that was the last time I had it right. That was the last time I felt like I could do anything I wanted to. After that, it was all downhill, Alex. On roller skates. Before I went down for good, I had to come back one more time. Just to see if I could be that person again."

I just shook my head.

"And Maria. This is kind of crazy, but I may be the only person in the world who can understand her now. After everything I've done, you know what? You can love somebody, Alex. You can really love somebody, even though you *know* you're using them."

"Randy, that's the most depraved thing I've ever heard."

"It's true," he said. "I've been there. My family will never forgive me, Alex. And I don't blame them. The people I've hurt, the people I've taken money from. They'll never forgive me."

"She barely remembered you," I said.

"She remembers me."

"No."

"That's what she said to you. I know she remembers me."

"Yeah? You know that?"

"Yes."

"How do you know this?"

"Because we're the same," he said. "That's how I know. We'll always have a connection."

"A connection," I said. "That's good. That's real good. How about this instead? You know her so well, you gotta figure she's got a lot of money stored up after all these years. Am I right?"

He didn't say anything.

"You've worn out your welcome everywhere else. You know you're about to take your last fall, so you figure, Why not? You'll come back, see if you can tap into her again. After all these years."

"No."

"It was a long time ago. You don't have much leverage. But you *know* she's running something now. You get in on it. Or you threaten her, tell her you'll scare away the mark, or God knows what. You'd think of something. Am I getting warm here?"

"No."

"This was your last chance. Take her down, whatever you had to do. Take the money and run. Where else were you going to go, anyway?"

"You got it wrong."

"Give me one reason why I should believe you."

"Because I can't lie to you."

"You could lie to anybody," I said. "You could look God himself in the eye and tell him the sky is green."

"Not you," he said. "I could never lie to you."

"Why the hell not?"

"Because you're my catcher."

"Come on, Randy. Enough with that. It was thirty fucking years ago."

"It doesn't matter," he said. "I'm telling you the truth, and you *know* it. I've got no reason to lie to you now. In your bones, you know it. You just have to trust me."

I laughed. I couldn't help it.

"You believe me, right?"

"I don't know what to believe anymore."

"Tell me you believe me. I gotta hear you say it."

"Randy . . ."

"Say it, Alex. Tell me you believe me."

"Let me think about it," I said. "I get nervous when people tell me I have to say things."

"Is there really a cop outside?" he said. "Right now?"

"I'm surprised he hasn't come in yet. He must have heard us talking."

"Maybe he's asleep. Do you think we'd wake him if we sneaked out of here?"

"I think he'd wake up, yes."

"We could tie these sheets together," he said. "And go out the window."

"I hope you're not serious."

"I'm never serious," he said. He rubbed the bandages around his neck for a moment. "Is she safe?" he finally said. "Tell me that much."

"She's safe," I said. "Harwood's dead."

"Did you kill him?"

"No."

He thought about it. He didn't ask me anything more.

"You want me to get the doctor now?" I said.

"Yes. I need some water."

"You should call your family."

"Doesn't matter," he said. "You know. You talked to them."

"Call your son," I said. "Terry, the catcher. He'll want to know."

"Okay," he said. "I'll do that."

There wasn't much else to say. When I finally said good-bye to him, I wasn't sure how much I should hate him. In a way, he was exactly the same person I had known back in 1971. Now, almost thirty years later, after all the trouble he had caused me, I still couldn't make myself hate Randy Wilkins. No matter how hard I tried.

And I still didn't know if I believed him.

I drove home, four and a half hours straight north in the middle of the night. The sun was just coming up as I crossed over the Mackinac Bridge. There was still snow on the ground in the Upper Peninsula. As always, it felt like a different world. Maybe that's why I came up here in the first place. And why I've stayed so long.

I went to my cabin and slept a few hours. When I got up, I found my old catcher's mitt and wrapped it up in a cardboard box. I addressed it to Terry Wilkins, care of the UC–Santa Barbara Athletic Department. I got myself cleaned up and took the box to the post office.

And then, of course, I went to the Glasgow Inn for lunch. Where else was I going to go? Jackie was there waiting for me with a cold Canadian. He asked me about everything that had happened. I spent the rest of the afternoon telling him about it.

Around dinnertime, a wheelchair came through the front door. For one sickening second, I thought it was Harwood's ghost come to get me. It was Leon, both of his ankles still in casts, his wife pushing the wheelchair.

We all had dinner together, and I got to tell the whole story again, this time for Leon. After dinner, I told Jackie to mix me up a vodka and root beer. "One slinky, coming up," he said. It was truly awful.

We drank to the past. To money and to lies. To youth. To crazy left-handed pitchers.

We drank until the sun went down again on another day, keeping the fireplace fed and staying close to its warmth. Even when it's springtime in the rest of the world, the nights are still cold in Paradise.

 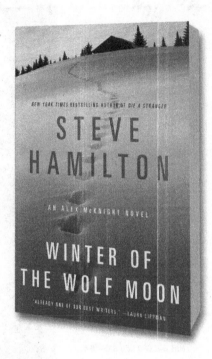

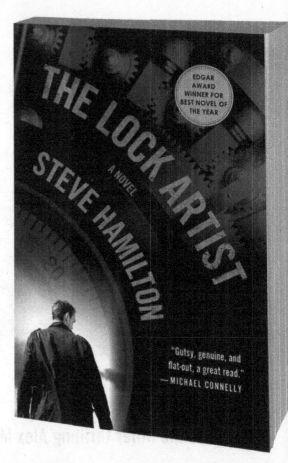